BRIGHTON HOVE LIBRARIES WITHDRAWN

SILVER STARDUST

Berris longs to be free of the Meredith Players, a travelling group of actors, and her chance of escape demands the performance of a lifetime. She is asked to take the place of a girl of high birth who bears a startling resemblance to herself. Berris's role is to last for one night—a night in which she must pretend to be the young beauty and become betrothed to the arrogant Sir Ellis Lennox. To Berris's dismay, fate dictates she play a longer role, when she unwittingly becomes the substitute bride of the handsome aristocrat...

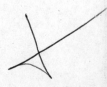

GW00750517

EQUAL ACCESS SERVICES CENTRE
HOLLINGBURY LIBRARY, CARDEN HILL
BRIGHTON BN1 8DA TEL: 296906

BRIGHTON & HOVE LIBRARIES

WITHDRAWN

Silver
Stardust

by

Mary Jane Warmington

BRIGHTON & HOVE COUNCIL	
02681700	
Cypher	30.04.04
ROM	£8.36
KZT	134013

EQUAL ACCESS SERVICES CENTRE
HOLLINGBURY LIBRARY, CARDEN HILL
BRIGHTON BN1 8DA TEL: 296906

Dales Large Print Books
Long Preston, North Yorkshire,
England.

British Library Cataloguing in Publication Data.

Warmington, Mary Jane
Silver stardust.

A catalogue record for this book is
available from the British Library

ISBN 1-85389-826-0 pbk

First published in Great Britain by Macdonald & Co.
(Publishers) Ltd., 1982

Copyright © 1982 by Mary Cummins

Cover illustration © John Heseltine by arrangement with
P.W.A. International Ltd.

The moral right of the author has been asserted

Published in Large Print 1998 by arrangement with Mr
William G Cummins

All rights reserved. No part of this publication may be
reproduced, stored in a retrieval system, or transmitted in any
form or by any means, electronic, mechanical, photocopying,
recording or otherwise, without the prior permission of the
Copyright owner.

Dales Large Print is an imprint of
Library Magna Books Ltd.
Printed and bound in Great Britain by
T.J. International Ltd., Cornwall, PL28 8RW.

CHAPTER ONE

The play ended to a faint spattering of applause and one or two catcalls. Berris Meredith walked forward to curtsey to the audience, her left hand clasped in that of her stepbrother, Sebastian Grey, and her right hand by her stepfather, actor-manager Brendan Meredith.

'My friends ...' began Brendan in his great sonorous voice.

A variety of rotten fruit rained on to the stage, soiling the flounces of Berris' gown. Normally it was worn by the leading lady, Mistress Mirabelle Grey, Sebastian's mother, but Mistress Grey had contracted chicken pox and Berris had been obliged to play her part. The gown was much too large, and Sebastian was amusing himself by removing one of two pins so that it billowed out around Berris' slender waist.

'Do stop, Sebastian,' she muttered through her teeth.

'Loosen up then,' he commanded. 'Sweep them a pretty curtsey. I declare you are a poor actress, Berris.'

Brendan Meredith tried once more to hold his audience, but a piece of cold potato hit him on the cheek and thankfully he gave the signal for the curtain to be lowered.

It was their final performance at the Revelry Theatre in Leeds and now they were moving on to York. The travelling Meredith Players had rarely visited this part of the country, and they had no following, but Berris could see that her stepfather was dismayed and angered by their reception, and that she was about to be allocated the lion's share of the blame. She hated the elaborate posturing and over-dramatic acting which was supposed to typify a fine performance on the stage, and was strongly advocating a more natural form of acting, but sadly, it had not been appreciated by the Revelry audiences.

'Go to the dressing room and change your costumes,' Brendan Meredith bade her and Sebastian. 'I'll bring our travelling wagon to the stage door and you'll help me to load up the scenery and costumes, Sebastian. Your mother is already resting in the wagon. Berris, I would like a word with you.'

The last words were spoken in an ominous tone and the girl shivered a little. Her stepfather was a reasonably good-tempered man, but he could also be frightening when he was angered. Her performance that evening had pleased neither Brendan Meredith nor herself.

He led her into a small ante-room, then grabbed her arm, turning her to face his anger.

'Have you learned nothing, girl? Have you not been trained and taught how to appeal to your audience, how to project your voice, how to show that you understand every nuance of the play and to teach the audience to understand your every gesture?'

She ran a tongue over her dry lips.

'I only seek to make the part appear more natural, Stepfather,' she defended. 'I have heard that Mrs Siddons approves of the overall developing of a character rather than emphasizing isolated parts ...'

'Mrs Siddons was hissed off the stage when she was your age!' he roared. 'She has learned her truly fine acting through experience. You try to bring new ideas, yet you succeed in making it a nonsense. One can be *too* natural, child. I might as well have asked one of the street women from a green box to play the part. Now you will do as I say!'

His anger, so quick to rise, was equally quick to leave him. He sighed, then put a hand on her shoulder.

'Change your costume. I have much to ponder and we should be on our way. Go now.'

In the dressing room Sebastian had gone behind a screened-off portion used by the men and Berris thankfully removed the great blonde wig, allowing her own shining chestnut-brown hair to tumble about her bare shoulders in a riot of curls and ringlets. Swiftly, she removed the stage make-up, leaning forward to look at her face in the cracked looking glass. Her features were unusual, the almond-shaped eyes slanting above delicately-formed cheekbones. Mirabelle Grey had declared that she was plain to the point of ugliness, but Brendan Meredith had laughed. Already it was Berris who turned heads when they walked in the street. She was like her mother, Brendan's first wife, who had been the most beautiful woman he had ever seen. In Brendan's opinion, Berris' beauty was her one asset to the company!

Slowly Berris moved behind the screens to take off Mirabelle's cheap garish dress. She hated playing Dorcas in *The Miller's Lament*. It was a stupid role, she decided, and she hated the elaborate costume. She tried to reach all the pins which held it together, then was forced to ask Sebastian to remove one between her shoulder blades. He did so, and the gown fell to Berris' feet. She stepped out of it thankfully, and threw it on top of the other costumes in the hamper.

As she reached for her own gown, Sebastian picked it up and held it behind his back.

'Give me that, Sebastian,' she said crossly. 'You have been irritating me all evening.'

'You looked very beautiful as Dorcas, Berris,' he told her. 'You are growing up.'

'I'm sixteen, as you very well know. Now give me my gown.'

He hung it over the screen and reached out to pull her into his arms. A moment later he was kissing her as she struggled to be free. What had happened to Sebastian this evening? Then she caught the smell of ale on his breath and her heart lurched. He had been drinking! He'd brought cheap ale into the theatre.

'Leave me alone, Sebastian,' Berris panted furiously. She hated the smell of ale on his breath. 'How dare you kiss me! You're my brother!'

'Stepbrother, my dear Berris. We're not related. My mother married your stepfather. He was your mother's second husband. Perhaps you have not noticed, but I am a man now and you are a grown woman. Why should I not kiss you?'

'Because ... because I think of you as my

brother,' cried Berris, her heart beginning to hammer with fright. He was slender, but his arms were as strong as steel. And what was he thinking about? He had pulled down her shift and was trying to fumble with the private parts of her person.

'Sebastian!' she cried, beginning to struggle wildly. 'What are you trying to do?'

His face had grown scarlet and his eyes were hot as they rested on her.

'You've got to let me try, Berris,' he whispered urgently. 'I know I can, with you. You've got to let me ...'

'Let you what?'

'Make love to you. You are the only one who means anything to me. I need you, Berris ... I *need* you!'

He was pulling at her underwear and she began to make a low moaning sound of protest, her eyes appalled by what was happening. She wanted to scream. This was Sebastian who was attacking her ... Sebastian ... her brother!

Suddenly the screens were jerked aside and Brendan Meredith stood there. He wore his great black theatre cloak, lined with red silk, and his eyes showed more fury than anything Berris had ever seen. She was used to his rages but this had quite a different quality. Almost as if it was mingled with fear.

'Sluts!' he yelled. 'Animals! Cannot I trust you to behave decently towards one another even for a few moments? Have I taught you no better than this? Sebastian, if you touch Berris ever again, I will kill you. I swear it. Is that understood?'

Sebastian's chest was heaving, but he stood up stiffly and faced his stepfather. Looking at him Berris' fears faded and she wondered why she had ever been afraid of him. He was always a clown, full of pranks. Now he just looked like a boy who had been caught stealing apples.

'Sebastian was only playing the fool, Stepfather,' she defended. 'It was nothing.'

Brendan threw her gown towards her, his eyes resting on the torn threads of her shift.

'Cover yourself decently, girl,' he said, contemptuously. 'If Sebastian plays the fool, I do not. From now on you will stay away from one another. I will not warn you again. Boy! You will carry out these baskets and trunks to the wagon, and take charge of the horses. I will escort Berris when she is ready.'

'Yes, sir,' said Sebastian, much subdued.

He avoided Berris's eyes as he hastened to do his stepfather's bidding.

Berris hated Saturday nights. It was then that the Meredith Players were required

11

to travel in the wagon which Brendan Meredith had designed and commissioned to be built many years ago especially for the purpose. As a younger actor, he had foreseen a bright future for himself on the London stage. He had played parts at Drury Lane under David Garrick and might now have been more famous than John Philip Kemble and Mrs Siddons, since he had many years more experience than either, but his bouts of drinking and gambling had eroded his money, his health and finally his career. Finding the most famous of the theatres barred to him, he had formed the Meredith Players and had begun to tour the provinces, earning himself a sufficient livelihood to provide his company with a reasonable standard of living.

Berris could remember the time when they owned two wagons, the second looked after by a manservant, Thomas Grey. In those days her mother had been still alive and, although she was not one of the Players, she was a fine needlewoman who delighted in keeping the costumes in good repair.

Thomas Grey's wife, Mistress Mirabelle Grey, became their leading actress, and Sebastian joined the company as soon as he grew old enough to learn small parts.

Bad luck had dogged the Players

two years before when they appeared in Manchester during an epidemic of fever. Brendan and Berris had contracted a mild infection, but Mrs Meredith had died within two days and Thomas Grey a few days later. Brendan had indulged himself in a severe bout of drinking and, when he recovered, he had been forced to sell one of the wagons, and had married Mistress Grey as a matter of expediency.

Berris was considered old enough to join the Players, playing the part of a child, boy or girl. In recent months, however, her figure had formed and Mistress Grey had watched this development jealously. She was not yet ready to give up the heroine parts to a younger girl.

Other changes had also been made. The wagon was divided by a curtain into two compartments. At one time Brendan Meredith occupied one compartment with his wife, whilst the children, Berris and Sebastian, slept in the second. Now that Berris had grown up, she was forced to share one compartment with Mistress Grey, whilst Brendan brought Sebastian's bedroll into the other. The proprieties must be observed.

As Berris climbed into the wagon beside Mistress Grey, she could see that the older woman had been informed about her performance that evening.

Chicken pox was rife in the area and, unfortunately, Mistress Grey had not suffered from the ailment as a child. Now her face was marked with spots, although her eyes were brilliant as she looked at the girl.

'So you were booed off the stage,' she said with satisfaction.

Berris said nothing. She was suddenly very tired. The wagon had been loaded up with their hampers and the rolled-up backcloths and Sebastian was taking charge of the horses, a task which normally gave him pleasure though he deplored their slow plodding gait.

The wagon began to sway, the horses' hooves resounding on the cobbled streets as they made their way through the darkness towards the roadway to York. In York they would live in cheap lodgings for a week but tonight, as on practically every Saturday night, they would all sleep for a few hours in the wagon.

Berris lifted a small flap of the canvas cover. It had rained heavily and the streets were running with water. There was a heavy odour of wet garbage and rotting refuse, mingling with warm animal dung newly deposited on to the streets.

Presently the roads narrowed, traffic lessened, and the last of the scudding clouds drifted away. Berris looked up at the bright stars and thought about her favourite play, *Silver Stardust*. She played well in that. She felt that she had the potential to be a great actress if only she had the right audience who could appreciate what she was trying to do. But the audiences had to be educated away from the heavy dramatic acting they expected.

The wagon had stopped in a quiet side road, and Sebastian loosed the horses and came inside to rest for an hour or two. Brendan had climbed through into the women's section at the insistence of Mrs Grey, who would not settle until they had talked. Berris could hear their low voices, arguing.

'What is your objection to Sebastian?' Mrs Grey was asking. 'Why should Mistress Berris be thought too grand for my son? I tell you, husband, it is the finest solution for them to marry. I could say *she* is not good enough for Sebastian!'

'Enough, woman,' Brendan growled. 'You know nothing about my plans. As a virgin, the girl is valuable to me.'

'Since when does an audience insist upon virginity? I, myself, have played virgins and have been appreciated by audiences.'

'I told you it must be as I say. If Sebastian spoils her, she is worthless. As

15

it is, she can make money for us.'

'How?'

'That is my affair. Now get to sleep. I have much to do tomorrow.'

Listening to Brendan Meredith's whispered words, Berris' heart lurched, then raced with apprehension. His voice, trained to reach the furthest seats of any theatre, came to her clearly as a bell. She pretended to be asleep, though she longed to rain questions upon her stepfather.

But something in his voice had put fear into her heart. What did he plan to do with her? And why must she remain a virgin? Did he plan to *sell* her to someone?

Brendan Meredith was a strange man. He was so consumed by all the parts he played that it was difficult to reach the true man underneath the play actor. She feared him, yet she loved him as the only father she could remember.

Berris could hear Sebastian settling down on his bedroll and her body began to glow with heat. He had kissed her as a man might kiss a woman. He had laid hands upon her person, and though she had fought him off with revulsion, she could not help remembering that her body had stirred under his fingers. She had never thought of Sebastian as a possible husband, but now she wondered what it would be like to lie with a man, to lie with Sebastian. He

16

was tall but delicately made and he behaved like a clown, though he could also snarl with bad temper when he was frustrated. Would he turn against her if Brendan denied them to one another? Sebastian could be exciting but there was also a dark side to his nature.

Berris looked up at the stars against the soft midnight velvet of the sky, then her eyelids dropped in sleep. She had learned to live her life one day at a time.

CHAPTER TWO

It was Berris's first visit to York. She looked out at the old walled city with its magnificent cathedral and fine cobbled streets, and her heart was stirred. Somewhere, a long time ago, she had seen a city just like York and the memory still lingered to tease and delight her.

But why did it remind her of something precious and fragile, which splintered into a thousand gems when she tried to recall its significance? But of course, Brendan Meredith had told her many times about the famous theatrical manager, Tate Wilkinson of York, who had built up the reputations of many fine actors and actresses. Perhaps it was the knowledge of this which made the city seem so exciting.

Their lodgings were in a mean hovel near the river, but the Meredith Players were used to such accommodation. The theatre, however, was fairly new and had been granted a license to present plays. It was much more opulent than many of those in which they normally played.

Brendan Meredith had agreed to present

Silver Stardust, a lovely old fairytale which gave Berris her best part as a fairy princess. Sebastian played the Water Prince and Brendan the King of the Forest, but Mistress Grey hated her part as the Twilight Fairy. She was growing plump and it did not suit her, though she declared herself well enough after her chicken pox to return to playing parts.

For the first day or two Berris was nervous and apprehensive despite the fact that she enjoyed looking at new scenes and mingling with crowds of energetic people. There was interest and excitement in the very air she breathed, and she would have relished spending many hours wandering the streets and gazing in the windows of the fine shops had Brendan allowed her to do so. But he made it a rule that she should be well chaperoned at all times, and she was never allowed to see anyone who called to ask for her at the stage door after a performance.

The play should have appealed to their audiences, but the numbers were disappointing, and Mistress Grey constantly took her husband to task.

'Why did we have to come to York when we have no following?' she demanded peevishly. 'For years you will not set foot in the place, and now you are determined to come when we can ill afford poor houses.'

'Be quiet, woman,' he growled. 'I have my reasons.'

He did not appear to be worried that the houses were so badly attended, and walked about deep in thought. Even his performances were abstracted, a sure sign that he was deeply disturbed. Berris watched him fearfully. Occasionally he would stand perfectly still, his eyes resting on her almost unseeingly, then he would sigh and pace the floor. If only she knew what he had in mind.

Sebastian had got over his sulks and once again he was smiling at Berris behind their stepfather's back, and seizing every opportunity to run his hand caressingly over her so that she shivered to his touch. He did not dare to kiss her but his eyes were hot and, in spite of her feelings of insecurity, her heart beat suffocatingly whenever their bodies touched.

On Thursday morning, as they ate breakfast in their lodgings, Berris' cheeks began to colour prettily. Under the table, Sebastian's knee pressed against hers and she grew suddenly aware that Brendan was staring at her with intense concentration. This time he was in full possession of his thoughts.

'Put on your best gown, Berris,' he commanded. 'Be ready by two o'clock. We have to make a journey.'

'A ... a journey? Where do we go, sir?'

'You will accompany me. That is enough.'

Her heart had leapt then plummeted with fear. Once again she could hear his resonant voice as he informed Mistress Grey that she was worth money to him, as a virgin. What was he going to do with her?

Mistress Grey had been about to ask questions and remonstrate with her husband, but something in his eyes stilled her tongue. There was much in Brendan Meredith's life which she did not understand.

Berris' best gown was made of soft brown velvet. Mistress Grey had wanted her to choose burnt orange, but Berris preferred plain, dark colours. Her stage clothes were so bright that she found the quieter colours restful. Her bonnet was also plain with a plume of matching ostrich feathers.

Brendan looked at her critically and nodded his satisfaction.

'Your mother had good taste,' he said. 'You are very like her, my dear.'

He had hired a closed carriage which looked very grand to her as it waited outside their shabby lodgings. Once Brendan had handed her into its gloomy interior and climbed in after her, he

21

called sharply to the coachman and they took off at a spanking pace. Mingling with her apprehension, Berris was beginning to glow with excitement. This was the greatest adventure which had ever befallen her, but she would have given much to know where they were going, and why.

She peeped out of the window of the carriage and saw that they were once again negotiating narrow country lanes, and a signpost told her they were on the Harrogate road. Soon they were driving between great wrought-iron gates and up a long narrow drive which led to the front entrance of the finest house Berris had ever seen. Her knees were trembling as Brendan Meredith handed her down from the carriage, but he kept his hand firmly on her elbow as he pulled the doorbell.

'Where are we?' Berris whispered through stiff lips. 'Where is this?'

Brendan Meredith shook his head, then he drew himself up proudly as an elderly butler came to the door.

'Mr Stephen Ashington, if you please,' he said in his most ringing voice.

The butler looked at him then turned to Berris, his eyes widening a little.

'Mr Stephen is dead, sir,' he said. 'Mr Mark Ashington is the master of Birkridge now.'

'Oh.'

For a moment Brendan looked crest-fallen, then he glanced at Berris.

'Present my compliments to Mr Mark Ashington and ask him to receive me,' he told the butler, handing him a card.

The butler's eyes again travelled from Mr Meredith to Berris, and he nodded slightly.

'You may wait here, in the hall, sir,' he invited, and Berris found herself being escorted into the largest room she had ever entered. It was dimly lit and great ornate pictures hung from the walls. Settees, chairs and tables had been placed round the room in a fashion more orderly than welcoming.

She sat gingerly on the edge of a very uncomfortable chair, but her stepfather was quite at his ease, leaning forward nonchalantly to rest his chin on a silver-topped cane.

Presently the butler came to find him, and Berris was asked to wait. A door had opened and shut further down the hall, and soon she could hear Brendan Meredith's deep resonant tones mingling with other, higher-pitched voices which might have been raised in argument.

Unable to control her nervousness, Berris rose to her feet and walked about, her feet making no sound as she slowly paced a rich, but faded, Chinese rug. Suddenly her eye was caught by one of the pictures as a shaft of sunlight lit up the hall, and her eyes became glued to the face of the woman in the portrait. It was her own face! She stared at the slanting eyes and the delicate cheekbones. The hairstyle was that of a previous generation, but the rich chestnut colour was still the same.

Greatly disturbed she sat down again, then suddenly a door was thrown open and the sound of voices grew very loud.

'I tell you it is impossible,' a woman was saying imperiously. 'The girl is already ruined. It is too late.'

'And I tell you it is not too late,' shouted Brendan Meredith. 'I have seen to that, ma'am.'

'You have indeed, sir,' a man's voice broke in. 'You have seen to it. That is why it is too late ... for us!'

'You insult me, sir, but one day you will be sorry!'

The door banged shut once more and there was the sound of quick heavy footsteps mingling with a lighter tread as the butler hurried once again into the hall.

Berris could see that her stepfather was in a towering rage as he strode towards her. She had risen to her feet and he grasped her arm, ignoring the butler, then steered her out of the main door and handed her

24

back into the hired carriage. Without a backward glance, he leapt into the carriage and once again they were on their way towards York.

Berris's mind was full of the painting she had seen.

'Stepfather,' she began. 'I saw a portrait in that hall which I found very curious ...'

'Stop chattering, child!' he snarled, turning away from her. 'We must get to the theatre. We have wasted time enough already. I may change the play to *The Miller's Lament* once more. It will please Mistress Grey.'

'Oh no, Stepfather! Just for one week, let us do *Silver Stardust*. The audiences have been small, I grant you, but appreciative. We will have more people when they spread the word. You will see. But ... cannot you tell me about that portrait?'

He turned a face of such anger towards her that she recoiled, then sat quietly until the carriage reached their lodgings. She had learned when to hold her tongue.

Brendan Meredith's anger smouldered as he prepared for his theatre performance. He was still infuriated by the attitude of the Ashingtons of Birkridge. He had loved his wife deeply and now he loved her daughter. Berris was dearer to him

25

than anything in this life, even if he rarely showed her his true feelings. He had always felt that he must return her, one day, to her own people.

He had educated her so that she could take her place beside the highest in the land, and had forced himself into making the effort to part with her. But the Ashingtons had rejected Berris. How could they reject her?

Brendan's anger went very deep.

CHAPTER THREE

Audiences improved but Brendan Meredith had retreated within himself and remained depressed and surly. Berris suspected that his finances were at a low ebb, and she was apprehensive that he might risk their remaining fortunes on gambling and drink because of his miseries.

Quick to take advantage, Sebastian began to waylay Berris, guiding her into a quiet corner to kiss and fondle her. At first she would fight free of his embraces, but now she was eager for them and trembled at his touch.

'He has changed,' Sebastian whispered, nodding towards Brendan. 'He no longer scowls when he sees me. Perhaps he will not deny you to me. Why should he?'

'I do not know, Sebastian.'

'You are not like other women, Berris. They do nothing but revolt me with their cheap scent and tawdry petticoats. I hate their mountains of soft flesh and vast bosoms, but you are delicately formed and your body is beautiful and slender as a reed. With you I can love. Let me love you, Berris.'

27

She pulled away. Loving Sebastian was exciting, but she did not want to feel his searching hands upon her. She was not yet ready for his sort of love.

On Saturday evening a lady and gentleman of distinction occupied one of the boxes. Sebastian, peeping from behind the curtain, brought this news to the dressing room where his mother was trying to arrange her blonde wig on top of her own greying hair.

Brendan Meredith had already changed into his King of the Forest costume, and he followed Sebastian to assess the audience. Moments later he was back in the dressing room, his eyes more alive than Berris had seen them since their journey to Birkridge. He hurried towards her.

'You must give the performance of your life, Berris,' he said, taking her hand. 'It is very important. Someone has come to see you.'

'Who?' she asked.

'What are you talking about, Mr Meredith?' Mistress Grey demanded. 'Who has come to see the child? Why, the play depends upon all of us to give of our best, and not just Mistress Berris.'

'Then we must *all* do our best,' he said, magnanimously. 'But ... Berris ... remember all that I taught you about good speech, and good diction. Every

28

word must count and every syllable must be pronounced correctly. I was fortunate to be given this advice when I was a very young actor by the great David Garrick. I have never forgotten. Sebastian, you will not touch her. Leave her alone, I say.'

'Yes, sir,' Sebastian agreed, his eyes dancing.

Berris was nervous and her performance was poor, much to the disgust of Mistress Grey.

'You are like a block of wood,' she hissed.

Berris bit her lip as they acknowledged the perfunctory applause, but Brendan Meredith was in no mood to take a final curtain call. He hurried Berris along to the dressing room and ordered her to remove her make-up without delay. A short time later he came to find her and she was conducted to a small ante-room, then shown in by Brendan in his grandest manner.

'This is the young lady, ma'am,' he said, proudly. 'Berris, my dear, will you please curtsey to Mr and Mrs Ashington of Birkridge.'

Berris' mouth was dry as she curtseyed prettily. She looked at the couple from under her eyelashes and saw that they were staring at her fixedly.

'Turn your head to the right, child,' Mrs Ashington commanded.

Slowly, Berris obeyed and again there was silence.

'I think she will do.' The woman's voice was very deliberate. 'What do you think, Mr Ashington?'

'She will do, my dear. We have no other choice.' He had a high affected voice and appeared to be restless and uncomfortable in his surroundings. 'Fetch the girl now, Louisa. We can see to everything at Birkridge. The details of the matter can be discussed then. It is time that we return home.'

'No!'

Berris' voice rang out and the couple, who had risen preparatory to departure, turned to stare at her.

'I will not go anywhere until I know why you wish me to accompany you,' she said, clearly.

'The voice will not do,' Mr Ashington muttered, but Mrs Ashington had returned to her chair.

'It is an important acting role, Mistress ... ah ... Meredith. You are astonishingly like our niece, and we would like you to stand in for her at her betrothal party. Unfortunately Lora has contracted chicken pox. It is very rife in this area ... but it is essential that the betrothal party should not be cancelled. You understand, Mistress ... ah ... Meredith?'

Berris looked from one to the other. Her stepfather was hovering in the background, assuring Mr and Mrs Ashington that all would be well and that Berris could play the role perfectly.

'I do not think I could do so, sir,' she said, clearly. 'What about ... about the fiancé?'

'The *gentleman* who is my niece's affianced husband is Sir Ninian Andrew Lennox. He is travelling from London to his family home at Massingham especially for the betrothal ceremony. It will inconvenience too many people if the ceremony does not go according to plan. You need only appear for a short time and you will wear Miss Ashington's gown. You can excuse yourself very speedily, on account of a headache. If you smile prettily and say nothing, all will be well.'

'But ...'

'And the fee is surely gratifying.'

Mrs Ashington glanced at Brendan Meredith with a raised eyebrow and he stepped forward.

'It will offset our losses for some weeks, Berris,' he said in a low voice. 'You know it has not been easy recently.'

She nodded then turned again to look

at the Ashingtons. Some deeply-ingrained instinct made her want to refuse this commission and to stay as far away from the Ashingtons as possible. For a brief moment she experienced a great surge of excitement, quickly followed by apprehension and a strange sense of desolation. Only rarely had she experienced such emotions, but she felt that somewhere there was great sadness waiting for her if she did not take care. But she was given no time to ponder. Mr Mark Ashington had become increasingly restless and now he stood up and held out his cane.

'We have no time to argue,' he said, impatiently. 'Are you coming, Mistress, or do you refuse the commission?'

Brendan Meredith looked at her beseechingly and Berris nodded her agreement. Although not her own father, he had always been kind to her and had never forced her to do anything against her conscience. Now she felt she had no choice. Her stepfather needed the money.

'I will pack my clothing,' she said.

'There is no need for that,' said Mrs Ashington. 'You will be given something to wear which is ... ah ... suitable.'

'We are moving on to Harrogate,' said Brendan to Berris. 'I will come for you when this is all over. This might be a fine chance for you, child.'

Mrs Ashington withered him with a glance.

'The girl is only needed for this one event, Mr Meredith. Make no mistake about *that!* Come, child, out to the carriage with you. It is time we left for Birkridge.'

Once again Berris made the journey in a closed carriage to the mansion on the outskirts of York. This time she found the house well lit with maids scurrying here and there. A bedroom had been prepared for her and one of the maids, a tall strong girl in her late twenties, conducted Berris upstairs and arranged a bath for her before she was clad in a nightgown of finest lawn, daintily embroidered and frilled with lace, and she was helped into bed. The maid servant had looked at her closely, her eyes devouring Berris' face.

'It's uncanny, that's what it is,' she said, eventually.

'What is?' Berris asked.

'Not for me to say but I have never seen anything like it. Pull that bell if you want anything, ma'am.'

Berris had already eaten a light supper and would have welcomed more food. She was always ravenous after a performance. However she felt too shy to ask for anything else, and the bed was easing her tired body.

'I want nothing,' she said.

'Goodnight, ma'am.'

Her hair was still damp from the bath, and she looked around her bedroom, which was predominantly decorated in green and gold. She was not happy about the acting role which lay ahead. It would be very different from a stage role. On the stage everyone knew she was an actress, playing her part. But it appeared to her that she was going to be asked to deceive the guests at the betrothal party, and she did not care at all for that.

And what about the fiancé? Surely she would not be asked to deceive *him*.

CHAPTER FOUR

Berris was dreaming that Sebastian was bending over her. She tried to thrust him away because a capacity audience was watching their every movement. Her eyes flew open and she stared into the widened eyes of a young maidservant. As she struggled up in bed, the girl backed away.

'I am just pulling your shades, miss,' she said. 'Madam is coming to see you in a minute.'

'Madam?' asked Berris, stupidly. She had slept very deeply and she felt quite bewildered by her surroundings.

'Mrs Ashington.'

Berris sighed and lay back on the pillows. Memory returned full-fold and she pulled herself up once again, then leapt out of bed, searching for her clothes. They had been removed. Anger began to boil in her. How dare they remove her clothes!

Minutes later Mrs Ashington strode into the bedroom and once again she and Berris surveyed one another.

'Where is my gown?' the girl asked. 'I wish to dress.'

'Presently, presently,' the woman murmured. 'Masters, my own personal maid, is going to attend you. We will see what she makes of you.'

The personal maid was the older girl who had attended Berris on the previous evening. She walked into the bedroom carrying a new white muslin gown, sprigged with rosebuds, and dainty white kid shoes. Another bath had been prepared and once again Berris was soaked in warm scented suds before being dressed in the new clothes.

When she was ready, Masters conducted her downstairs to a large drawing room, greatly over-stuffed with ornate furniture, but very grand in Berris's eyes.

'Wait here near the fire, ma'am,' said Masters. 'I will tell Madam.'

Mark and Louisa Ashington arrived a short time later, and Louisa studied Berris very frankly through a lorgnette.

'Very promising,' she said. 'Very promising indeed. Masters has done well.'

'Make the girl walk. And talk,' added Mark Ashington and Berris's chin came up. He spoke about her as though she were a performing animal.

'Walk across to the window, Mistress ... ah ... Berris,' Louisa commanded. 'Tell me what you see in the garden.'

Berris did so, remembering her part

36

as Lady Cynthia in *The Torn Shoe*. She described the garden as accurately as possible and Mark Ashington turned away and shrugged his shoulders.

'See what I mean? The girl is hopeless.'

'She is an actress. She can learn. We have two more days.'

'It is unbelievable that there should be such a difference,' Mark Ashington muttered, then he strode out of the room as a maidservant appeared with a tea trolley.

'We will take tea together, Berris,' said Louisa Ashington. 'I must see how well you can take tea.'

Berris had grown nervous again. The teacup rattled against the saucer and a large splash of tea descended on to her pretty gown, the napkin having slipped from her lap.

'Have you had chicken pox, child?' Mrs Ashington demanded, after she had testily dealt with the tea stain.

'Yes.'

'Then we will go to my niece's bedroom. You will have to keep her company for the next two days, and since you claim to be a good actress, you will learn to be Miss Lora Ashington of Birkridge. You will copy Lora in everything she does. After that we can only hope you will earn the money I have paid for you. Come with me.'

Berris was conducted out of the large drawing room and once again she mounted the wide staircase in the wake of Mrs Ashington. They walked along a broad corridor, then Mrs Ashington threw open a bedroom door and ushered Berris into a large sunlit bedroom. A four-poster bed occupied the centre of the room and Louisa Ashington stepped forward and looked down at the girl who lay there, then she drew Berris forward.

The two girls stared at one another. For Berris it seemed as though she were looking into a slightly distorted looking glass. The other girl's face, with its unusual bone structure and slanting eyes, was exactly like her own. The delicate skin was beginning to blemish with the pox, but the amber eyes and rich chestnut hair was exactly like her own. Only the haughty, petulant expression was different.

That expression was changing, however, as Lora Ashington looked at her visitor, into a look of contempt. The girl was very like herself, but she was brash and no doubt cheap. She was, after all, only a third-rate actress. Lora's lip curled as she lay back on the pillows.

'Why have you brought her here, Aunt?' she drawled.

'She has a lot to learn in two days,' said Mrs Ashington. 'She can only learn from you, Lora. She must remain with you and you can teach her.'

'In two days! She is hardly a silk purse, Aunt Louisa.'

'That is quite enough, Lora. You know how important the betrothal party is to you ... to *all* of us. I would not instigate such a charade if it were not necessary. I will remain with both of you. Now, Berris, you will repeat everything which Lora says. You will have to match her voice exactly.'

Berris had been completely ignorant of the fact that her accent and mannerisms were considered inferior by the upper echelons of society. It came as a shock to learn that she was such a low class of person, but Mrs Ashington left her in no doubt as to her status as she held up her hands in horror, and asked her to repeat certain words over and over again, altering the vowel sounds so that the words sounded languid and affected in Berris's ears.

She also had to learn how to dispense tea from a silver teapot, and drink it gracefully from the finest of china cups. The teapot had a small hole near the top of the handle, and into this boiling water must be poured in order to keep the tea hot. The gap between the double layer of silver from which the teapot had been made was very narrow and Berris found this task, alone, irksome. She did not care for the insipid liquid. She was more used to drinking weak ale from a pewter mug.

Lora was vastly entertained as she watched this training programme, and sometimes her eyes showed a distinct lack of ease and even revulsion when Berris, in her fatigue, lost all traces of a proper accent and complained that she could do no more.

When Mrs Ashington was called away to receive a distinguished visitor, Berris leaned back in her chair and rubbed a weary hand over her face.

'It is too much,' she said. 'There isn't enough time.'

'You poor creature. I am very glad that Papa kept me and Mama took you when she ran away with Mr Meredith,' Lora remarked, languidly. 'I am appalled by what I might have become.'

Berris had closed her eyes, but as the words began to sink into her mind, she sat up and stared at Lora.

'What did you say?' she asked, '... that ... that Papa kept you and Mama ... *Mama* took ... took me? I ... I do not understand. What does this mean?'

Lora's hand had gone to her mouth.

'I ... Forget what I have said,' she told Berris, sharply. 'I was merely teasing you.'

The warm colour had crept into her cheeks and Berris looked at her closely.

'No, you spoke the truth,' she said, flatly, 'and I want to hear more.'

'There is nothing to tell. I thought you knew ...'

Again Lora's hand flew to her mouth.

'There *is* something to tell,' said Berris swiftly, 'and I will hear it, *all* of it, or ... or I shall destroy your betrothal party for you. I wouldn't not hesitate.'

'No, you would not,' said Lora, her eyes contemptuous again. 'You could easily destroy it by being yourself! You are just a common actress.'

Berris had slowly risen to her feet, her eyes blazing with amber lights.

'And *your* sister ... your *twin* sister,' she said in a ringing voice, her cheeks now scarlet as the implications of Lora's remarks began to penetrate. 'I am not so stupid that I cannot see the truth of our relationship. I always knew that Brendan Meredith was not my father, and that my mother had been married before. She must have been married to ...'

'She was married to our father, Stephen Ashington,' said Lora. 'Now that you have fathomed so much, you will hear it all. She loved the theatre and when she went with Father to London, he took her to see a play at Drury Lane, and

41

... and Mr Meredith performed in the play. Mama found excuses to remain in London, and somehow she contrived to meet Mr Meredith. She became completely fascinated by him, and decided to leave Papa to go to Mr Meredith, even though she had twin daughters. You and me. She took you and Papa kept me. How lucky I was! Now I am Lora Ashington of Birkridge, and you are a theatre player.'

Berris felt that the blood had drained completely from her face, as though her whole body was weak with sickness. There was a strange heavy feeling in the pit of her stomach and she had to fight against faintness.

'So I am as well-born as you,' she whispered. 'I, also, was born a ... a lady.'

Lora's laughter was almost wild.

'You are too ruined, ever to be a lady,' she choked. 'You can only *act* a lady, and that very badly.'

'Tell me more about this man you are going to marry,' Berris commanded, ignoring the jibes. Her eyes had narrowed into slits. 'Are you in love with him? Does he love you?'

'Love!' cried Lora. 'How little you know, Mistress *Meredith.*' She emphasized the name. 'He is Sir Ninian Lennox. My father arranged the match when I was twelve years old. Sir Ninian's aunt is

Lady Truscott of Massingham who was godmother to Sarah, our mother. She is a very rich woman and she will make Ninian her heir, if he marries Sarah's daughter.'

'But you would not marry for such a reason if you did not love one another!' cried Berris.

For a moment Lora's face crumpled.

'Do *you* have a lover?' she asked, huskily, 'some young man who is a delight to you?'

Berris's cheeks grew warm.

'Only Sebastian, son to Mistress Grey, Brendan Meredith's second wife. She still wishes to be called Mistress Grey because she is an actress.'

'And you would be happy with him?'

'Perhaps.'

'Then you are better off than I. You are not a pawn in the marriage game. No, forget I said that,' said Lora with her quick change of mood. 'Lady Truscott will settle money on me when I marry Sir Ninian and Birkridge needs the money. My Uncle Mark has gambled away most of his fortune. All gentlemen like to gamble but he does so to excess.'

'And does Sir Ninian also need the money?'

Lora looked reflective. 'I do not know. He is a devil and he frightens me. He tried to cry off last time he travelled north from London and came to visit

43

Birkridge. That is why Uncle Mark is so set on the betrothal. Lady Truscott, also. She was most fond of our mother and looked upon her as a daughter. Ssh! Here comes Aunt Louisa ...'

Mrs Ashington came hurrying back into the room, complaining loudly about her recent visitor. Berris was sitting upright in her chair. Her amber eyes were almost feverishly bright. Something rather strange was happening to her. Mrs Ashington had almost completely destroyed Berris's confidence in herself by the horror she had shown at her mannerisms, but now that confidence was returning tenfold. She was not a cheap actress to be sneered at by this haughty woman. She was every bit as well-born as Lora. They were twins. They were as one person, separated only by a short time at birth, not by a whole social stratum.

'Now let me see,' Mrs Ashington said. 'I think you had better have a bad cold which prevents you from using your voice. Your movements, at least, are graceful enough, and you can be conducted home before you have to partake of refreshment.'

'I think not, Mrs Ashington. Or perhaps I ought to call you "Aunt Louisa", as Lora does?'

Mrs Ashington's face turned bright puce, then slowly paled.

'You told her!' she said, accusingly, to Lora. 'I specifically instructed you to say nothing.'

'I forgot,' said Lora, sulkily.

'In any case, it means nothing,' she went on. 'You were no longer a member of the Ashington family from the moment Sarah took up residence with Mr Meredith, and took you with her. You belong to him now.'

'I belong to myself,' said Berris, 'and if I was born Berris Ashington, why then I am *still* Berris Ashington.'

'Do not think you can insinuate yourself back into Birkridge. I have already made this very clear to Mr Meredith.'

'My thoughts are my own,' said Berris, 'but you need not be afraid, *Aunt* Louisa. I would not seek shelter under your roof. Mr Meredith may be a *common* actor ... is that the expression? Why, yes, a *common* actor in your eyes, but he has treated me with kindness, and he made my mother happy. He is capable of love and that is worth more than social standing. I will take Lora's place, and I shall do it well, now that I know we are akin. Afterwards I shall live my own life. I shall be *myself.*'

The dull red colour had crept into Louisa Ashington's cheeks and she longed to slap the cheek of the girl whose eyes challenged her so defiantly. How dare she, the little nobody!

Then slowly her anger left her and she looked at Berris with something like relief and not a little awe. It was uncanny. The girl had suddenly become Lora, who could also be imperious when it suited her. When she had agreed to marry Sir Ninian, there had been just such an expression on Lora's face. They were remarkably alike and Berris would make a perfect stand-in for her sister.

It was essential to formalize the engagement and hurry on the wedding. The financial situation of Birkridge was not good, and soon it would be desperate. Sir Ninian had proved elusive in the marriage market and he might well weigh his freedom against the Truscott money. Lora would be lucky if she saw much of him after they were married. He had kept many mistresses in London and rumour had it that he might have married an Italian contessa if the lady and her husband had not been Catholic.

'After tomorrow you may do as you please,' she said, indifferently. 'We must be thankful that you are now a little more ladylike in your behaviour, whatever the reason. I think you should rest, Lora my dear. Your face is really quite blemished now with pox.'

CHAPTER FIVE

The following evening was one of great enchantment, mingled with apprehension, for Berris. For most of the afternoon a bevy of servants had worked hard, ironing and crimping the flounces of her gown, and her many petticoats whilst she was bathed, soaped, rinsed with rosewater, dried, perfumed and her hair combed into great curls which were twisted round fat pads, then allowed to hang around her shoulders as ringlets.

Lora watched sulkily. Her chicken pox was now at its height, the pustules blemishing the soft skin of her face and neck. There was little disappointment in her, however, that she would not see Sir Ninian. Her sulks were only because she was missing the ball.

Aunt Louisa had assured Berris that Lora and Sir Ninian were barely acquainted and she need not worry on that account, but Lora knew this was not so. He was a strange man and he had made opportunities for them to be alone in order that they should try to know one another a little better. Lora had found him frightening in his perception. He appeared to read not only your mind, but your very soul.

She lay back on her pillows and looked at her twin sister. How beautiful she was! Was she, Lora, as beautiful when she was well-gowned for a special occasion? But of course she was. They were as alike as two peas, and both of them favoured their maternal grandmother, who had been Lady Truscott's great friend.

Berris came to stand beside the bed.

'I am sorry you are ill,' she said with warm sympathy. 'It must be disappointing to you that you cannot attend your own betrothal party.'

'I am hardly presentable,' said Lora.

'I could give you a lotion to cool the spots, if you so wish. It helped Mistress Grey when she was similarly affected and your maid could very quickly make up the recipe.'

'It will be better soon,' Lora said indifferently. 'I had no engagements other than this evening.'

Suddenly she caught at Berris's hand.

'I had better warn you, sister. Sir Ninian is not a man to be trifled with. If he finds out that he has been deceived, his rage could be terrible. I cannot explain to Aunt Louisa because she thinks I do not know him. But I do! He would kill us both if ... if he thought we were trying to make a fool of him. Be careful. Try not to be alone with him ...'

'Ah, so you are ready to leave, Berris,' said Mrs Ashington, loudly, as she sailed into the room. She wore grey satin and many diamonds which Berris now knew to be paste replicas. 'We will not be gone long, Lora, my dear. It grieves me that you are confined to bed in this fashion, but we must do our best to see that no damage is done. I will plead a cold and fatigue for Berris, after the formalities are over. The guests will enjoy everything without her. The Massingham tables are always well-laden at these functions and there are those ill-mannered enough to be principally concerned with the food. Try to rest until we return.'

'I will rest, Aunt Louisa,' said Lora, wearily, but her eyes looked fevered, and she reached out towards Berris.

'Be careful,' she whispered again.

'Rest easy. I will take every care.'

Berris smiled at her, and on impulse bent down to kiss her cheek. In different circumstances, it would have been great happiness to her to have a twin sister, but she saw Lora recoil a little, and quickly straightened, fighting down her hurt.

'I am ready to leave,' she said, quickly.

Massingham Hall was the nearest estate to Birkridge, but the house dated back to Queen Anne times and the land was better tended. The long drive, after passing through the huge wrought-iron gates, wound through parkland which had grown beautiful through constant attention, each tree and shrub trained and cared for to perfection.

The great hall was ablaze with the lights of many candles and Mrs Ashington had timed their arrival so that they were just a little later than expected, but early enough for them to receive the other guests along with Sir Ninian Lennox.

Lady Truscott had planned to sit beside her nephew, but her health had deteriorated over the past few days, and she had been obliged to keep to her own room. Her door would be left wide open so that she could hear the festivities, and after the formal betrothal, she would receive her nephew and Lora in her bedroom.

All this Berris learned within a few minutes of her arrival. Mrs Ashington did not intend that she should be allowed to spend very much time with Sir Ninian, and had primed Berris well as to how to greet her affianced husband, smiling and setting him a fine curtsey. The betrothal ring, the great Lennox diamond, had already been made to fit Lora's slender finger.

But as they entered the great house, Berris felt as though she had walked into a dream, and at any moment Sebastian would peep from behind one of the great pillars and start to pull the pins out of her hair. She was glad that the elegant style forced her to hold her head high, however, since it reminded her constantly that she was playing a part. But it was one thing to agree to play this charade, and to make plans in the comparative safety of Birkridge, and quite another to walk into this magnificent house, and to pretend to be another girl even if it *was* her twin sister. Berris knew a quick moment of such terror as she had never before experienced, and but for the Ashingtons following closely behind, she might have run, like Cinderella, from the ball.

Suddenly she was aware of a tall man walking forward with easy, swinging strides to greet their party. Fervently, she hoped that Sir Ninian Lennox would not wonder at the shock on her face when she first caught sight of him. Lora had not prepared her for such a handsome, polished man. She had never seen anyone so well-groomed and sophisticated; a man who wore an air of quiet expectation that his slightest wish would be gratified immediately. He would only need to snap his fingers, and servants would rush to do his bidding.

He was very tall and slender, and wore

his own black hair neatly queued. His mulberry velvet with silver buttons fitted him to perfection, but his eyes were the coldest she had ever seen. Sir Ninian looked as though he had lived through a thousand such assemblies as were gathered here this evening, and that he had long ago decided that they were a trial to be borne with all the fortitude at his command.

He had glanced at Berris briefly and acknowledged her greeting, holding out a slender hand to clasp her own. With a courtly bow he carried her fingers to his lips, then apparently reminded himself that this woman was going to be his wife, because he looked at her more attentively, and swept her another bow.

The girl was more beautiful than Sir Ninian remembered. The warm glow of candlelight lit up her dark hair which shone like polished chestnuts, and her strange slanting amber-coloured eyes had a new quality which intrigued him. The child had become a woman. She had grown tall, slender, and well-formed, but the difference lay in the carriage of her head and the air of dignity and reserve which had been lacking when he last saw her. Then she had been a simpering, affected child, but this young woman was worthy of more attention.

'The guests are arriving, Sir Ninian,'

said Mrs Ashington, clearly, noticing his close scrutiny with misgivings. 'You had better stand beside me, Mr Ashington, and I will stand just a step behind Lora. It is her night, and Sir Ninian's.'

Berris's heart beat to suffocation point and she could feel perspiration clinging to the small of her back. She had feared that she might feel cold in Lora's lovely creamy satin gown embroidered with gold buttercups, but the heat from the huge log fires and the candelabra, combined with her own body heat, made her feel faint from lack of air. Small theatres could be stuffy and airless, but she always knew how long a performance would last and how soon she would belong to herself once more. She had no such guidance this evening.

She knew that the betrothal ceremony would be performed after all the guests had arrived, and that the food already piled on the great long tables would be consumed with lack of ceremony. Aunt Louisa had complained that honoured guests often forgot their manners at such a spree, especially if gaming tables had not been set out, and a betrothal ceremony was not considered a suitable occasion for gaming.

Berris need not have worried about her voice and accent. As the crowds arrived and a small four-piece orchestra began to play, the noise grew louder and louder. She made one or two small errors when she smiled warmly at guests, as though they were old friends, only to learn that they were Massingham acquaintances and strangers to the Ashingtons. Others looked curious at her lack of recognition, teasing her on her grand manner now that she had grown up, and her alarm caused the discomfort from her body heat to become even more acute. How soon would it all end!

She might have enjoyed part of the evening had not Sir Ninian remained so close to her. She managed to smile at him now and again, and her cheeks warmed as she met his lazy, speculative scrutiny, and his own answering smile. His eyes devoured her, raking her from head to foot so that she blushed as she strove to remain calm.

Aunt Louisa was constantly behind her whispering to her so that she would avoid making too horrendous a gaffe and she was thankful that she had not been obliged to hold a cup of tea as well. It was wine which flowed freely and Berris, her arm clasped in Sir Ninian's long delicate fingers, began to mingle with their guests, laughing and chattering, responding to good-humoured chaff.

Soon Mr Mark Ashington called for everyone's attention, and loudly pronounced the betrothal of his dear niece, Lora Ashington, to Sir Ninian Andrew Lennox. The betrothal ring stuck on Berris's finger and for an awful moment her widened amber eyes met the black opaque gaze of Sir Ninian. Her fingers must be slightly larger than Lora's! It was something which had been completely overlooked!

'Sir, my hands sweat a little ... perspire ...' she said nervously, and once again he took her hand and almost rammed the great diamond over the knuckle so that she winced slightly. Again he raised her hand to his lips, his eyes boring into her own.

Cheers and well-wishes rang out as glasses were raised. Sir Ninian picked up his own glass.

'To my affianced bride, Mistress Lora Ashington,' he called, and drank the contents at a gulp. Again his eyes swept over her.

'Come, my dear,' he said. 'Lady Truscott, my Aunt Elizabeth waits to offer her very good wishes. We will visit her in her bedroom now.'

She ran a tongue over her dry lips, then slowly walked beside Sir Ninian towards the great sweeping staircase. Mrs Ashington would have fallen into step behind, but Sir

Ninian merely turned with a raised eyebrow so that she fell back.

For the first time Berris was completely on her own, with this tall arrogant stranger.

CHAPTER SIX

Berris had never seen anyone so old and so near to death as the frail, feeble woman who lay on the bed. Her own mother had died of a severe illness which had only lasted for a few days, and she had seemed young and vibrant up until the moment of her death. But Lady Truscott had skin like parchment and a thin scattering of hair underneath her bed cap which had slipped sideways. Only her black eyes, so like Sir Ninian's, were alive and snapping with excitement.

'Come, let me see you, child,' she croaked as Sir Ninian conducted Berris into the bedroom. 'You are only a little like Sarah now that you have grown up, but you are very like Caroline, your grandmother, and Sarah's mother. She was my friend, my great friend. She would be proud to see her grand-daughter bride to my nephew, Ninian. Our families are united at last ...'

The words began to come out in laboured gasps and Ninian stepped forward.

'Be easy, Aunt Elizabeth,' he said, gently.

'There is plenty of time for you to talk. You need not hurry. Miss Lora and I will not leave you until you wish us gone and ask to rest.'

Her black eyes gleamed as they looked into his own.

'I am dying, Ninian,' she said, painfully. 'There is not such time left ...'

'Nonsense, Aunt Elizabeth. If you rest now, you will regain your strength.'

Lady Truscott's lips firmed.

'Enough, Ninian. There is no need to humour an old woman. Come here, child.'

She beckoned with a bony finger and, her knees trembling, Berris walked over to the bed, then knelt down so that the claw-like hands could caress her face.

'You will be a fine bride for Ninian, dear child,' she whispered, then darted a powerful look at her nephew. 'I have decided to see you both wed before I die, so I have asked that a priest should be brought here, tonight, and he will perform the ceremony ...'

Again her voice faded as she gasped for breath, and slowly Berris rose to her feet, her heart hammering wildly with fright. Had she mistaken the whispered words? Surely Lady Truscott could not mean the marriage to be performed this very evening.

All colour drained from her face as she looked at Sir Ninian, seeing that he also viewed the prospect with horror, though she was unaware that her own revulsion had shaken and disturbed him. Why should the Ashington girl be so ill against the match when it was the Ashingtons who so much desired to support Lady Truscott in joining the two families? Yet the girl obviously had no liking for the match, judging by the naked look of shock and dismay on her face. He had never seen such pallor, she was completely ashen-faced and her hands were shaking.

'But ... but I have no wedding gown, ma'am,' she protested. 'My Aunt will be against such haste.'

Sir Ninian's lip curled. So it was all a matter of fripperies! She was like all other young females, only concerned with her appearance and the niceties. Her revulsion was against the lack of ceremony in such a hasty wedding, and her fear was for her aunt's displeasure.

'Your gown is fine enough for any wedding,' said Lady Truscott. She motioned to a hovering serving woman. 'Desire Mrs Ashington to come to me.'

'Yes, my lady.'

Once again the old woman turned to the girl.

'You will wear my wedding veil, Lora. I

59

have already arranged everything. I know, in my heart, that there is no time for me to prepare for another occasion like the one I have arranged this evening. It will have to serve as your wedding celebration as well as your betrothal. The priest will say the words over you both. I have sent for your aunt, my dear. She will help you to prepare.'

Once again her voice faded and Berris looked round wildly, wondering how she could escape. The door opened and Louisa Ashington, closely followed by Mark, walked into the room. Their faces too were ashen in the pale candlelight and Berris knew that they believed their charade had been discovered, and all was lost to them. Aunt Louisa's eyes were diamond-bright with accusation as she flashed Berris a look of anger and contempt. What had the girl said that her true identity had been so immediately exposed?

She was about to plead her cause when the old woman spoke again, her voice now amazingly strong.

'I desire that my nephew and Miss Ashington be married straight away,' she said. 'This is my wish because I feel that my death is near. I wish to see them wed before I die. A priest will perform the ceremony in my bedchamber. Later the assembled guests can celebrate the wedding.'

Colour rushed back into Mrs Ashington's cheeks, then drained away, leaving her as sick and shaken as Berris. She looked at the girl whose anguished eyes entreated her to make everything clear, but already Mark Ashington was stepping forward.

'I shall be glad to witness the marriage, Lady Truscott,' he said in his high affected voice. 'It is also my wish to unite our two families.'

Mrs Ashington moved towards Berris and made a pretence of kissing her cheek.

'Go through with it,' she whispered. 'We can arrange everything later.'

Berris made no reply but her look of contempt caused Mrs Ashington to drop her gaze, then Berris turned to look at Sir Ninian who stood, stiff and unyielding, beside her.

'You do not care for such haste, Miss Lora,' he muttered. 'That is not difficult to see, yet you have not always been so reluctant.'

'I dislike force, sir,' she said. 'I like to choose my own time.'

'As I do,' he returned, swiftly. 'I have considered the matter and one time is as good as another for a match such as ours. Aunt Elizabeth desires that the knot be tied now. I beg leave to go and see to the arrangements, and I would fain see a smile upon your face. This is an occasion for rejoicing. I may remind you that your family had been very busy in bringing this about.'

His eyes glittered like black ice as he turned from her and bent over the old lady on the bed.

'I shall go and find the priest, Aunt Elizabeth,' he said, formally. 'We will give my bride a short time to prepare, then everything will be as you wish. I will marry Miss Ashington so that you see the ring on her finger this night.'

A maidservant had arrived bearing the beautiful lace bridal veil which had been worn both by Lady Truscott and her sister-in-law, Lady Lennox. Now it was to be worn by the new Lady Lennox.

Mrs Ashington claimed the privilege of robing her niece, and they were conducted to a nearby bedroom which was already aglow with candlelight and had a warm fire burning in the grate. Giggling maidservants rushed about, preparing the bedroom and, with dawning comprehension, Berris realized that they had entered the bridal chamber. Cold sickness gripped her stomach and she turned to Mrs Ashington as soon as they were alone.

'I cannot go through with it, ma'am. Surely you must see that I cannot! We must tell Sir Ninian ...'

'Are you mad, girl?'

Louisa Ashington had already received a warning nod from her husband and now she grasped Berris's arm.

'What do you think would happen if you confessed to this farce? I tell you, for everyone's sake and more especially for the sake of your own skin, you *must* go through with it. Sir Ninian Lennox is no milksop. He would not hesitate to use a whip on you.'

Berris put a hand to her mouth.

'But there will be no time to exchange me before ... before morning.'

Her cheeks flushed with colour as she looked at the bed, and Mrs Ashington's eyes grew remote.

'I need hardly remind you that you are an actress, Miss Meredith. You have no reputation to lose. It will be a simple matter for you to ask to remain at Massingham should Sir Ninian wish to return to London, and for you to visit your relatives at Birkridge. You will come to Birkridge and Lora will return here to Massingham.'

'But *she* will not be wife to Sir Ninian. *I* will be his wife.'

'You will *not* be his wife. Even now Sir Ninian is drawing up marriage papers and Lora's name will be put on the papers.

63

You will sign anything required with Lora's signature.'

Her eyes suddenly widened with dismay.

'Can it be that you cannot read and write?'

Berris's lip curled. 'You certainly do not know Mr Meredith,' she said. 'He has taught me my letters and in addition I have been made to study the plays by William Shakespeare and the history of World Theatre.'

'Oh, the theatre!' said Mrs Ashington, witheringly. 'Hardly an education! It is well that you can write your name, however. You will sign everything with Lora's name and you will be, in fact, a substitute bride for her, or a stand-in bride if that is the theatrical term. I tell you, it is working out better than I thought. Lennox has always been slippery as an eel, and Mark suspected him of crying off should Lady Truscott die before the match could be made.

'He has estates in Scotland, as well as the house in London, so he is wealthy in his own right and does not need her money. It would go to a distant Truscott cousin if she does not make Lennox her heir, and he is practical enough not to wish it to slip through his fingers.

'He might not be so very well feathered, though, because he has been known to do diplomatic service and to undertake art commissions, but one cannot ever get to the bottom of Lennox's affairs. He will be unfaithful to Lora. She understands that. But he must marry some time and an Ashington is good enough, even for a Lennox.'

'Then why does he want to cry off?' asked Berris as the gossamer-soft wedding veil was pinned to her hair.

'He enjoys his freedom, like all men. Perhaps he enjoys his even more than most. He travels abroad and no doubt enjoys the women of foreign countries as well. Stand still, child! There! Lady Truscott is quite right. That cream silk brocade gown with embroidered buttercups is as fine as any wedding gown. The veil is perfect for you. You are Lora to the life. I declare that even your voice is changing.'

Berris said nothing. She had a quick ear along with her acting ability so that she was inclined to be a chameleon, and could adapt quite quickly to her surroundings. But that did not include the marriage bed. Would she be expected to share such an experience with the hard-eyed stranger, the man who enjoyed many women, even women from foreign countries?

But there was no time for further speculation. A young maidservant had entered the room, bobbing a curtsey, and

65

telling them that everything was now ready in Lady Truscott's bedroom. The priest had been found and was waiting along with the bridegroom.

'We will come straight away,' said Lady Ashington, briskly. 'Come along, my dear Lora.'

There was an air of excitement throughout Massingham. Sir Ninian had informed the assembled guests that they were now about to attend a wedding, and after the initial surprise, there was a great deal of rejoicing and well-wishing for the young people.

They mounted the stairs and assembled in the corridors outside Lady Truscott's bedroom. Berris's face was very pale as she walked on her uncle's arm into the room where the priest waited to perform the ceremony.

Sir Ninian had changed his coat for a handsome black velvet with diamonds flashing in the buttons, and now he stood, tall and straight, waiting for his bride.

Berris could remember little about the ceremony other than that it was Miss Lora Ashington who married Sir Ninian Andrew Lennox. Later, at a small table, she had many papers to sign, one or two of which would make her ... Lora ... a rich woman and another which freed Birkridge of crippling debts. Wryly she wondered how long it would stay free with the fever of gambling in Mark Ashington's blood.

Old Lady Truscott held out her arms and again Berris knelt in front of the bed and received her blessing. Sir Ninian knelt at the other side of the bed and the old lady joined their hands, and asked God to bless their union with many children.

Berris's heart froze, then hammered wildly. She could not ... *must* not have a child! She thought about the marriage bed and wanted to tear off the veil and rush out of Massingham to find Brendan Meredith. Even the thought of the hated travelling wagon was like a sanctuary.

Her hands had fluttered in Sir Ninian's grasp and she felt his fingers closing like steel upon her own. Should she confess everything when they were alone? But no! Lora, as well as Mrs Ashington, had warned her that he was not a man who could be made to look foolish, and he would take a very jaundiced view of this deception. She could imagine his rage would be terrible and she could feel those steel-like fingers closing about her throat.

Berris almost fainted with nerves and the old lady reached out to stroke the dark curls which fell from under the bridal veil. The girl's face clearly showed the strain of the past few hours.

'The child is tired,' she said. 'It has been

a long exciting day for her, as it has been for all of us. Be kind to her, Lennox. She is young.

'Now all has been done that I wish to be done, and I can rest easy. If God sees fit to summon his servant to eternal life, then I shall make the journey happily. Massingham is secure. I have kept faith with my dearest Caroline and Sarah.'

Berris got to her feet as the old lady's voice croaked into silence and her eyes closed. Her heart gave a great bound. Was Lady Truscott dead now that she had achieved her heart's desire? And what about her own eternal life? Would she not be punished for deceiving the old lady in this, her last dying wish?

'Is ... is she ...?' she began, trembling in every limb. This had been the most frightening day of her life and she had no courage left.

'No, she is only asleep,' said Sir Ninian. 'She will live to be a hundred, the old schemer! If the good Lord has any sense, he will not bid her to His Kingdom until he has no choice but to scrape her up.'

'Sir!'

Berris was scandalized, but a mixture of relief and amusement caused her to smile and Sir Ninian's hand gripped her arm.

'That's better,' he said. 'Now you look more like a bride and less like a Tragedy

Queen in some cheap theatrical play.'

She recoiled as though he had struck her. How could she forget that she *was* just an actress, playing a part?

'I declare you are a creature of moods,' he said, intrigued. 'We will join the guests to receive their congratulations, then you will retire, Lady Lennox. I think you have earned your rest.'

Lady Lennox! She had signed some of the papers as Lady Lennox, but it had meant nothing. Now, hearing the name on Sir Ninian's lips, she had a sense of unreality once more. Just for a little while she could be a titled woman in real life. Other actresses had married men of title and distinction. Not all actresses were considered cheap and common, as Mrs Ashington had impressed upon her. Even when she rejoined the Meredith Players, she would always remember that for a little while she had been a true, well-born lady, with maidservants to attend to her every need ...

Sir Ninian held her hand lightly as they walked down the length of the Great Hall, acknowledging the good wishes of the assembled guests, every face that of a stranger to Berris, even though many were Lora's friends. Already she had forgotten those who had made themselves known to her and teased her a little, and she hoped that her smiles to the company in general would suffice. Again glasses were raised to toast the bride and bridegroom and the noise became deafening once more as the guests began to join in the dancing.

Soon she was being conducted back up the great broad staircase of polished black oak, and once again she entered the bridal chamber where the wedding veil was removed, and two fresh-faced maids unhooked her lovely brocade gown, and helped her out of her petticoats and nether garments. There had only been time for a brief farewell to her aunt and uncle, and a whispered word that all would be well in a day or two.

From somewhere a fine cambric gown, lace-trimmed, had been found for her to wear. It was too large and voluminous and once again the maids stifled their giggles, then looked at Berris respectfully, aware that they were robing the new Lady Lennox. She said nothing, and allowed them to remove the pins and pads from her hair, and to comb out her shining curls.

Brendan Meredith had always insisted that she look after her hair, since the wearing of wigs could be harmful, and she had washed and brushed it regularly. Now, with Joan Masters's added attention, it fell in shining folds about her shoulders, and the maids were full of admiration.

'Oh, my lady, your hair is beautiful,' the taller maid said, shyly, brushing out the soft waves.

My lady! Berris's mouth felt dry when she remembered Lora. It was Lora who was now a titled woman.

'That will do,' she commanded, crisply. 'I wish to rest. It has been a long day.'

The maids recognized the note of authority and were no longer inclined to linger. They helped Berris into the great soft bed with the crisp linen sheets well-warmed by the use of warming pans, then tidied away her clothes. Day clothes were being sent from Birkridge as soon as Mrs Ashington returned home.

Some of the candles were snuffed, but a log from the fire fell sharply, sending up a shower of sparks and new bright flames which cast great giant shadows on to the ceiling.

Berris waited in fear and trembling, then the bedroom door opened and Sir Ninian Lennox came quietly into the room. He closed the door and turned to stare at the girl on the bed, her face now white as paper and her eyes glowing orbs of liquid amber.

Slowly and deliberately he began to remove his clothing, garment by garment, until he stood, naked and unashamed, in the red glow of the firelight. Berris wanted to hide her eyes, but she could not. She had never seen a man completely naked before, even though Sebastian had almost exposed his more private parts in his efforts to love her. Now she saw that this man, who was a stranger to her, yet who might have been closer to her than anyone in this life had she not been a substitute bride, was beautiful in his powerful body.

If only he were her true husband, there could be ecstasy and excitement in giving herself into his keeping. There could be peace and love in her heart, that she belonged to someone so fine, so strongly masculine.

But she dared not allow herself to accept him. He did not belong to her. She had a great terror that he would take her and leave his child within her. What would happen to her then? How could she ever marry another man, even Sebastian, if she carried another man's child? How could she continue to earn her keep with the Meredith Players if she became great with child, and what about the child? It would be a bastard child and would be marked by that shame for the rest of its life.

Sir Ninian was snuffing the candles, then there was only silence in the room, and the warm rich glow of the firelight as he walked over to the bed and climbed in beside her.

'Well, my lady?' he whispered. 'Are you prepared to do your duty by your husband? I recollect that your eyes have not always been so forbidding. Why so coy now that the knot is tied?'

'I ... I am afraid, sir,' she muttered, shivering to his touch.

He was removing the nightgown and Berris had a vision of the maids giggling as they slipped it over her head. It was easy to understand their amusement now as Sir Ninian threw the garment to the foot of the bed.

'We have no need of such clothing to keep our bodies warm,' he said, practically. 'I will provide all the warmth you need, my dear wife.'

He leaned over and claimed her lips with his own, and Berris's heart hammered loudly enough for her to hear. She had not known that a man's lips could be so strong, yet so soft. He seemed to draw all resistance out of her body, so that she became acquiescent in his arms. She no longer belonged to herself. She was part of this strong man who had begun to explore her body with light, sensitive probing fingers, so different from Sebastian's clumsy advances, as he caressed her young breasts and gently kissed her white throat. She could not

73

believe that he was so gentle and she relaxed against him.

Then swiftly his probing fingers rippled down her body to her thighs, pressing her legs apart.

'You know what a wedding night means,' he said, very softly. 'You are no ignorant child, my dear Lora. Why do I feel that you are now resisting me?'

'I ... I do not want to bear a child!' she gasped. 'I ... I am too young as yet to be mother to a child.'

The soft gentle fingers stopped probing for a moment and his laughter turned harsh in her ears.

'That is more like it,' he said, roughly. 'Always the vain little bantam. Thinking about her figure and spoiling her pretty looks, and her pretty clothes. She must not swell with child until she has had her fill of amusement and entertainment. She is horrified, not because marriage is sprung upon her, but only because it might result in planting a child in her body. That was the true reason why you shrank from the wedding ceremony, was it not? I knew there was something behind that white face and that fluttering heart.'

Berris lay shivering. His tone had completely changed and she could hear contempt in every word. His fingers, which had been so gentle and loving,

74

suddenly became talons as they dug into her soft flesh.

She gasped again, even as her body leapt with the intensity of her feelings as he joined his body to hers, and for the first time she knew what it was to be possessed by a man, and to suffer pain which was at once tortuous and exquisite. She found herself clinging to Ninian, even after he was spent, and as he rolled away from her, his hand brushed his forehead in perplexity.

'What are you that you can become two women?' he asked, roughly. 'Are you a witch? You're selfish and cold, yet you can become a warm, passionate woman in a trice. You're a child, primping and simpering in a new dress, then a woman who could love a man more than she loves herself. You refuse my children, yet you could be a fine, loving mother. What are you, Lora? Are you my wife?'

'Your wife,' she repeated in a whisper.

She felt that her body had been transported into a strange new world. He pulled her into his arms and once again she felt his lips on hers so that she forgot about everything else other than that they were man and woman, and belonged together.

'Are you in pain, little wife?' he asked, tenderly. 'Did I hurt you? I was impatient to possess you because you had driven me to desire you.'

'It is nothing,' she whispered.

She forgot that she was Lora and that she would lose him in another day. She forgot that she did not want a child who might face a life of suffering because she desired this man. He was like no one she had ever known and the ecstasy of sharing her body so closely with another human being was unbelievably wonderful. She would never be lonely again with him by her side. She could lose herself in the love of such a man.

Once again she was drawn close to him and once again she felt him taking possession of her body, and her passion rose as great as his own and joined both of them in a great wave of shared excitement. Her arms were round his neck, and his hands held the silken waves of her hair.

'By God, you *are* a witch!' he said. 'By God the bargain is good, better than I ever dreamed. I could love you, little Lora, better than any woman. I have found me a true woman this night.'

Slowly she came out of her dream world and realized that it had been only a dream. Slowly the difficult tears began to form in her eyes and to wash down her cheeks. The past few days had been such a mixture of dreams and nightmares that her emotions

76

had completely drained all resistance, all strength.

'No,' she whispered. 'It has all been just a dream, a dream.'

He pulled away from her.

'What now? Tears? She weeps because she has become a wife! Love! Passion! Tears! It is too much for me this one night. Go to sleep, wife. We will both feel better in the morning.'

He turned over and minutes later his slow gentle breathing told Berris that he was asleep. She got out of bed and recovered the cambric nightgown, putting it on once more. She had no wish to catch any maidservant giggling in the morning, even though the bed linen told its own tale.

Her cheeks grew warm with embarrassment when she thought how she had behaved with Ninian, at the height of her passion, and not a little dismay when she remembered that she was supposed to be Lora, not Berris. Lora would not have behaved with such abandon. Lora would have remembered that she was a lady. She had puzzled Ninian, and little wonder. It was so easy to forget.

She crawled back into bed and lay for a long time, thinking deeply. She was neither wife nor maid. What was to become of her when she changed places with Lora? She would never be the same girl she had been. Whatever happened she would always hear Ninian's tender words in her ears, and her heart would be stirred with love for him. Sighing, she gave herself up to sleep.

CHAPTER SEVEN

Berris was alone when she woke next morning. A young maidservant had unlatched the window shutters whilst another stood shyly by her bedside with a tray of breakfast food.

Slowly she pulled herself up on the pillows, a hand pushing her tangled hair out of her eyes. She had slept very deeply and for a moment she forgot that she was Lora and had just been married at Massingham.

' 'Struth, but I still dream,' she said in her most theatrical voice, and both maidservants giggled unashamedly.

'Oh, my lady, you *are* a mimic,' said the girl with the tray. 'Sir Ninian has gone out riding. He said to tell you. And when your riding habit comes from Birkridge with your other garments, he would like you to join him at the stables.'

'My ... my riding habit?' Berris repeated rather faintly. Memory returned full-fold and her cheeks were stained with colour as she realized her mistake. She was thankful that Ninian had been out of the room.

But ... riding habit. She could not even

sit a horse, and yet no doubt Lora had been riding since childhood. Ninian was sure to suspect that something was wrong if she went to the stables then refused to ride with him.

Swallowing her nerves, Berris thanked the maidservant for the message. She learned with a mixture of relief and frustration that her gowns had not yet arrived. She hated being confined to bed, though it was pleasant to eat a hearty breakfast of kippers, slices of beef and eggs. She had an excellent appetite and the food at Massingham was so much more delicious than the fare she was normally obliged to eat in their cheap theatrical lodgings.

She had barely eaten the last mouthful when the servants arrived once again, followed by a red-faced man bearing a trunk full of clothing. No doubt Mrs Ashington had sent most of Lora's clothing, Berris decided, in preparation for her move to Massingham.

'I will hang these garments away for you, my lady,' the taller girl said. 'Bess is fetching water for your bath.'

'What is your name?' asked Berris.

'Jessop, my lady. Hebe Jessop. Bess Orthwaite and I will lay out your riding habit, ma'am. I think we had best hurry. Sir Ninian does not like to be kept waiting.'

Berris bit her lip. She moved to get out

of bed and found that she ached a little. Her slanting eyes glittered. No doubt the warm bath would soon put her to rights.

She said little as Hebe Jessop soaped and rinsed her, then helped her into her nether garments and slipped the lovely amber velvet riding habit over her head. It must have been newly made for Lora, thought Berris, as Hebe hooked it firmly into place. The hat, which exactly matched the riding habit, suited Berris to perfection.

'Oh, my lady, you *do* look beautiful,' said Hebe when Berris put the final touches to her toilet, pulling the folds of lace and velvet into position.

'Thank you, Hebe,' she said, graciously, though her mind was racing in an effort to think of possible excuses. She wondered whether she dared visit Lady Truscott. The old lady might detain her for long enough to bring Sir Ninian back indoors with news that her morning ride had been cancelled.

'Has Lady Truscott slept well?' she asked Hebe.

'Very well, ma'am, though she still wishes to remain in her bed. She grows weaker by the day.'

'Would you present my compliments and ask her if she would see me?' said Berris. 'I would give my time to her happily.'

81

'She expects you and Sir Ninian at eleven, ma'am, and refreshments will be served in her room. Sir Ninian will be waiting for you now.'

Berris slanted a glance at Hebe Jessop. She was an older girl who had no doubt served at Massingham for some years. She appeared to be very familiar with the running of the huge old house. Berris would have liked to inspect every room, but that privilege must be left to Lora, who would no doubt arrange everything to suit her taste, when they changed places.

Again she pondered on how on earth this might be accomplished, but no doubt her aunt, Mrs Ashington, had her plans well laid. In the meantime her husband ... the man who had married Lora ... was waiting for her at the stables and Bess Orthwaite hurried into the room, offering to conduct the new Lady Lennox to the cobbled yard at the back of the house. Sighing, Berris said no more, but followed the maidservant down the wide stairs, along endless corridors, and out into the pale cool sunshine.

She had no more excuses for wasting time.

Sir Ninian walked forward to take her arm and to kiss her cheek.

'Ah, there you are, my dear,' he said,

briskly. 'I have had this mare saddled for you. Her name is Black Velvet and she is as soft and elegant as her name suggests. I think you will be pleased with her.'

'I shall not be pleased with any mount this morning,' said Berris, coolly. 'I would prefer not to ride, Sir Ninian.'

His brows drew together and she could see how formidable he would look if he were crossed too often. Her own manner was calm and composed, but underneath the amber velvet, her knees were trembling with nerves.

'Why so, madam?'

'I would not be comfortable sitting a horse,' she replied with absolute truth, but allowed an imp of mischief to dance in her eyes, and a smile to play about her lips. For a moment he was silent, then as he caught her meaning, he threw back his head and laughed immoderately.

'By God, Lady Lora, but you are not such a shy young woman,' he said, his eyes dancing. 'So our first night of wedlock has left its mark upon you. The finest cure, until I find a better, would be to ride out on Black Velvet, but I will humour you. Instead we will walk together across the park. The snowdrops are in bloom and the daffodils are as young in heart as your self. Only their buds are showing.'

He caught her hand in his firm grasp

and she wandered along beside him. The horses, his own grey stallion and Black Velvet, were being led away by a stable boy, and Berris had looked up at the fine-boned creature, acknowledging that the mare was a beautiful animal. But how tall she looked and how powerful. Brendan Meredith and Sebastian had always attended to their slow-plodding animals. Berris had had as little to do with the creatures as possible.

They walked slowly across the park and Sir Ninian put an arm round her waist and drew her to him as they paused to look at an ancient beech tree whose branches resembled the limbs of a huge giant.

'Tomorrow we leave for a Grand Tour,' he said, running a teasing finger along her fine cheekbones.

Berris's heart leapt, then hammered madly. She could not go away with him! Mrs Ashington considered that two more days would be necessary before the blemishes would fade from Lora's cheeks, but suppose she, Berris, were whisked away from Massingham, then how could Lora take her place?

'I ... I do not care for a ... a Grand Tour,' she said, nervously.

'What's this?' Again he frowned. 'Why so? It is essential we spend some time together on our own so that we become used to marriage. I confess I have never

wanted the shackles of it, but now ...'
Again he ran his finger down her cheek.
'... it is not such a prison when the jailer is
young and beautiful and a willing lover.'

Berris's cheeks warmed. She had completely lost her head on her wedding
night, and had not behaved at all as
Lora might have done. She had forgotten
to be ladylike and to allow Ninian his way
without behaving like ... like a wanton!

'I would prefer to become used to
Massingham,' she said feebly.

His eyes narrowed.

'So you fancy yourself mistress of
Massingham already, madam?' he asked.
'I must remind you that my Aunt Elizabeth
is not yet in her grave.'

She flushed. 'You mistake my meaning,
sir. It is *because* Lady Truscott is so ill that
... that I would not care to leave her.'

'Hm. She has been ill before and
recovered her health after being allowed
her own way. We will take tea with her
at eleven. I will be surprised if she is not
already gaining strength.'

'She was very feeble last night, sir. I was
afraid she would not survive the excitement
of ... of the wedding.'

'It is nourishment to her spirit. Even
today, as the servants set the house to
rights, she will be guiding and instructing
them into ensuring that every knick-knack

85

is back in place. We had better return to the house. She will not be pleased if we are late.'

His hand was very firm on her arm as he guided her towards the house and Berris knew that she had little choice but to obey him.

In fact, Lady Truscott was still very frail and tired-looking when she received Sir Ninian and his bride into her bedroom, and Berris hardly knew whether to be glad that her argument against a Grand Tour was sound, or sorry that the old lady was not, in fact, rallying as quickly as Ninian had predicted.

'When do you return to London?' the old woman whispered.

'Tomorrow,' he told her, almost casually. Berris stared at him and shook her head as she turned to the old lady.

'I do not care to leave you,' she said. 'I would like Sir Ninian to leave me at Massingham to attend to you.'

'Bless you, child. It will make no difference to my lifespan whether you go or stay, though it is a pleasure to me to have you here. I will see that you become acquainted with Massingham. It is a fine property.'

The old lady's eyes had softened as she looked at the girl and Berris blushed as she glanced at Sir Ninian and caught his eyes resting upon her, the black eyebrows raised. Why must he make her feel like a fortune hunter? Yet it appeared that he had cause. Had not Mr Mark Ashington's debt been paid on their marriage? Lora had inherited money from their father on her marriage and she had a settlement from Lady Truscott. Berris thought about her own circumstances and could not help feeling a pang of envy for her sister.

She looked again at Sir Ninian who was gazing thoughtfully out of the bedroom window and across the wide lawns and green pastureland which surrounded Massingham. She admired the strength of his features and the well-informed firm outline of his mouth which had sent such fire through her body as it claimed her own.

His head sat well on his fine shoulders and there was elegance in his movements as he wandered around the bedroom. He disdained tea and Lady Truscott insisted that if Ninian did not care for tea they drink a glass of Madeira to warm their blood. Berris sighed with relief, remembering that she had not yet mastered the teapot.

She was so intent on her admiration of Ninian that she failed to notice his eyes upon her and blushed when she looked once again up to his face. Lady Truscott's black eyes were tender and she sighed inwardly with contentment.

She need no longer concern herself for Ninian's happiness. Sarah's daughter was right for him. She was a warm-blooded woman such as the boy needed in his life. They would breed fine children together.

'I wish to rest,' she said, clearly. 'I will talk to both of you later.'

'I beg to take leave of you, ma'am,' said Berris, swiftly bobbing a curtsey, and Ninian bent over the frail body.

'You old fraud,' he whispered. 'You will be up and ordering the household to your liking before the week is out.'

'Did you take care of the child?' the old woman asked.

His eyes slowly lightened and he smiled, then laughed.

'What child?' he asked. 'My wife is all woman. You can believe that I speak the truth.'

'Then see that she is enough for you.'

His face grew cool.

'I do not take your meaning, Aunt Elizabeth.'

She sighed as they left the room. He took her meaning very well. He was pleased with his wife, but did she yet hold that wayward heart of his?

Berris tried to remember that she was Lora as she lay in Ninian's arms that night and he found her ladylike and rather prim when he wanted her to partner him in taking pleasure from one another.

'What ails you?' he asked. 'Why so stiff when you have already suffered the pain and put it behind you. You are like a piece of wood!'

Berris's heart lurched. The words found an echo in her mind as she remembered Mistress Grey's high voice complaining about her acting.

'You are like a block of wood,' she would say. 'You are a poor actress, Berris.'

She was a poor actress. Tonight and tomorrow night might be the last she would spend in Ninian's bed, and suddenly the anguish of the situation was upon her and she wanted to weep because she would lose him all too soon. She could see the dark colour of his face and neck in the firelight, yet his skin, where it had not been darkened by wind and sun, was as soft and white as her own.

'I will not hurt you again, little Lora,' he was whispering. 'Do not shut me out.'

His fingers were as fine and gentle as a musician's, playing upon a favourite instrument. He stroked her breasts and kissed the soft white flesh of her neck so that her heart began to beat strongly with a strange new excitement, which was making her body throb with pleasure.

She felt his hand moving down to caress

the satin smoothness of her flesh between her thighs, then she caught her breath in a sob as she put her arms round his neck. Once again they mingled their love and passion for one another so that Berris reached a new plane of ecstasy and was unaware how strong her young body could be, as she clung to Ninian's neck and sought his lips with her own.

Once again his delighted laughter brought awareness of her duplicity and she pushed away from him.

'No ... no ...' she whispered, urgently. 'It is wrong. I ... I must not love you like this. It is wrong.'

'Wrong? My dearest wife, it is all that is right. I had never thought to marry a real woman. I had thought you were merely another female, bred to grace the salon but not the bedroom. I cannot believe even now that I have been so fortunate. Tomorrow ...'

He paused.

'Soon I must go to Italy, and you will accompany me. Sometimes I undertake a small commission for certain personages, and I wish to look at paintings. The Italian cities are the finest in Europe for their culture, and we shall meet great writers, painters, musicians and actors and actresses who perform plays of great merit.'

She had stiffened in his arms. Had he

emphasized the word 'actress'? Did he know her for an actress? But no, he could not. He would not be planning to take her for a Grand Tour if he knew she was Berris.

But Lora had said he was a devil! Could it be that he was playing with her, believing that she played with him? Could he be pretending that he knew nothing whilst at the same time amusing himself by preventing her from changing places with Lora? In this way he could be punishing both Lora and herself.

He had leaned up on one elbow, and was looking down into her face in the faint glow of the firelight.

'Do you not care for the theatre, or for splendid music? Have you no interest in the Arts? Can it be that our bodies crave to love one another, but our minds are as far apart as the poles?'

What did Lora enjoy she wondered, wildly. Would it be music, or painting? She must have been taught both. It would be part of her education.

'I ... I enjoy music and the Arts,' she said, hurriedly, 'but I should not enjoy any of it until Lady Truscott shows signs of returning strength.'

'Upon my soul, you put me to shame,' he said, gently. 'You are a young woman with more thought for an old woman than for yourself. There is heart in you, my Lora. But cannot you see that if we hang around the bed curtains and look with concern into the face of poor Aunt Elizabeth, she will think herself at death's door and might nudge herself through? She is very old and we both know, she and I, that she will be meeting that Maker of hers one day soon. It would hasten the hour if I spend every one of them hanging by her bedside. My concern for her would be reflected in herself and she might give up the ghost before her time. Now if I leave her, and show her I see well that she is still full of life and spirit, then she will pull herself out of bed and be haranguing the servants in no time.

'Nor will you show interest in managing Massingham whilst she is alive. Jessop knows every inch of the place and his daughter, Hebe, is a fine competent young woman. She was born at Massingham and has lived here all her life. They will give the reins into your hands and make sure you hold them properly.'

'Jessop?'

'The butler. Did you not know he was father to young Hebe and that her mother is the cook?'

'I did not.'

'Strange. I was sure that you knew Jessop.'

Again her heart hammered when she realized she had made another blunder.

'I had forgotten,' she said, carelessly. 'I cannot remember the names of servants.'

He withdrew himself a little and she heard his small indrawn breath. His voice grew chilly.

'They are people, just as we are, my dear Lora. They work the happier if they think the mistress of the house takes an interest in their lives. You must try to do this. I rarely have trouble with my servants.'

Her face burned in the darkness. How could she possibly explain that she did not consider herself above the servants with regard to her own station in life. That she was not the snob she appeared to be.

'Do not show such heavy concern for Aunt Elizabeth,' Ninian was saying rather wearily.

'Very well, sir,' she agreed. 'I will take care.'

Seconds later he was asleep and in spite of her problems, Berris too slept soundly. Somehow she would deal with everything tomorrow.

CHAPTER EIGHT

Hebe Jessop was packing a trunk for her when Berris woke up. Sir Ninian was already up and dressed, and he came to smile at her as she struggled out of sleep.

'Come on, Lady Lennox,' he said, sitting on the bed and pulling at her hair. 'Wake up! Young Orthwaite is bringing your breakfast, and Hebe Jessop is packing for you. We are leaving for London before noon, then we will make plans to travel to Italy.'

Her face paled visibly.

'But ... but I cannot!'

'Cannot?'

The good humour left his face abruptly. 'We have discussed this before, madam, and I will have no more of your moods. Aunt Elizabeth is much improved in health this morning and I can waste no more time. Why are you so coy about going to Italy? I know many women who would be glad to make the journey.'

Her wits were working more sharply now that she was awake, and she saw that she could only agree to his plans for the moment. Somehow she must find an excuse for them to call at Birkridge and perhaps something could yet be accomplished. She could *not* go to Italy with Ninian. It could well involve a journey of some weeks.

'I have no doubt at all that you know many women who would be delighted to accompany you, sir,' she said lightly. 'I mean that I *cannot* ... do not *wish* ... to take all of those garments on such a journey. To my shame I am growing out of them. I was not full grown when they were made for me, but I am a woman now. Could I not buy one or two gowns in London?'

She could not take Lora's clothes away from Massingham, she thought in a panic. Her figure was better developed than her sister's and already a stitch would be needed on the amber velvet riding dress. Lora would expect all her fine garments to be hung away and waiting for her at Massingham. Berris had accepted her role of impersonating her sister, but something in her rebelled against wearing Lora's clothing.

'Fripperies again,' said Ninian, witheringly. 'Just when I think you different, I find you are as trivial as any other woman, under the skin. Buy what you want in London, and the rest in Milan.'

'Is that where we go?'

95

'Milan and Venice, then perhaps we will travel south. I will take my own coach ... *our* own coach, my dear wife. Everyone in Italy must travel in their own coach. I will say that travelling there is not easy, but by God, one is not bored! I have invitations to stay with friends I have entertained in London from time to time. You need not fear the inns, which are poor hostelries.'

'I do not fear them,' said Berris, thoughtlessly. 'I'm well used to poor accommodation.'

'Do you say so?'

He swung round to stare at her with an eyebrow raised. 'I should not have thought you old enough to have travelled far. I did not know the Ashingtons enjoyed making the Grand Tour.'

'Oh, just a little travelling in England,' said Berris, hurriedly.

'Inns and coaching houses are not quite the same as the homes of friends. They would not enjoy hearing that they had offered you poor accommodation.'

'May I supervise the packing ... of my clothing?' she asked, almost desperately.

'No, Hebe, not that gown.'

'It is very pretty, my lady.'

It was much too pretty. It must surely be one of Lora's favourites, thought Berris, as she looked at the rich cream silk gown sewn with tiny seed pearls.

'It will spoil with travel,' she said. 'My best gowns must be kept at Massingham.'

'I will supervise your purchases in London,' said Ninian, frowning. 'I have no wish to be thought tight-fisted over my wife's wardrobe, although you have a fine appetite for adornment, my love. But it makes a pretty wife.'

'Then I shall certainly leave these at Massingham,' said Berris, her cheeks dimpling in a smile.

He caught a handful of her hair and pulled her into his arms.

'We are going to Italy to enjoy a Grand Tour,' he said, 'whether you want it or not. I will decide where we are going, how we travel, and where we are to stay. Is that clear?'

'Yes, sir,' she whispered, and the black opaque eyes lightened with laughter.

'I do not understand you, but I confess that it is no bad thing. Now I must make arrangements for our carriage to be made ready.'

He kissed her lightly. 'Wear your travelling gown and cloak. It is not yet warm enough for early spring.'

Berris chose so few gowns to take with her that Hebe Jessop showed her surprise.

'They will hardly last the journey, my lady,' she said.

'No matter. There are others still at

Birkridge more suited to travelling,' she said with sudden inspiration. 'I shall ask Sir Ninian to call there when we leave for London and they can be packed for me. I will be able to say my farewells to my aunt and uncle.'

'Birkridge is not on the London road, my lady,' Hebe reminded her. 'You will have to make a special journey.'

'Then we must make a detour. I will inform Sir Ninian.'

Now that she had found a solution to her problem, Berris sighed with relief. She was exhausted with the strain of playing her role. She dreaded spending a great deal more time in such close intimacy with Ninian. She feared that he could wield great power over her which both attracted and frightened her, and she was afraid of the many traps which could expose her deception as Lora. How many more would she have to face?

Lady Truscott was indeed a great deal better when Berris, accompanied by Ninian, went along to her room to say their farewells to her. She had commanded the maids to help her out of bed, and now she sat on a large chair near the window. A wig had been placed on her scanty hair and her hands sparkled with fine diamond rings. She still looked very old and frail, but there was a vigour in her which had been lacking on the day of the wedding.

'Ah, so you are ready for your journey, my dear,' she said, as she reached out to take Berris's hand.

Her voice, too, had strengthened and Berris knew a twinge of alarm as the bright black eyes scrutinized her in the strong light of morning. Lady Truscott must have been familiar with Lora since childhood. Suppose ... suppose she saw something different in Berris.

'The marriage bed has improved you, child.' she said. 'You have less *ennui* in your eyes.'

Berris blushed and heard a deep chuckle in the old lady's throat.

'She will do, Lennox. You have made a woman of her, but she can still summon the roses to her cheeks. How long will you be gone?'

'A few weeks, perhaps. Lora has not yet made the Grand Tour. She must have this experience before she settles down to breed.'

'Quite right. A man must always be taking enjoyment from life, and a wife is a poor thing if she allows him to do it alone. Give me a kiss, child. I will have the bridal chambers arranged properly for you before you return.'

Obediently Berris kissed the old lady's cheek, then saw a hint of tears in the dark eyes as she turned to Ninian who also kissed her cheek, then her hands, the diamonds sparkling with a myriad points of light. His face had grown almost hard, but his eyes showed distress. He was afraid to leave his aunt, thought Berris with insight, but also afraid to stay in case it destroyed that bright spirit.

Outside a fine carriage, drawn by four horses, was waiting in the cobbled yard. The harsh look was still on Ninian's face as he handed Berris into the carriage and supervised the final loading of their luggage. Two servants travelled with the coach, but there was no woman servant for Berris. Ninian had decided that he was quite capable of attending to her needs until they reached his London home, where one of the maidservants who had been born in Italy would accompany them on their journey.

'I would like to call at Birkridge before going to London,' said Berris, as Ninian entered the carriage.

He stared at her coldly.

'I do not see any need for you to call at Birkridge.'

'I have to pick up some of my clothes and ... and I would like to say my farewells to my aunt and uncle.'

Ninian's mouth curled. 'It is barely two days since you last saw your relatives. They were not loath to part with you, so I do not feel obliged to waste my time in prolonged farewells. As to your clothing, madam, you need have no worries. A sufficiency will be provided for you in London, as I have promised. The Italian women do not slavishly follow fashions as do the English and French.'

Berris's mouth went dry, and the blood drained from her face. She had been so confident that Ninian would do as she wished that she had not thought what to do if he decided otherwise. Now she saw that unless she did something very quickly to prevent it, she would be forced into remaining in Lora's place for some weeks.

'But you must!' she cried in panic. 'I ... I *cannot* go with you unless I see my aunt and uncle first of all!'

'Cannot?' repeated Ninian, very quietly. *'Cannot?* Need I remind you, madam, that you are now my wife? You will do as *I* wish, Lady Lennox.'

His eyes sharpened as he looked at her. 'Upon my soul, Lora, I do *not* understand you. Are you afraid of travel? Is *that* what you fear?'

He was looking so keenly into her eyes that she shrank away from him. Since their marriage he had been kind to her, had even shown delight in her. But now she could glimpse the other side to his nature, the side which would insist upon her obedience and which would not be challenged. Had she been his true wife, she might have found this domination exciting, though she would have fought against it. She refused to be completely dominated by anyone.

Brendan Meredith had a certain respect for female theatre players, and although he had made most of the decisions, he had not been brutal in his domination. Even though he could be bad-tempered when crossed, Berris had rarely been afraid of him, but now she acknowledged that she was afraid of Sir Ninian Lennox.

He called out to the coachman, and the horses took off at a spanking pace. Berris put out a hand as though in a feeble attempt to stop the coach, and Ninian came to sit beside her and to draw her into his arms. He was intent on soothing her fear of travel which he believed was at the root of her reluctance to leave Massingham, and Birkridge, and he kissed her gently. In her nervousness she was unresponsive and after a moment he drew away.

'You will grow used to it, Lady Lennox,' he said, indifferently. 'That I *promise* you. You will be a well-seasoned traveller by the time we reach Milan.'

'Milan is ... is very far away.'

'Far enough. We will travel through the French provinces and enter Italy via the Alps Maritimes. France has been ravished by its own strife, but that need not concern us. I have no interest in their affairs and my papers will ensure our safety.

'I hope you find your carriage comfortable, my dear wife. You will grow used to it, I assure you, in the weeks to come.'

Berris found it exceedingly comfortable after the wagon which Brendan Meredith had converted for the use of his theatrical company. She was well used to travel and, if circumstances had been different, she would have been filled with excitement and delight at the prospect of such a journey. She loved London and had always been very happy when the Players returned to its outlying villages and from there, journeyed into the city.

Now she ran her tongue over her dry lips and tried to relax. She felt sick and confused. What would the Ashingtons do when they learned what had happened? Would they inform Lady Truscott? And what about the Meredith Players? There were few plays which could be performed without her and the excerpts from the plays of Shakespeare were not always well received by their class of audience, who much preferred comedies, melodramas, or the pretty light fairytales. The audiences were also beginning to enjoy a variety of lighter entertainment in the theatres with music, dancing and burlesque. There was a great deal of competition for a group of players.

She bit her lip nervously, unaware that Ninian watched her closely from the corner of his eye. What ailed the girl? He had been beginning to take a delight in his marriage, but he knew he would grow very impatient with such lack of response and such obvious preference for the company of her relatives than for himself.

Firming his lips he looked out of the window and began to think about Italy. He had given Lora one or two reasons for his journey, but the real one was deep in his heart. Before travelling north for his betrothal, he had promised the beautiful Fiorenza Michiel that he would return to Venice. He had acted as her *cicisbeo* when he was last in Italy, conducting her to galas and the opera when her elderly husband preferred the gaming tables. His great friend, Carol Faliero, was cavalier to Fiorenza, but Carlo had been injured in a duel and had asked Ninian to take his place. Fiorenza had been very happy to accept his attentions and Ninian had found her the most exciting woman he had ever met, even though he knew he could never possess her.

Ninian scarcely saw the passing country-side. His thoughts were now with Fiorenza who must surely be the most beautiful woman in Italy. Her delicate features had the perfection of a flower, and he had often sat in her bedroom in the mornings, attending her toilet and watching whilst her hair was dressed. He knew that her beauty owed little to artificial aids. It was her own.

He had promised to return to her very soon, but he had not promised to bring a wife. Yet Fiorenza jealously guarded her reputation, and Ninian had recognized that his marriage would not displease her. To return to Italy with a young wife was no bad thing, though it might make a difference to his freedom to enjoy life there to the full.

For a moment Ninian's eyes darkened as he thought of that other woman whom he also kept locked away in his heart. Fiorenza appealed to his ascetic tastes, but it was Sophia Mario who could soothe and refresh the demands of his body. She was younger than Fiorenza, but her fathomless dark eyes and lazily smiling mouth were ageless. Together they had shared many nights of laughter and pleasure. Sophia would not care whether or not he now had a wife, so long as his purse was emptied as generously as she offered her love.

Ninian could present his wife to Fiorenza, but not to Sophia. For the past few days Lora had enchanted him and had even made him put both Fiorenza and Sophia to the back of his mind. He had glimpsed, in his wife, a beauty and passion which could become enchanting and, almost, he thought he had found in her what he sought in both other women. But the enchantment would probably not be lasting. It was, as he had supposed in the first place, a mere colourful bubble. She was young and bred to the narrow life of appearance and convention. She was acceptable as a wife, but it was Fiorenza who could give him joy in living and delight his eye with her beauty, and Sophia who could make him relax when he grew weary.

Yet ... Lora was also beautiful. She was unusual, with her strange slanting eyes and well-defined cheekbones. What would Fiorenza think of her? Ninian experienced a tiny twinge of doubt, and then he shrugged. Lora would have her place in his life, just as Fiorenza also had her place, but Lora's sulks because she had not been given her own way would never be tolerated for long by him. He hated sulking women.

'Come, my dear, show me your dimples. It is not such a tragedy that you now have a husband instead of an aunt and uncle.'

Berris had been looking out at the passing countryside. Already Birkridge had been left far behind, even further than Massingham. With a sigh she leaned back in the coach. There was now no hope of changing places with Lora until after her return from Italy. Somehow the Ashingtons would no doubt adjust to what had happened and her stepfather would be informed.

She smiled at Ninian, a smile of such enchanting pleasure that he was startled once more. She was an enigma, this strange child who had become his wife. A short time ago she had appeared to be gazing on the face of Tragedy itself, and now her joy and radiance were lighting fires in him once more.

'Are not the trees beautiful without leaves, when one can see their shapes?' she asked, 'yet when spring comes into full bloom and adorns them with new leaves, they can be exquisite. Do you not think the countryside is beautiful to look upon?'

'As beautiful as a woman,' he said, softly, 'and for the same reason.'

She coloured again and laughed.

'I long to see London once more.'

'Once more? Did your aunt and uncle take you to London? I thought you recently out of the schoolroom.'

She caught her breath. 'Sometimes,' she said, nervously. 'Not often enough.'

'We will see enough of London in the years to come. We will not linger long in the London house.'

He reached out and once again drew her into his arms. This time there was no resistance in her and she responded so warmly to his kiss that he spared a thought for the first coaching house where they would spend the night. Once again the Italian women slipped far away into the back of his mind.

'What are you thinking?' he asked, lazily, as he traced out the lines of her nose and cheek with his fingers, a favourite gesture.

'I am thinking that I am hungry.'

He slanted his dark-eyed glance at her, then he began to laugh.

'We will make a traveller of you yet. I had expected that food would not attract you until you became used to the swaying of the coach.'

'I always find food attractive,' said Berris, ruefully.

She had eaten little that morning, her nerves driving away her appetite. Now that she had passed the point of no return, she relaxed and decided that every minute of her time with Ninian must be enjoyed. The touch of his lips on her own was finding her body more and more responsive to him. That she was falling deeply in love with him did not seem to matter for the moment. The next few weeks were to be a magical time in her life when she could be Lora. She could forget Berris. She was Ninian's wife, and she loved him devotedly.

'I am happy,' she whispered.

He held her lightly, then the thought of Italy came back to torment him. This young wife was offering him her love and trust. Would her eyes still glow with such happiness when she met Fiorenza? Would she understand what it meant to be a *cicisbeo?* And how could he visit Sophia Mario without her knowledge? He had no wish to cut the luscious Sophia out of his life.

With a quick change of mood Ninian thrust her from him, and returned to his own corner of the carriage.

'Have patience, Lora, and you will be fed all in good time,' he told her. 'Meantime, I wish to rest. We have a long journey ahead.'

CHAPTER NINE

The London house was situated in a quiet tree-lined square within easy distance of the clubs of St James'. It was a tall house, solidly built behind iron railings, the rooms well-proportioned and elegantly furnished, the walls hung with fine portraits and paintings.

Berris entered the house shyly, greatly awed by what she saw. Massingham had been very fine, but this town house was magnificent in its splendour. Here, looking at the evidence of wealth and nobility, the whole well-ordered by many servants, she could well understand the lack of interest in Ninian's eyes from time to time as they rested upon her. She had sensed that he was distrait and wondered why he should suddenly wish to shut her out of his thoughts. For a brief moment she felt an inadequate sort of wife for such a man. Then she remembered that of course, Lora was a well-born lady from an old family, even if the Ashington wealth had become depleted over the years. The thought gave her courage, and she walked forward with quiet dignity.

The staff had assembled to greet the new Lady Lennox and the elderly butler assured Sir Ninian and his bride that all had been done to ensure their comfort. Dinner would be served at whatever time pleased Lady Lennox in the dining room.

'Ask Maria Bibiena to attend her mistress,' Sir Ninian commanded and the butler bowed and withdrew as servants carried in luggage, attended to fires and ensured every form of comfort for Sir Ninian and Lady Lennox.

Soon an older woman, dressed in black and wearing a starched white cap, appeared and curtseyed to Berris. She looked into the woman's dark eyes which gazed back at her sombrely and for a brief moment she felt that this woman had pity for her. Although she attended to Berris with swift efficiency, there was little servitude in her manner and Berris began to feel young and rather gauche.

'We leave for Italy in a few days, Bibiena,' Sir Ninian informed her, carelessly. 'You will be required to accompany Lady Lennox on the journey. I shall inform Johnstone.'

'Yes, sir.'

The dark eyes came alive, though Berris could see that the woman had been taken by surprise. Perhaps she had not expected Berris to be making this journey.

'See to it that madam has clothing fit for the journey,' he went on.

'It will be as you wish, Sir Ninian,' the woman said, her English heavily-accented. 'Will you dress formally for dinner, my lady, or will you wish to wear a house robe?'

'Lady Lennox is tired. A house robe will be sufficient,' said Sir Ninian.

Berris's chin lifted. She *was* tired, but she also disliked her life being arranged for her in this fashion. She would not have decisions made for her.

'I will dress,' she said, clearly, 'and I wish you to attend to my toilet, Bibiena. This is my first evening in our London home, and it must surely be made an occasion.'

'Yes, ma'am.' The black eyes had sharpened and now they regarded Berris with more respect. Ninian, too, shrugged and smiled.

'Appearances again, my dear Lora. Ah well, perhaps you are right. We must make this an occasion. So you approve of your London home? I will see that Johnstone makes you familiar with it tomorrow. It has had no mistress since my mother died, but you should find that the house runs smoothly, even though my only female relative is Aunt Elizabeth.'

'And your wife,' put in Berris, smoothly.

'And my wife.'

A half smile played about Bibiena's lips and again Berris sensed that she was being humoured. It occurred to her that Maria Bibiena knew Ninian so much better than she did herself. Had they been lovers at one time? Had he brought the woman home from Italy as his mistress? Berris experienced a stab of jealousy, then dismissed the idea. The Italian woman was older than Ninian and not physically attractive, but her eyes were full of knowledge.

'You look tired, my lady,' she said, softly, after she had finished Berris's toilet. 'I will have your bed made ready for you when you return from dinner. The master has given orders for his bed also to be made ready.'

'*His* bed?'

Maria Bibiena nodded. 'The master thinks you should rest well after your journey. He desires his own bedroom.'

'I see,' said Berris.

Inwardly she was gripped by a great rage. It was scarcely a week since the wedding, but already she was being asked to spend a night on her own. And it had been her new maidservant who had informed her of this. Ninian had not even troubled to discuss it.

Berris looked at the reflection of a

pale tired-looking young woman in the gilt-framed looking glass. She knew that Ninian did not love her. He loved her body as he would appreciate the charms of any fresh young woman, but there was no deep abiding love in him. She had not touched his heart.

She forgot that this should not matter to her, and tried to remain calm as she allowed Bibiena to drape a soft shawl round her shoulders. Ninian loved another woman and this maidservant knew her identity. Mrs Ashington had remarked that he had loved many other women and would be unfaithful to Lora, and she should not be hurt by this knowledge. But she, Berris, was both hurt and angry.

Berris rose to her feet when Ninian came to find her, looking splendid in his black velvet.

'We will no doubt entertain many guests here,' he informed her, 'but for tonight there will only be the two of us. Does that please you, my lady?'

'Does it please *you*, sir?' she asked with a touch of asperity.

His eyes sharpened. The child was not in the best of tempers.

'I have no doubt that the cook will have done her best for you. *That* should please you,' he said, and escorted her downstairs.

Dinner was exquisite and served so daintily that Berris was almost afraid to do more than pick at her food in case her robust table manners made her appear uncouth. This, too, had been pointed out to her in no uncertain terms by Mrs Ashington, but she had learned quickly how to be gracious at table.

Tonight, however, with only herself and Ninian being served at the beautifully-polished dining table with tall, scented candles in silver candlesticks lighting up the lovely room, Berris felt nervous again. She must not show ignorance of the delicate sauces and the dainty meats which she had never before tasted. What on earth was the darkly-coloured meat with the strong flavour and the texture of chicken? Which knife and fork must she choose from such an array? She could only watch Ninian and follow his example, but she was so intent on her table manners that once again she made a silent companion for him. He was discussing the merits of the various paintings in the room, and she knew nothing about Art and could not appreciate the brushwork adopted by the various painters. Lora would know, but Berris was too tired to disguise her ignorance.

'Are you fatigued that you remain so

silent?' Ninian asked after he found her so lacking in response.

She was glad of the excuse.

'It has been a tiring journey for me, sir.'

'I understand. I will not disturb you this night, ma'am. I will see that you have your rest.'

'Oh, but ...'

She was about to protest that she had enough life and energy in her for sharing his bed, then blushed at the thought of making such an admission. It was very hard to be a lady.

'Yes? You were saying?'

His dark eyes were in shadow as the candles flickered.

'It was nothing. I am willing to abide by your wishes.'

'That makes a pleasant change,' he commented drily. 'However, you had better gather strength over the next few days. We have a long journey ahead.'

Ninian spoke absently. Now that he was home in London, his thoughts were leaping ahead once more to his arrival in Italy. The thought of Sophia stirred his blood. All other women were pale shadows against her when she offered her love, even the child he had married. He enjoyed her body, but even that, in his present mood, did not stir him unduly. She would be there when he needed her. Meanwhile, he just wanted to dream about the beautiful Italian women. He preferred his own thoughts as company for the time being.

After dinner he joined Berris in the drawing room, noticing the droop of her mouth and the withdrawn look in her eyes. For a moment he felt disturbed and ill-at-ease, as though he had made a misjudgement. Then he rang the bell for Bibiena.

'Lady Lennox is tired,' he said. 'See that she is allowed to rest in the morning.'

'Yes, sir.'

Berris rose quietly, concealing her anger, and followed Bibiena to her room. Ninian had not troubled to conceal the fact that he was bored with her. Already his thoughts were on some other woman. It was not difficult to read the signs.

'I will make him forget her!' she vowed, as she punched her pillow that night and tried to still her trembling body which ached for his love. 'She will not have him! She *shall* not!'

The next few days were filled to overflowing for Berris so that, in fact, she was grateful that her nights were undisturbed as she sank into sleep the moment her head touched the pillow.

Sir Ninian spent most of his days at his club, and Berris had expected him to be absent in the evenings, no doubt visiting his paramours—but in this she was wrong. He appeared to take pleasure in dining with her, even though he was often silent and preoccupied. He no longer made any special effort to entertain her with his conversation.

To her relief, also, she found herself indisposed and was profoundly thankful that Ninian had taken account of her plea to postpone the conception of a child until she was ready to settle down in marriage. This had been her biggest nightmare, and she grew once again lighthearted in her relief.

Maria Bibiena had sent for the seamstress and silk, satin and velvet gowns, trimmed with lace and ribbons, were added to Berris's wardrobe. In addition there were simple travelling gowns and cloaks in warm wool, but of such charming colours that she was delighted with the choice.

'Not so long ago all ladies in Italy wore black,' said Maria, 'but now the fashion changes and they bedeck themselves with elaborate gowns and wear wigs.'

'I prefer my own hair,' said Berris, proud of her beautiful ringlets.

'Yes, my lady, but in Italy you will wish to dress as others do.'

'That would please Lora,' said Berris thoughtfully, and saw immediately that she had made a mistake as the Italian woman's black eyes swung round to look at her curiously.

'Lora? I do not understand, ma'am. I ... surely you are Lady Lora ...?'

Berris almost fainted with dismay, as she tried to laugh lightly.

'I was referring to that side of me which enjoys dressing up,' she said, but she knew that the Italian woman would not forget her slip of the tongue. She must take much greater care from now on.

She wondered if she would like Italy. Ninian now had an eagerness and an air of suppressed excitement about him as he prepared for the journey which, by contrast, made her feel so uneasy. Sometimes he looked at her as though he found it difficult to remember who she was, and although that should have pleased her because of this deception she was perpetrating, she could not but want him to put her first, to consider her before anything, anyone else.

The final days of preparation were completed, however, and they left London one dull morning as soft relentless rain washed the cobbles and soaked the clothing of luckless pedestrians.

Berris looked out from the carriage at the tall, beautiful house which she had come to love. How long would it be, she wondered, before she saw it again?

CHAPTER TEN

The journey through the French provinces to the north of Italy was at once a delight and a torment to Berris. Being well used to travelling, she did not succumb to the usual bodily upsets of those less used to venturing abroad, and it was she who had to administer soothing remedies to Maria Bibiena when the serving maid turned white and ill because of the swaying of the coach and the food they were obliged to eat.

Berris had not been pleased by Ninian's decision to take Maria with them.

'I do not require a servant,' she said. 'I can attend to my own needs and I only require a little help from you.'

'You astonish me, Lora,' he returned. 'You cannot know how inconvenient your life would be without a woman to maid you, you who have had servants to attend you all your life. Maria is Italian and can speak the language even as she can speak English. You will require her help when we reach Italy as much as you will need her on the journey. I arranged it this way for your benefit, madam.'

'We managed well enough between Massingham and London.'

'On such a comparatively short journey, it was not necessary to deprive Aunt Elizabeth of one of her maidservants.' His eyes grew cold and remote once more. 'Enough of your arguments. Bibiena travels with us. I would have expected you to insist upon a servant.'

Berris said no more, feeling that she had made another mistake. She was afraid of Maria's dark probing eyes, but perhaps she would be glad of a maid who spoke Italian since she, herself, knew not a word of the language.

'How did you come to join Sir Ninian's household?' she had asked Maria as they crossed the Channel, and she had sat beside the woman and held a cooling pad to her forehead.

'I was servant to the Signora Michiel,' the woman muttered.

'Who is Signora Michiel?'

'Fiorenza Michiel. Sir Ninian acted as her *cicisbeo* when he was last in Italy.'

'What does that mean?'

But Maria shook her head, and Berris saw that her face was now a pale sickly grey.

'I do not feel well,' she muttered, and Berris soothed her as best she could. But she remembered Maria's words and decided that she would ask Ninian about the signora. But not until his mood was more receptive to such enquiries. Sometimes he liked to listen to her chatter and to answer her questions, but at others he became a remote, dark-faced stranger who had to be left to his own thoughts.

Ninian had expected Lora to complain bitterly about the quality of the inns where they had to spend the night. France still lay wounded and bleeding from the effects of the Great Terror and the inns did not always offer the best of service. He was surprised when she accepted even the meanest of them without complaint, and the best of them with evident pleasure. Used as she was to theatrical lodgings, the inns were as comfortable as Berris could wish, and Ninian shared her enjoyment as they stopped each evening at a suitable hostelry and ravenously ate whatever meat the landlord could provide. The wines were not always rough, and even the hardest bed was a luxury when she shared it with Ninian.

As the days passed, she gradually forgot about Lora, and it was Berris who could love so passionately that Ninian found in her everything he could want in a woman. He saw beauty in her slanting eyes and her vibrant young body, and he was alternatively intrigued and amused as he watched the veneer of ladylike manners and behaviour gradually falling from her, leaving a warm, exciting and completely natural woman.

Like his wife, he began to enjoy each day as it came without thought for the future.

The northern French provinces were a wonder to Berris and the speculation and hint of compassion in Maria Bibiena's eyes began to fade so that she was treated with respect. She was, indeed, Sir Ninian's true lady and not just the wife who would bear his children.

As they journeyed towards the south of France, the weather began to grow warmer and the countryside gradually changed. Parts of it reminded Berris of England, but England was very remote now. She no longer thought about her life there, and the Meredith Players belonged to another world, faded far into the past. She became so used to being called 'Lora' that it was difficult to remember she was Berris.

'Ninian, what is a *cicisbeo*,' she asked him one evening after they had gone to bed, and he had held her body in his arms, gently stroking and kissing her soft flesh, then taking her so violently in love that she was left gasping. He had ceased to be the stern frightening man she had once thought him to be, and was now her beloved, and when his passion became a living flame she could meet it equally with her own generous love.

The question which she asked seemed to cut through the golden cord which had been gradually binding them together. As soon as the words were spoken she could feel his withdrawal from her, as though he had stepped into another world and closed a door behind him.

'Where did you hear that word?'

'From Maria. She said you were *cicisbeo* to an Italian countess.'

'Fiorenza Michiel is not a countess. She is a Venetian and a member of an ancient Italian family. She requires no title.'

'Then you are her ... her *cicisbeo?* What does that mean?'

'Bibiena's tongue clacks at both ends, but no matter. It is only a social custom in Italy and you need not concern yourself with such formalities.'

'But I should like to hear about it, and I should like to know all about the signora.'

He drew in his breath sharply.

'And I have no wish to be questioned,' he said, coldly. 'I have my friends in Italy. You will meet them in due course. I will expect you to behave in a ladylike manner, and remember your upbringing.

Sometimes I think you forget what you have been taught when your aunt is not here to discipline you, though the fault is mine that I should encourage you.'

Berris coloured. 'I will see that you have no cause for complaint, sir,' she said, quietly.

She felt hurt and rather soiled. Ninian made love to her with passion and her own love for him grew every day. She had believed that he shared that passion and revelled in the fact that she could meet it with her own. She had thought he was even coming to love her a little; but now she could see that if there was love in him, it was not for her. He admired the dainty manners of a lady, despite all he had said about her being a warm woman. Now that the novelty had worn off, no doubt her abandonment repelled him.

Ninian had no such thoughts. He'd thrust Berris from him in confusion. As they neared Italy, his mind was once again full of the lovely Fiorenza whose beauty he had admired for so long. But when he tried to imagine her exquisite face, it was the slanting eyes and smiling mouth of his wife who looked at him with love in her eyes. She was so open and frank in her enjoyment of life, and their love, that she puzzled him. She was like no other young lady he had ever met. Sometimes he even found her more fulfilling than Sophia.

Ninian wanted time to try to arrange the turmoil of his thoughts so that he would understand his own feelings. His wife's behaviour was what he would expect from a concubine! And the behaviour of Fiorenza Michiel was what one would expect from a delicate and charming wife.

CHAPTER ELEVEN

They entered Italy by the Alpes Maritime, and almost immediately Berris could sense a change, not only in her surroundings, but also in Ninian. Once again he became cool and remote towards her; a stranger whose dark opaque eyes were unreadable.

Maria Bibiena, on the other hand, grew more animated and watched every passing mile with pleasurable anticipation.

For Berris the delight in her journey had disappeared and she found the region at once so magnificent yet so desolate that she was reduced to silence as she looked out of the swaying coach. The weather had turned warmer in France, but now the nights were cold enough to echo the chill in her own heart. She was in Italy, and she was afraid of what was to come. She wanted to grasp Ninian's love with firm, possessive fingers; but she could only watch, bleakly, whilst he slipped away from her into a world where she could not follow. She was the stranger outside the gates.

The great snow-topped mountains up-lifted yet repelled her, so that she pulled her cloak closer round her shoulders and longed, almost desperately, to have Ninian's comforting arms round her. She felt rejected by his neglect.

For the first time Berris complained about the inn when they reached Tenda. No lodging had ever been more cheerless and filthy, and she shivered with cold, then sweated as though with fever, as she tried to gain a night's rest. She had strangely disturbed dreams, haunted by Sebastian and the beautiful but evil face of a stranger who teased Sebastian into laughing at her, so that she called out to him again and again, only to find Ninian shaking her awake.

'Who is this Sebastian?' he asked, after she was quiet. 'I understood that you are not acquainted with another man, yet you cry for him as though he were part of you.'

Berris pleaded for a cooling drink to ease her dry throat, and sought frantically for an explanation as realization dawned that she had been calling out in her sleep.

'I dreamed that I watched a play by Mr Shakespeare,' she said, tossing back her hair. 'I think I called out for the actor.'

'How fortunate to find such entertaining dreams,' said Ninian, drily.

'Fortunate indeed!' she returned, remembering that the best way to divert attention from herself was to offer him a few complaints. 'This inn must surely be fashioned to house the Devil and his minions. There is not even a window in our chamber.'

'It is no worse than others we have seen,' he told her. 'Besides, we will soon reach the northern cities which must surely please even you, Lady Lennox.'

'I have *never* been difficult to please,' she defended.

'That I grant you,' he agreed, but his icy tones did not make the words sound like a compliment, and she was silenced.

She wondered at his own ability to accept such discomfort and was jealous of the new eagerness in him as they travelled into the northern provinces of the country. Then, as they began to reach the larger towns, Berris forgot all the discomfort which she had endured and her eyes grew wide with wonder when they reached the outskirts of Milan. She had never seen such a city of splendour and great beauty.

The chill of the journey had been making her feel feverish and ill, but now all was forgotten as she gazed about her.

'We will remain here for a few days to give you time to rest,' said Ninian, his eyes noting the signs of fatigue on her face. Her journey through France had animated her so that she had glowed with health, but she had become quiet and subdued in recent days. He had been too impatient to trouble himself, but now that they had arrived in Milan, he had thought for her once more.

'The Barberno Palace, the home of my friend, Carlo Filiero, is in Milan and I have an apartment there. It should provide you with every comfort. It will be delightful to see Carlo again, though he may be in Venice. We shall see.'

Berris forgot her chills and fevers. Her eyes were feasting on such scenes as she had never seen before. Great tall buildings, richly ornamented, stood beside Roman basilicas, magnificent palaces and churches, the whole façade interspersed with new elegant buildings.

The streets, however, were filthy and as they proceeded at a slow pace, the water cart pulled by six men, passed by, scattering water in an attempt to clean the streets. They were shackled together and Ninian shrugged as Berris gazed at them, horrified.

'They are prisoners,' he said. 'It is their task to pull the water wagon.'

The contrast between such magnificence and such squalor took her breath away. But soon she was once more awed and entranced by the size and elegance of the palaces and by the great cathedral, and what surely must be a theatre. She had to know, and as she asked Ninian, bright colour once again warmed in her cheeks and her eyes glowing with amber light. He smiled at her indulgently. It was very pleasant to see the child so entranced by a city which he loved.

'It is indeed. That is La Scala, and is newly built. But there are certainly very many theatres in Italy.'

'I would love to go there,' she said longingly. 'Perhaps they will perform plays by Goldoni and I would love to see how the players handle such comedy.'

Ninian's eyebrows rose. Once again his wife was surprising him by her knowledge. Most educated young ladies knew the plays of Shakespeare, but he would not have expected her to know very much about the theatre and an Italian playwright, even if his comedies were now becoming well-known throughout Europe. He would almost have wagered that Lora had not been in the theatre in her young life!

'I am surprised that you should be at all acquainted with Goldoni,' he said.

Berris turned quickly from his searching gaze, scolding herself for yet another careless remark, spoken in the excitement of the moment.

'My ... my father saw that I was educated in such matters.'

132

Ninian sat back thoughtfully. Something stirred in his memory. Had there not been scandal involving Lora's mother and the stage? His Aunt Elizabeth had touched briefly on the subject, but had said that her dear Sarah was now dead and her one lapse must be forgotten and forgiven. But perhaps the same inclinations were now in Lora's blood, and he had no wish to encourage *her* to be stage-struck.

'It is doubtful that we will visit many theatres,' he said indifferently. 'Here is the Palazzo Barberno.'

The carriage had stopped in front of a magnificent palace. A great flight of steps led up to the entrance, and Berris was awed into silence as she descended from the carriage and looked up at the grand and ostentatious building.

The weather had grown warmer, but inside the great palace, as they walked through the portals, the air was like ice.

The first storey appeared to consist of a vast hall with marble flooring and many side apartments, but Ninian was already conducting her up to the second floor where a number of servants appeared from every direction. He was made welcome with many smiles and curtseys as though he were returning to a well-loved home.

The ceiling height of the second floor was not nearly so daunting and there were a great many smaller apartments. Ninian and Berris were conducted to a suite of rooms by a manservant in livery, and serving maids scurried about preparing the apartment.

'Carlo is not at home at the moment, but he should return shortly,' Ninian explained.

'But ... surely we are intruding ...' she objected, hesitantly.

'This is the apartment I use when I come to Milan,' he told her, coldly. 'It is usual for guests to be offered this hospitality. Maria Bibiena will attend you, but there are plenty of servants in the palace.'

The chill of the great halls below had found a echo in Berris's heart, and now, although it was warmer in this smaller apartment, she felt ill-at-ease. How rich and noble Ninian's friend must be. Again her own confidence began to ebb and she understood Maria's compassionate gaze when she was first introduced to her new mistress. She must have seemed an insignificant girl against such splendour, which Ninian accepted as part of his life.

The serving maids were chattering and smiling cheerfully and Maria had come to life as she conversed with them eagerly. Berris began to relax a little. Now she was thankful for Maria's presence as she was helped out of her dusty travelling clothes, bathed and then dressed in fresh garments. She was ravenously hungry, but she learned that Ninian would supply the food for themselves and their servants. Italian hospitality did not extend farther than hot chocolate and biscuits when it came to providing food.

Soon, however, a meal had been prepared for them and Berris was glad to eat the chicken and aubergines which had been quickly purchased from street stalls.

'Well? Do you feel better now?' Ninian asked her as Berris found a small square of linen with which to wipe her mouth. He was still restless and there was impatience in his manner, but he had been happy to relax while they ate and there was a lazy smile on his lips as he watched her frank enjoyment of the delicious food.

'Much better,' she agreed, 'though it is all so very strange. I would like to see more of Milan. I would like to see that new theatre you called La Scala. I would like to go there beyond anything!'

'And so you shall!' cried a lighthearted young voice behind them.

Berris twisted round as a young man, richly dressed in velvet with a short cape swinging from his shoulders, came striding into the room. He spoke English, even if it was heavily accented, and he swept them a deep bow as he entered the apartment.

'Ninian! My dear friend!' he cried. 'I welcome you on both cheeks.'

'It is good to see you again, Carlo,' said Ninian with evident pleasure. 'I had thought you would be in Venice with Signora Fiorenza.'

'In three more days. I have business here in Milan for my father, then I return to Venice before the Carnival is over. Why did you stay away from the Carnival? What pleasure there would have been for you!'

Quickly Ninian presented Berris as his wife and Carlo bowed low.

'So you were arranging a marriage, my friend? You are forgiven for neglecting us. I am honoured and delighted to meet a lady who is so enchanting.' He kissed both of her hands. 'I will be Lady Lora's *cicisbeo,* and you can be the cavalier of Signora Fiorenza once more, my dear friend,' he said, turning to Ninian. 'This I will do for your lady.'

Ninian looked disconcerted as he glanced at Berris.

'We have only just arrived, Carlo,' he said. 'My wife, Lady Lora, is not yet familiar with Italian customs and etiquette.'

'Then she will have me to help her and take her to the galas and receptions. My father and mother will have a great gala here in Palazzo Barberno before we go to

Venice, and the Lady Lora will wish to go to the opera and listen to music. Or perhaps she would like to see a play?'

'Is ... is the signora well?' asked Ninian.

To Berris's quick ear, trained to catch nuances of speech, there was an anxious quality to the words. Ninian cared very much about this Italian lady.

'She is very well and she looks forward to your arrival from England once more. We knew you would return soon, Ninian, and it will please her greatly that you have brought your lady.'

He turned again to Berris and she saw that he was taller than she had supposed now that he had removed his richly-embroidered cape and stylish hat. He wore a tunic, deeply pleated, and elegant silk stockings and shoes. He also chose to wear a powdered wig, but his whole appearance was graceful and elegant. She had never seen anyone whose appearance intrigued her more.

His face, however, was so engaging that Berris found herself smiling in response to his dark twinkling eyes and delightful smile. Carlo Filiero must surely be one of the handsomest young men she had ever seen. She could hardly take her eyes from him.

'Tomorrow morning I will attend Lady Lora's toilet,' he said, again sweeping her a bow. 'We have several guests in the Palazzo, Ninian, and there will be gaming, if you wish. It is better that you stay here for a few days and we travel to Venice together. You agree?'

'I agree,' said Ninian, rather reluctantly.

He looked at Lora and saw that she was already fascinated by Carlo and there was vague disquiet in him. She did not understand the custom of *cicisbeism* where a beautiful young wife could have the attentions of a man other than her husband, who was happy to squire her to galas and the theatre, whilst the husband was then free to follow his own pursuits. Would she understand that the attentions of a *cicisbeo* should be accepted lightly and gracefully? It enhanced the social graces of a woman to be able to handle such a situation, and Fiorenza was an expert.

But Lora's nature was quite different. She was a constant surprise to him, in spite of her upbringing. And he found the Ashington family more and more intriguing because of how well, and in some cases how badly, she had been taught.

Ninian moved restlessly round the room, wondering if his unease and reluctance arose from the fact that he was unable to proceed to Venice immediately to see Fiorenza. He was not a true *cicisbeo* to the signora, having only taken Carlo's place

138

now and again, and perhaps because of that he had been unable to prevent himself from becoming emotionally involved with her. He adored her. She was the most exquisite woman he had ever seen. She personified all that was beautiful in Italian art and sculpture; as though a Roman god had breathed life into the most wonderful of all works of art. Fiorenza was unique.

But Carlo's eyes had flickered and widened when he first looked at Lora, and Ninian had recognized deep admiration for her beauty in the eyes of his friend. Carlo would enjoy being her *cicisbeo,* but Lora must not allow her heart to be touched by Carlo. She was as yet so unsophisticated that she could easily be hurt.

'I will leave you to rest,' Carlo was saying. 'Until tomorrow, Lady Lora.'

He kissed her hands again, and Berris turned a delighted face to Ninian.

'Is he not charming?' she asked. 'I was afraid to meet this friend of yours who owned such a magnificient palace ...'

'His *father* owns Barberno.'

'But he is the son, and he has made us so welcome in his splendid home.'

'You should not be so impressed by a building!'

'And he is so handsome,' went on Berris, as though Ninian had not spoken. 'He has promised to take me to the theatre. Did you hear that, Ninian? He will take me to the *theatre*. Oh, Ninian, I think I shall like Italy *very* much!'

'A *magnificent* palace is certainly better than a filthy inn without windows,' Ninian agreed, bitingly. He felt unreasonably bad-tempered with her. 'You had better go to bed, madam. Your *cicisbeo* will arrive in the morning to attend to your toilet and you must not look heavy-eyed with lack of sleep. I shall leave you now.'

Berris was disappointed.

'You ... are you going out, Ninian? Cannot I come with you? I ... I do not care to be left on my own.'

'You have Maria. For me there are the gaming tables. Carlo has promised me a few fine games. Do not worry, I shall not disturb your sleep.'

He begged leave of her and strode out of the apartment. Maria disrobed Berris and once again there was the hint of sympathy in her eyes. Lady Lennox had a great deal to learn about society in Italy.

Ninian walked swiftly out into the street where his surly looks might have brought him trouble had not his broad, lithe body also acted as a warning to those who might have challenged him as he fought his way through groups of young men bent on pleasure.

If only Sophie were here and not in

140

Venice. How desperately he needed her this night when his anger against Berris made him restless and dissatisfied.

Then he paused and sniffed the air, and once again that special magic which embodied the very spirit of Italy took hold of him, and he turned to walk slowly back to the palazzo. He could wait for the delights which lay ahead. Meantime there were the gaming tables.

CHAPTER TWELVE

Berris slept well and was awakened the following morning by Maria, who informed her that Carlo Filiero wished to eat breakfast with her, after which he would attend her toilet.

'Oh no, Maria,' said Berris, sitting up in bed, 'not my toilet! I prefer to be already dressed when Signor Carlo arrives. Where is Sir Ninian?'

'He has gone out, my lady. He wishes to look at paintings.'

'*I* would have enjoyed looking at paintings,' said Berris, piqued because she had not been consulted as to her own plans for the day. 'Could you ask the signor to wait, and help me to dress, Maria?'

'He will not wish to wait, ma'am. It is the custom that he attends you now.'

When Carlo arrived shortly afterwards, Berris was coolly polite, but soon she found herself responding to his gaiety and charm; although having two maids attend her toilet with a man giving advice and instruction at every turn was a new experience for her.

'That gown will not be suitable,' he said, frowning. 'We must see that you have pretty gowns and that is too plain and dark in colour.'

'I like plain dark gowns.'

'They are not suitable for present-day fashion. My mother still wears her black from the days when all women were encouraged to look like crows, but you are young and beautiful and you will have a pretty gown over hooped petticoats and a small jacket made from Italian velvet. We will choose the colours of autumn leaves to match your eyes, and you will wear a fine wig, and look very elegant.'

'I do not wish to wear a wig,' Berris protested.

'Here in Italy you wear a wig. Everyone wears a wig. Yours will be blonde. Tonight I will take you to the opera and you will hear such music as you have never before heard, even in dreams, but you will also draw many eyes because you are an English lady, and beautiful. I will arrange it all.'

'Will ... will Sir Ninian also go to the opera?' asked Berris, suddenly nervous. What did the custom of having a *cicisbeo* really mean? Would she ... would she be expected to share her bed with Carlo after they returned from the opera? Would he also be her lover as well as her cavalier?

143

He had watched with interest, but in an impersonal fashion, as the maids tried on her gowns and set one or two aside to have adjustments made. Even in the travelling theatre, Brendan Meredith had insisted upon discretion and had afforded her and Mistress Grey as much privacy as possible. Berris's eyes crinkled with amusement when she thought about what her stepfather would say if he could see her now, being watched quite openly by an Italian gentleman as she stood in her petticoats.

'We will make an excursion round Milan,' Carlo decided, 'and as to this evening, Ninian will please himself about what he does. Perhaps he, too, will go to the opera. When I stay at his home in London, I also enjoy pleasing myself as to my amusement, and whilst you are in Italy, I will take you to many balls.'

'I shall enjoy the opera,' said Berris.

'I own a box at La Scala,' said Carlo, grandly.

'And I would like to see a theatre play,' she added, her eyes beginning to light up.

'There are many theatres, and if we grow bored with the plays, we can go to the gaming rooms, since they are *in* the theatres,' he told her. 'For who would pay the players if we did not have gaming?

I want all Milan to see that I escort a beautiful lady, and tonight, after the wig-maker has performed his art, you will be even more elegant and beautiful.'

Berris looked at her reflection in the looking glass, her face having been very delicately painted. The maids had exclaimed with pleasure that her skin was already perfect and should not be covered with paint. Ladies must not look like actresses or brothel keepers, but a little paint enhanced the beauty which was already there.

Now faint colour tinged Berris's cheeks as Carlo offered her his arm and escorted her down into an open carriage. There was no sign of Ninian and Berris felt vaguely uneasy. Did he *really* approve of her being escorted by another man? She sighed, then gave herself up to the enjoyment of her day.

Berris's visit to the opera that evening was an unforgettable experience. The cream silk gown which had been chosen for her had been enhanced with lace and embroidery, the sleeves widened to fall in a froth of lace over her elbows. The wig-maker had also worked steadily, and now a tall wig was set on top of her head with a great many gold and silver pins set into it. The pale gold of the wig altered

Berris's appearance considerably, and it was a stranger who stared at her from the gold-framed looking glass at her dressing table. Even Maria held up her hands with wonder and delight when she looked at Lady Lennox.

'But you are beautiful, ma'am,' she said with pride. 'You are just as beautiful as ... as ...'

'Signora Fiorenza?' asked Berris with some asperity, and Maria turned away, busy with tidying up the discarded day gowns. She had served the signora at one time and owed that beautiful lady her loyalty also.

Carlo arrived a short time later to supervise the finishing touches to the toilet, and for once he was entirely satisfied with what he saw.

'A small patch here,' he said, 'High on the cheek so that one sees the eyes ... such unusual eyes! ... and such fine beautiful bones of the face. Lady Lora, you are enchanting!'

He picked up both of her hands and kissed them fervently. 'Never have I seen anyone with such beauty.'

'Well, well! You have been busy, I see, Carlo,' said Ninian, sauntering into the room. 'I see that my wife is now a lady of fashion.'

He smiled at Berris, but she could see

that something had displeased him. She was beginning to know Ninian very well, and to recognize the fire which could kindle in his eyes, and the lines which formed at each side of his mouth.

'So you have lost at the tables,' said Carlo, laughing. 'Next time you will win, my friend. Now I am escorting Lady Lora to La Scala.'

'I will accompany you,' said Ninian. 'I am in the mood to be entertained.'

His eyes scarcely left Berris's face, then they travelled over her body, noting the lower neckline and the softly feminine fichu of lace on her gown. Her appearance was startling and again he felt unreasonably irritated and angry, especially with Carlo. Because of Carlo he had agreed to stay in Milan for a few days when he could even now be on his way to Venice. Now it seemed that the days were to be spent in entertaining Lora.

Besides which, Carlo had made a hothouse flower of her appearance. He had turned his garden marigold into an exotic bloom, and Ninian did not like it. It was not suitable that she should be so painted and powdered that she was unapproachable. She was like a delicate, dainty china ornament instead of the warm, loving, entirely natural girl he had come to know.

Berris wondered if Ninian had lost a great deal of money, but surely he could afford it. Yet he was not accepting his losses philosophically, judging by his black looks, for he was certainly in an ill humour. Nevertheless she was happy that he had decided to accompany her and Carlo to the opera. She would enjoy it the more with Ninian by her side.

It was dark when their coach eventually set out for La Scala opera house, but two runners, one in front of the coach, and one behind it, ran swiftly, lighted torches held aloft.

Berris had already admired the external splendour of the great opera house, but she was unprepared for the luxury which she found inside. The huge lobby had lateral walls with great marble fireplaces and arches decorated with garlands of flowers. The halls were furnished with gaming tables and carved armchairs, and were already occupied by gentlemen intent upon their cards.

Carlo had told them that his father owned a box, but Berris was unprepared for the most sumptuous of apartments, hung with silk, with a ceiling of gilded wood. The walls alternated Venetian mirrors and panels of landscape paintings, and the chairs and divans were covered with yellow silk.

'It is magnificent,' she said, her eyes dazzled by such grandeur. 'I did not know that such a theatre could exist.'

'It replaced one made of wood,' said Carlo. 'It burned down and, among others, my uncle lost his life. It was very sad.'

Her eyes widened with horror, then Carlo smiled reassuringly.

'Do not be alarmed. The great Piermarini who built La Scala has put reservoirs of water up there, above the stage. If there is a fire ... poof! It is out.'

Ninian had been very silent, but the atmosphere of La Scala was gradually lightening his mood as he and Carlo conducted Berris to a comfortable chair from which she could look down upon the stage lit with oil lamps.

The noise in the theatre was incredible. Many patrons had come to hear the opera, but for those who were disinterested in the music, the gaming tables were the chief attraction.

'When will they grow quiet?' Berris asked as the orchestra which was seated on a large platform, began to play an overture.

'When there is music enough to interest everyone,' said Carlo with indifference. 'It is then you will hear the music I have promised you.'

Berris had rarely spent an evening on

the audience's side of the footlights and now in spite of all the grandeur, she felt angry and upset for the singers who, after a great deal of scene shifting, had come on to the stage.

'I think I prefer the audiences of our own theatres who throw things. At least they do not ignore the artists,' she remarked.

Yet the haphazard changes of scenery and long recitations *were* boring, she thought, until the scenes ended and one singer began to sing an aria, and the beauty of the voice began to fill the great auditorium. Gradually the noises ceased and the attention of the audience had been captured at last, so that not a sound was heard except for the music.

Berris had never heard such singing. The female voices, even in the chorus, had a quality, an unearthly beauty such as she had, as Carlo promised, never heard before even in her dreams.

'Can it be that the design of the opera house makes the voices change?' she asked. 'The women's voices are so very unusual.'

'But they are not women; they are men,' said Carlo. 'We do not allow women to act upon the stage.'

Berris was astounded.

'Men!' she cried, 'but ... but the voices?'

'*Castrati,*' said Ninian. 'Sometimes the barbers oblige the young boys who would sing the female parts when they grow up.'

'It is so,' said Carlo.

It took Berris a moment or two to understand, but when she did, her great enjoyment of the evening began to fade and she turned a white face towards Ninian. Silently he poured a glass of wine from a table laid out with refreshments, and handed it to her.

'Thank you,' she whispered, and felt better after the wine had warmed her. So young boys were made to lose their manhood at an age when they did not appreciate the meaning of such a thing, in order that women's roles could be sung by men.

'Why do you not have women singing?' she asked.

'They would be attractive and would cause trouble,' said Carlo. 'In Venice it is different. Orphan girls and girls born out of wedlock are trained to sing and play music. They are very popular. But why concern yourself with such things, Lady Lora? Do you not see the eyes which are turning to you instead of to the stage? Everyone is admiring the beautiful English lady and I am proud to be her escort.'

The warm colour tinged Berris's cheeks as she became aware of her surroundings once more and saw that many heads had turned in her direction. She was unaware that in the soft lights of the theatre, her face looked ethereal in its strange beauty and that her interest in all that she could see and hear had brought an animation so often lacking in ladies of noble birth. Ninian had once again retreated within himself and when she looked at him, he returned her gaze with a stony expression. Why did he so dislike it when admiration was showered upon her? She could only assume that he was impatient of anything which might delay his journey to Venice.

Carlo conducted his guests to the door of their apartment after they returned home from the opera and Maria, who had been dozing sleepily, woke up and swiftly disrobed her mistress, carefully placing her new wig on a special stand.

Berris was glad to lie down between the fine linen sheets. She wondered which room Ninian had taken for his own and marvelled at this strange society which separated a husband and wife in their social life, and gave the wife a charming escort. Or a charming lover? How soon would it be before Carlo wished to share her bed? What would she do if he showed that this was expected of her?

Suddenly the door of her room opened and Ninian strode inside and closed the door once more with a resounding bang.

Berris was startled and raised herself on one elbow.

'Ninian?'

'Be quiet,' he said, sharply. 'I do not want to hear your prattle. I have already listened to enough this evening with all those questions about the theatre and the play actors. Why should you be interested in such people? I should have spent my time at the gaming tables and left you to Carlo, like any husband, but I thought you might feel a little strange in these surroundings. How little I need have worried!'

He was shrugging off his fine velvet coat and embroidered waistcoat, the light from the solitary candle throwing the reflection from his body into weird fantastic shapes upon the ceiling. His black eyes were lit with an inner fire, and his mouth had twisted with an anger she failed to understand. How had she behaved that evening in any way which was not absolutely proper? She had not made a single gaffe. Carlo had lingered over kissing her hands and had told her that all Milan must admire her beauty, but she had accepted such compliments with lightness and grace. She had appeared in many plays where compliments were showered upon the heroine in just such a manner. They were not meant to be taken seriously.

'It was only a game, Ninian,' she whispered, but he placed a cruel hand over her mouth as he leapt into bed beside her.

'Then learn to play the game,' he said. 'If you wish to act like a noble Italian lady, you must learn the manners of such a lady. Instead you grasped Carlo's hand as you watched the stage and moved in unison with the actors. Indeed, you might have been one of them. You behaved like a stage creature, and that is how I intend to treat you!'

He had grasped her body in his strong hands, then he pulled her to him, running his hands over her breasts, then across her stomach to her slender hips and long legs. Next he grasped her most tender part so that she gasped as his thin fingers began to caress her, yet there was no intimacy or love in his exploring fingers, and she felt angered and degraded.

'Do not touch me like that!' she cried, and for answer he covered her mouth with his own, then rolled on top of her and took her body so violently that she cried out with pain. Then he lay panting beside her as the difficult tears began to form in her eyes.

'Lora ...' his voice was hoarse, 'you should not provoke me. I do not know ...' He grew silent.

'You do not know why it should matter to you since you do not love me,' she finished in a harsh, choked voice.

'Do not put words into my mouth.'

'You have made your meaning very clear, sir. You were forced to marry me, just as ... as I was forced to marry you.'

She caught her breath. *Berris* had been forced into the marriage, but what about Lora? She must say no more. She could not speak for her sister.

'But you *are* my wife,' he told her, 'and you are not an Italian woman. You are English. Do not become influenced into behaving like the Italians.'

She was tired, and her body had been disappointed. Ninian's love-making had not awakened her response. She longed for tenderness, but could not ask for it. Now she only wanted to rest.

She sighed and he said no more. But she could not forget that he had used her as though she were 'a stage creature'.

CHAPTER THIRTEEN

They left for Venice two days later and once again Berris found herself journeying through the Italian countryside. She had been withdrawn and coolly polite to Ninian, and even Carlo could not tease her out of her mood. She only wanted to endure the rest of her stay in Italy with patience, then return to her old life with the Meredith Players, as soon as possible after her return to England. Perhaps it was better that she should not be too close to Ninian. In spite of his dark moods, she could not tear him from her heart. Yet because of her love for him, she was vulnerable and he could so easily hurt her.

The journey to Venice, however, was a delight and their welcome, by friends of Carlo, in the cities of Verona and Vicenza, was heart-warming. Apartments were always made available in fine houses and the journey between Vicenza and Padua was unforgettable because of the beauty of the vines which were trained on trees. They covered the branches, then hung down to entwine with other vine shoots from neighbouring trees. Later,

Carlo told her, they would be even more beautiful when the fruit began to ripen.

The roads were in poor condition and caused Carlo to mutter under his breath and to call out sharply to his coachman. But a smile played about Ninian's lips. As each mile passed, he had begun to wear an eager expression once more.

Berris would have enjoyed a visit to the Olympic Theatre in Vicenza, but she did not dare to ask for the journey to be delayed for yet another day. Her eyes grew cool as she watched Ninian's impatience for the journey to be at an end; but once again her sight of the splendours of Venice put everything else to the back of her mind, when they arrived in the great city. The great white marble palaces on the Grand Canal were surely the most magnificent buildings she had ever seen.

The Carnival of Venice had lasted throughout the winter season, having begun at Vespers on Twelfth Night, and even now when it was almost over, the city appeared to be on holiday. Jugglers, singers, entertainers of every type gathered crowds around them, the elegant ladies and gentlemen wearing masks as they watched bullfights, boxing matches, clowns, acrobats and shrieked with excitement when the fortune tellers, palms well crossed with silver, promised long lives and many children.

Berris's eyes were round with wonder as they slowly made their way through the crowds, even as Ninian's lips tightened with impatience that anything should impede his progress when he was so close to seeing the woman who now haunted his every thought.

The home of Fiorenza Michiel was smaller than the Pesaro Palace but no less magnificent. Once again apartments on the second floor had been set aside for them, but the fact that Ninian, Carlo and even Maria Bibiena treated the great palace almost as their own home, only served to make Berris feel more alien. She was dirty and dusty from the long journey, and again many servants hurried to attend to her needs, and to do so with such eagerness to please that she might have been warmed by her welcome had she not been nervous of meeting the Italian lady who meant so much to her husband.

Ninian had been given his own room and soon he came to her, wearing more elaborate clothing than his normal dress. His short cloak was lined with scarlet silk and embroidered with flashing stones.

Berris wore apricot velvet which enhanced the glowing colour of her amber eyes. She had laid aside the blonde wig and once again had insisted that her maids dress her own hair with silk ribbons to match her gown. The anxiety in her eyes gave her a vulnerable look, and for a moment Ninian paused to put his arm about her shoulders.

'What is this? You are very subdued, my lady.

'It is all ... all very strange to me ...'

'Are you afraid of Venice, then? Do not worry, you will not tumble into the Grand Canal and you will soon become used to the gondolas.'

'I am not afraid of *Venice*,' she said, quietly. 'I think it is beautiful. I am afraid of ...'

She paused when she heard a commotion, then a small party of people arrived at the door of the apartment and Carlo swept open the door and bowed low as Signora Fiorenza Michiel glided into the room.

'Ninian!' she cried. 'My dear friend! I knew you would return soon and I was delighted to hear that you were with Carlo in Milan. How wonderful to see you again.'

Ninian's face had come alive and he, too, bowed low and kissed the tiny dainty hands which were held out to him. Watching, Berris's heart was stabbed with pain when she saw the naked adoration on his face. He was oblivious to everything except this

159

woman. He had never looked like that at her.

Then she was face to face with the Italian woman and her heart shook as she looked at the exquisite face, the elegant but well-shaped figure, the smooth perfect complexion, and the bright sparkling eyes which were an astonishing shade of blue. She watched the eyes widen as they rested on her.

'But you have chosen well, my Ninian,' she said, graciously. 'The bride is quite charming. You are very welcome, Lady Lora. I hope that you are going to enjoy your stay in Venice. Carlo has already told me so much about you.'

Berris curtseyed with elegance. She wanted to hate this woman, but instead she had only admiration for her. No wonder Ninian had found her unforgettable.

'It is all very beautiful, ma'am,' she said, huskily.

'I think we will be friends, and you will call me Fiorenza, and I shall call you Lora. We will not be formal with one another.'

Somewhere a bell rang resoundingly and Fiorenza turned to Carlo and Ninian.

'We must go to the coffee room,' she said. 'My husband will be waiting for you and will wish to welcome you before the soup is served. Antonio will want cards later, Ninian, and claims his revenge. You

160

were too good for him last time you stayed here, when you took my dear Carlo's place as my *cicisbeo*.'

Ninian held out his arm to her as Carlo claimed Berris's arm. Other guests appeared from various apartments and made their way to the large apartment which Fiorenza had described as the coffee room. Mirrors sparkled everywhere, the ceiling was frescoed, and the walls hung with draperies. The gilded armchairs were of elaborate shapes, and Berris experienced a strange inconsequential longing for Massingham which managed to combine comfort with elegance. She was finding the great rich palaces of Italy too exquisite to be comfortable, yet she acknowledged that she had never seen such fine carving or such delicacy of line in the cabinets which stood against the wall.

Signor Antonio Michiel was a man almost twice the age of his wife. He wore a massive wig which had twisted sideways and his coat of black velvet, long and pleated, was much less elaborate than that of most of his guests. He looked rather untidy until he turned to greet Berris, then she forgot about his appearance as his twinkling dark eyes searched her face, and a smile played about his lips. He could speak little English, and her own Italian was halting, though she had asked Maria to teach her a few simple phrases.

'Charming,' smiled the signor. 'Charming. You are very welcome.'

'Thank you,' said Berris, huskily, and again she could see laughter in his eyes. She found herself responding with a delighted smile.

'We do not have conversation while we eat our meal,' said Fiorenza. 'Soon you will grow used to the routine of the day, and we will take excursions together. We have a private chapel where you can attend Mass if you are Catholic, and there are billiards for the gentlemen and the ladies may see the dressmaker when they wish. Carlo will advise you on that.'

Her eyes swept over Berris.

'You love your new husband?' she asked, almost carelessly.

Berris was unprepared for the question, and the hot colour flooded her cheeks. Then her chin lifted. Why should she not tell the truth?

'Yes, signora.'

Fiorenza studied her with her head on one side.

'You are young, Lora, yet I see age in your eyes. You have seen more in your life than I would have believed. It is Ninian who sleeps, but soon he might be awake and that will be interesting. He is not a simple man. That is why I enjoy having

162

him as my cavalier.'

'As your lover, signora?' asked Berris.

The charming face grew cool and the eyes narrowed to slits. Berris was already regretting her impulsive question, but it was too late to recall the words.

'You have much to learn, child,' Fiorenza murmured after a long silence. 'Perhaps it would be amusing to teach you. You must excuse me. I have other guests.'

The night Ninian did not come to her bed and Berris was wakeful in spite of the luxury of her surroundings. In the early hours of the morning she could hear men's voices as the male guests returned from the gaming tables, then fatigue overcame her and she slept.

She did not know that Ninian had dressed himself in plain dark clothes, and only Maria Bibiena saw him leave the apartment, and her dark eyes were troubled and sad when she came to attend to Berris.

Ninian stole cat-like through the narrow streets, accompanied by two servants who were used to the desires of gentlemen, until he reached a shabby old building which teemed with life and warmth.

Having climbed the rickety stairs, he knocked on the door of a room and was admitted at once. Sophia Mario was expecting him. Ninian had not made the mistake of taking her by surprise as he had done once before. On that occasion his fury at finding another man in her room had only succeeded in making him appear foolish, after she had shrugged a white shoulder and reminded him that he did not have any exclusive claim to her time.

Ninian had already sent his servants with gifts of flowers and fruit, and now he found the apartment reasonably clean and Sophia clad virginally in white, as though waiting for her marriage night.

'Ninian!' she cried. 'How I have counted the hours and the minutes for you. It has been an eternity.'

He laughed with delight, his eyes sparkling as he held her at arm's length. She had grown more plump, and her skin was not quite so fine as he remembered. Or could it be that he was now used to the exquisitely soft white skin and slender body of his young wife?

Ninian put Berris firmly to the back of his mind and drew Sophia Mario into his arms. The dull glow of the candles threw a mysterious warmth round the room as he removed his outer garments. Again Sophia slipped into his arms and the soft white garment fell to the floor.

'I have waited for you, my Ninian,' said Sophia.

164

Laughter bubbled in him as her eyes met his in widened innocence. They both knew that Sophia would wait no longer than a day for any of her lovers. But her warmth and humour were already enveloping him, and he welcomed her attentions as she helped him to remove the dark clothes, then pulled him into her arms, her breasts pressed against him.

Yet although she was as generous and lovely as ever, Ninian felt vaguely dissatisfied as he ran his hand over the plump whiteness of her naked flesh, and felt how eagerly she responded to his every touch. He made love to her as he had always done, with an eagerness for the body of a woman who had completely abandoned herself to his every need. But it seemed to him that he had grown away from her. Surely he had not been young and callow when he last appreciated her charms? She no longer satisfied him like ... like Lora.

Almost angrily, he turned away from Sophia and, quick to sense his mood, she began to laugh softly. Her fine Englishman was not now so easy to please.

'We must be friends,' she suggested, 'and share some wine together. You will tell me what you have done with your life since we last met and what you are now doing in Venice.'

165

She had found a heavier garment and her black hair fell about her shoulders so that she looked young and fresh once more.

'I have come to buy a few pictures,' he told her, easily.

'Pictures? Paintings? Ah now, I entertained a young artist ... just a friend you understand ... and he wants to paint me when I only wear ... ah ... so little, but I say I will not unless he remembers that I am a lady.'

Once again her eyes, wide with innocence, met Ninian's and suddenly they were both laughing helplessly.

'Sophia, you rid me of my vapours,' he assured her. 'You do not ask if I bring you any presents.'

'You know I *never* ask,' she said, with dignity.

He reached deep into the pocket of his coat and brought out a slender jeweller's box. Inside was a bracelet which sparkled with gems. Fiorenza would have shuddered at the poor taste of such a gift, and Ninian had doubts whether Lora might also have found it too flamboyant. But Sophia accepted it with squeals of delight. Swiftly she tucked away the notes which went with the gift, but the bracelet was immediately fastened on to her wrist.

'Ninian! It is *so* beautiful!' she cried.

'Thank you millions.'

Suddenly his eyes were sad as he looked at her. She was young, almost as young as Lora, yet already he could see the signs of age in her.

'You should marry, Sophia,' he said abruptly.

Her eyes flew to his and there was a hint of fear in their depths.

'You are not coming back?'

He shrugged then bent to kiss her.

'Oh, I shall come back, but you must think about yourself.'

He picked up one of the flowers he had sent and stuck it playfully into her hair before letting himself quietly out of the door. Slowly Sophia removed the flower and crushed it against her lips. Only then did her eyes fill with tears.

Berris loved Venice. Despite the fact that Ninian could not hide his joy and pleasure in Fiorenza and she had to watch, silently, with a smile on her lips but a continued ache in her heart, she found the beautiful city a constant delight.

Nor could she hate the lovely Italian woman, even if she found Fiorenza difficult to understand. Long dark eyelashes would sweep over her brilliant blue eyes and sometimes she would raise a fan in front of her face so that Berris was never sure whether or not she pleased the older woman when they talked together. That Ninian pleased her was very evident.

They laughed and talked together by the hour, discussing the relative merits of Canaletto, Tiepolo and Francesco Guardi. Fiorenza had purchased a new piece of sculpture by Canova, and she and Ninian spent many hours discussing the mythological subjects beloved by the sculptor and how far Italian art would influence the rest of Europe.

Berris silently deplored her own lack of formal education. Only in the theatre could she hope to match Fiorenza's knowledge of the arts, but Fiorenza did not care for talk of the stage and the subject apparently bored her, so that Berris was obliged to watch Ninian being completely captivated by Fiorenza's bright mind as well as her glowing beauty.

Carlo was determined that Berris would not be neglected, however, and he attended her on every possible occasion. At first she had decided that she preferred to dress in her own fashion and to use the courtesies most natural to her, but always there was the echo of Ninian's voice in her head, advising her that she should learn how to conduct herself like a noble Italian lady. She could not hope to match Fiorenza, but she must learn to please him as best she could. Used as she was to learning a part, she began to emulate Fiorenza, and sometimes Berris caught a sparkle of amusement and approval in the bright blue eyes as she unconsciously mimicked a gesture and learned to walk with the carriage of a duchess.

From the first she had to observe the routine of the great palace. At nine o'clock a bell would ring to summon the gentlemen guests to be shaved and have their hair dressed. The ladies' toilet was carried out in their chambers. At ten o'clock another bell summoned all guests to the coffee room, where the Signor and Signora Michiel entertained their friends and everyone drank chocolate.

In the afternoons, after a rest, the signora insisted upon an excursion in the barouche, or in a gondola along the Grand Canal, and in the evenings they attended a theatre where Berris was completely captivated by the Goldoni comedies, even though her Italian was still not good enough to ensure complete understanding of the dialogue. The signora was, in turn, intrigued to see the absorption of her guest and was gracious enough to try to enjoy the comedies for her sake.

Yet the Venetian society felt strange and unreal to Berris, and she seemed to have exchanged her husband for Carlo, and had to accept that Ninian belonged to Fiorenza. At the opera it was Ninian who draped a silk shawl over the shoulders of the beautiful Italian woman, whilst Carlo held Berris's fan and handed it to her when she required to use it.

Her clothes were now elegantly fashioned, and she had succumbed to wearing a wig on every occasion. Soon her mannerisms were equally elegant, and she acquired a grace and poise which aroused Carlo's open admiration.

Gradually Berris began to enjoy her new life and, as she accepted Carlo's attentions, she became aware once again that Ninian was becoming less satisfied than he had been with this state of affairs. Sometimes he came to her bed after they returned home from a gala evening, though he was rather silent and she found it difficult to discuss anything with him. He took her body as though he had need of her, and nothing more.

Sometimes he would tell her, carefully, that his host had requested his attendance at the gaming tables and Berris allowed a small smile to play about her lips.

'We must not keep you from attending your ...' she hesitated very slightly, '... host.'

'It is unlikely that you will be bored without me,' said Ninian, almost harshly.

'It has not escaped my notice that you enjoy Carlo's favours.'

'As you do Fiorenza's,' she returned, crisply.

She seated herself in front of her dressing table, and he leaned over and suddenly pulled the blonde wig from her head, throwing it into the furthest corner of the room. The pins flew in all directions and she stifled a small cry.

'I knew that it was a mistake to bring you here,' he said, furiously. 'You have no idea how to conduct yourself.'

'Perhaps I conduct myself only too well,' she said with dignity. 'You want me to have the manners of an Italian lady. Very well, that is what you will have. Now I must ask you to excuse me. I am fatigued.'

She waved a fan in front of her face, stifling a pretended yawn. Slowly he rose to his feet, his eyes challenging hers. She saw that he was greatly angered, yet she had not protested against his attendance on Fiorenza, nor could he accuse her of being unfaithful to him with Carlo. Everything had been entirely proper between them.

At first Berris had wondered if Carlo would wish to slip into her apartment when Ninian was absent, but his attentions always stopped short of such intimacies.

But as Ninian began to show more signs of ill-temper towards her, Berris began to lose her new-found confidence. Her husband did not always want her, yet Carlo showed no signs of being attracted as a lover either. Could it be that she was physically unattractive? she wondered. What made Fiorenza so desirable? Surely her own appearance and manners were now as exquisite as was possible? In her own way she might be thought as attractive as the older woman, and her very youth was one of her chief assets. She had a vitality which kept her glowing with life long after many of the other ladies had retired to rest.

When Carlo returned home with her one evening, and bent to kiss her hands and to tell her that she was the most enchanting woman in Venice, Berris stared at him rather sadly.

'But not enchanting enough,' she said, sighing.

'I do not understand you,' said Carlo. 'What is enough?'

Berris forgot that she must always be delicate and dainty in her conversations. In her nervous state she reverted to her own natural direct approach.

'You have never asked to be my lover, yet my husband is the lover of the signora. Why is that? Am I so unattractive? Perhaps

I would not care to have a lover, but I wonder why you do not desire me, yet you wish to be my *cicisbeo*.'

Carlo's face had slowly coloured to a deep rich red, and his eyes were full of distress as he stared at Berris.

'I would give much to be your lover, Lady Lora,' he said, hoarsely, 'but how could that be? I could not insult you so grossly. Do you not know that a *cicisbeo* is *never* the lover of his lady? He is the dear companion of his friend's wife, but he must be trusted to look after her honour at all times. Such a thing could never be!'

'I ... I see,' said Berris, faintly. 'I did not understand. I ... I thought ...' Her eyes grew round. 'Then ... then Ninian is *not* the lover of the signora?'

'But never!' cried Carlo, horrified. 'He is a guest of Signor Michiel. He would be called out if he insulted the signora. Each night Signor Michiel desires him to play cards or billiards, and he is cavalier to Fiorenza during the day, just as I am when Ninian returns to England. It is the custom.'

'I ... I can only ask pardon,' said Berris, hot with shame. She had practically invited Carlo to her bed!

'You did not know. I will say goodnight.'

He rushed out of the apartment with all possible speed and Berris tried to cool her warm cheeks. She had now made the biggest mistake of all. She had never felt so ashamed.

The next few days were difficult. She could no longer relax and enjoy Carlo's company. The indiscretion of her behaviour seemed to lie between them like the torn petals of an exquisite flower. Now, more than ever, she began to understand the true nature of the game which was played in this society and to appreciate how delicately relationships must be handled in order to delight everyone concerned.

And although Carlo had appreciated that she had spoken to him out of ignorance of the true situation, nevertheless her words had destroyed the delicate grace of it all. No longer could they talk and laugh together. Now there was only awareness and lack of ease with one another. No longer was he even disposed to dally a little at the door of her apartment when he returned home with her in the evenings.

Berris retired early and spent some time in quiet thought before retiring to bed. How long would this state of affairs last? Surely Ninian must make plans to go home to England some time soon.

She was unaware that he had entered her room until he spoke.

'Things have gone wrong between you and Carlo, have they not?' he asked harshly, as he closed the door firmly behind him.

She jumped then turned to face him, distress in her eyes. He grabbed her wrist.

'He has fallen in love with you, has he not? It is plain that he is no longer happy merely to be your cavalier. And what of you? Have you encouraged him? Has he broken his trust and taken you?'

'No!' she cried. 'He is my *cicisbeo*. He would never be my lover!'

Some of the anger left Ninian's eyes.

'So you understand what it all means?'

'I understand.'

He was silent for a short while then his eyes narrowed once more.

'If you are lying to me, by God I will beat you.' His breath hissed between his teeth and his mouth twisted. 'Perhaps you do not know, Lady Lora, that I have just seen Carlo rushing away from this apartment after having escorted you home. He would not even wait to talk with me, nor could he look me straight in the eye. He has been avoiding me for several days and I can think of only one explanation. What has passed between you? Have you fallen in love with him?'

'No!' she cried again. 'Let me be, sir, you are hurting me.'

Berris had become Signora Fiorenza as she stared at Ninian haughtily. The role slipped over her shoulders perfectly and she had little idea as to its effect on Ninian. Deeply he was beginning to regret the loss of the lovely, warm-hearted natural girl who had been his wife. Now he had a beautiful, elegant Italian lady.

Ninian's need of her overwhelmed him, but reluctantly he released his hold on her wrist.

'Very well. I will leave you now. I must go ...'

'I know, sir, to the gaming tables,' she said sweetly.

'To the gaming tables,' he repeated.

He strode out of the apartment, his thoughts now turning towards Sophia Mario. This was one night when he needed the comfort of her body above all else. Swiftly he changed into the plain dark clothes he wore when venturing abroad at night, then left the apartment to find his servants, almost knocking down Maria Bibiena in his haste.

Maria, on her way to attend to Berris, looked after him fearfully. She had no illusions as to Sir Ninian's destination and her eyes were sad. So often she had thought that he would forget Sophia Mario after he married the Lady Lora. At first she had thought the lady too young to hold such a man, but she had changed her mind as she watched Lady Lora grow in maturity and beauty, yet still retain a warmth and capacity for love which was not always given to ladies of such breeding.

Maria deplored visits to such women as Sophia Mario, and crossed herself surreptitiously as she entered Berris's chamber and hurried to help her mistress prepare for bed. Lady Lora looked distressed and there were signs of tears in her eyes. Her face was white and she regarded Maria gravely for a few minutes as the maidservant helped her out of her elegant gown, and placed her tall blonde wig on its stand. Quickly, Berris removed the pins from her own hair and it tumbled in shining curls to her shoulders.

'Could you find Sir Ninian for me at the gaming tables, Maria?' she asked, huskily. 'I ... I think I have made a mistake.'

She should not have rejected him when he came to talk to her. It had hurt her pride that he did not love her, but only wanted the solace of her body. She had tried to accept the fact that his heart was already given, but sometimes, as now, her desire to possess him completely overcame her good sense. She should accept what he had to give, and not ask for more.

Soon, when they returned to England, she would have nothing.

Maria was acting strangely, making a great show of hanging out her gown.

'Maria?'

'Yes, my lady ... but ... Sir Ninian is not at the gaming tables. He has gone out. I ... I saw him go as I entered this chamber.'

'Gone out? Why should he go out? Surely he has every form of entertainment he needs inside the palazzo ...'

Her voice trailed off. She caught sight of Maria's averted face in the looking glass and saw that it was highly coloured and bore that same expression she had seen once before. Maria was sorry for her.

'Come here!' she commanded. 'Stand here where I can see you, Maria. Now tell me where my husband has gone, if not to the gaming tables.'

'I do not know, my lady,' said Maria, uncomfortably.

'You cannot lie to me,' said Berris. 'You cannot hide your thoughts, Maria. I have read them on your face in the past. Now, tell me. Where has he gone?'

'I cannot!' cried Maria, wildly. 'He would beat me.'

'I will most certainly beat you if you do not tell me.'

There was a glint in Berris's eyes and the other woman swallowed convulsively.

'He ... he has gone to Sophia Mario.'

Berris started. 'Who is Sophia Mario?'

'She is a lady of ... of leisure ... who entertains gentlemen ...' said Maria, painfully. 'I know because one of the

178

servants who often accompanies Sir Ninian is my cousin.'

'So he has visited this lady often in the past? When he last stayed in Venice?'

'Oh yes, my lady, she is not a new acquaintance,' said Maria, eagerly. She must assure her young mistress that Sophia Mario was an old friend.

Berris's hammering heart began to steady as she questioned Maria closely, learning everything she could about Sophia Mario. She was beautiful, but of poor family. She was trash, said Maria, crossing herself again. She had an apartment within walking distance and when she walked abroad she decorated herself with great fabulous jewels which were gifts from her admirers.

Berris listened and allowed the slow anger to rise in her. She had accepted Ninian's love for the beautiful Fiorenza. After meeting the signora, she had known that she could not match the Italian woman for beauty and grace. She did not blame any man for being moved with admiration, and she had accepted that her own role must be that of a wife who gave bodily comfort to her husband.

But even as he came to her, Ninian had also been visiting another woman. Many times she had thought him fulfilled, but she had believed that he was going to Fiorenza in great secrecy and discretion.

Having learned that such a thing was unthinkable, Berris had felt a great relief. A short while ago, when he came to her room, she had rebuffed him because she was still playing the role of Fiorenza. But immediately she had regretted it, and longed to feel his arms round her.

Now she felt betrayed. Ninian had betrayed her, and he had also betrayed the signora. He had been stealing like a cat through the night to this woman ...

'Find my darkest gown, Maria,' she said, urgently, 'and help me to dress.'

Maria's mouth fell open.

'But, my lady ... what do you intend ...?'

'I go to visit Sophia Mario, of course. You will come with me and we will also take two menservants.'

Maria's eyes widened with horror.

'You cannot do so, ma'am. You *cannot* go to see Sophia Mario. Such a thing is unthinkable!'

'*Cannot?*' repeated Berris, coldly. 'Do as I tell you, Maria. Stand aside and I shall select my own gown. This plain dark one is suitable. Help me into it. I will wear that cloak also.'

Maria did so automatically when Berris turned to face her, her amber eyes glowing with a strange light. Maria did not argue further. Without a word she hurried to find her own cloak and to bid two of the many servants attend them. If the men were surprised by the errand thrust upon them, their impassive faces did not show it. The behaviour of ladies and gentlemen was often beyond their comprehension.

Maria ordered a vehicle to take them to Sophia's apartment, and Berris found the whole of the old building well lit when she arrived. She understood at once, that there must be many apartments in the house, which had an air of neglect as if it had seen better days. One of the menservants directed her to Sophia's door, where Ninian's two servants stood guard.

'You will wait for me here in the carriage,' Berris commanded Maria.

'But my lady, you do not know what you risk.'

'And you risk a beating if Sir Ninian lays eyes on you. He will soon guess how I have discovered his secret. Remain in the carriage out of sight.'

Maria needed no second bidding and Berris made her way to the apartment and haughtily commanded the menservants to stand aside. Recognizing her, they obeyed, and Berris rapped imperiously on the door.

A notice stated that Sophia did not wish to be disturbed and it took three rappings before she came to the door, clad only in her white wrapper. She peered at her caller.

'Cannot you tell when I am not free?' she asked. 'Where are the guards? Tonight I have a guest. Who is it? ... Oh!'

'Perhaps it is your guest I wish to see,' said Berris, pushing past the girl and walking into the room. Ninian lolled at his ease on a rickety chair, his outer garments removed and his shirt open at the neck.

His smile froze when he saw Berris. They stared at one another, and very slowly he rose to his feet.

'Who is the visitor, my dear friend?' Sophia was asking in her rich, husky voice.

'Lady Lennox,' said Berris, succinctly.

'Another potential lightskirt or she would not be abroad at this hour,' said Sir Ninian, 'and in such an apartment.'

'In which you are so much at home, sir,' she said, sulkily. 'So this is what you need, is it?'

She grasped the white wrapper and whipped it from Sophia's body. The girl gave a cry and Berris threw it back at her disdainfully.

'And *this* is what *you* need, madam,' repeated Ninian and with a quick movement he pulled her over his knee and spanked her with all the fury she had aroused in him. Berris willed herself to remain silent even though a low moan escaped her lips as he threw her to the floor.

'That will teach you not to follow me,' he told her, 'and do not call yourself Lady Lennox whilst you are under this roof. It is an honourable name.'

'I have never besmirched it, sir,' she said, quietly, rising once more to her feet. Her tender flesh was burning unbearably.

She walked towards the door.

'Goodnight, sir. I shall not spoil your entertainment further.'

She swept out and hurried downstairs to the waiting carriage, no longer able to control the angry tears which coursed down her cheeks. Gradually they turned to soothing tears but she felt exhausted as Maria once again helped her to prepare for bed.

'The gentlemen lead different lives from their ladies, ma'am,' said Maria. 'I should never have told you about Sophia Mario. I could be dismissed from Sir Ninian's service.'

'I had to know,' said Berris. 'You will not be dismissed. I shall see to that.'

But would she? she wondered as she lay on her bed. Would Sir Ninian be so furious with her that he would no longer accept her as his wife? He had spanked her with fury in the heat of the moment, but after he had time to think, would not the punishment be even greater? And what would happen if he found out she was not really his wife, but only a play actress?

Berris shivered beneath the covers. Her life might not be worth a farthing. Lora would never have done as she had this night. Only Berris was unafraid to venture forth in the dark, and to argue with a lightskirt. That sort of life was not such a mystery to Berris as it might be to Lora.

As she turned the events of the evening over in her mind, she saw again the voluptuous woman who had held her husband's attentions. She was beautiful, yes, but she was no longer so young and fresh. Berris's small hands caressed her own smooth body. Sophia was no more beautiful than she was. The thought gave her some small satisfaction.

It might have pleased her to know that Ninian spent very little more time in Sophia's apartment.

'So that was the young wife,' Sophia said, pouting provocatively. 'She is not such a lady, is she? I think you should teach her better manners, dear Ninian. How did she find out? Perhaps you stole her bracelet to give to me ...'

'Be quiet, Sophia,' said Ninian harshly.

His anger was smouldering, born of a sense of shame that Lora should see him in such surroundings. How could she be so ... so brash as to come here like this? Surely it should have been bred in her that she must not enquire too deeply into her husband's affairs? She had behaved outrageously and he felt humiliated beyond belief. If he had her soft neck between his fingers, he felt sure that he would snap it like a twig.

His hands clenched as though he could feel her delicate skin, and even as he thought about her, great waves of revulsion swept over him for the woman who sauntered around the room, chattering lightly about Lora. How dare she even speak her name in this room!

He felt soiled and besmirched as he quickly donned his dark garments. Pulling out his purse, he placed gold coins on a table so that Sophia's eyes widened.

'So it is goodbye, my friend?' she asked, rather sadly.

He nodded. 'Perhaps it is best.'

She began to laugh, a low throaty chuckle.

'I tell you, Ninian, I would not leave such a wife. She is a real woman. She has courage.'

He said no more, but kissed her briefly on the forehead. Sophia sat down, her eyes sad, then she began to laugh once more as she thought over the events of the evening, and soon she was rolling helplessly on the bed, hardly able to breathe. She had never been so amused. She had entertained many gentlemen, but never before had their ladies come to winkle them from her bed.

Wiping her eyes she rose and counted out her gold coins. She would miss the tall English lover, but she would never forget his lady!

CHAPTER FOURTEEN

It was a stranger who looked out of Ninian's eyes when he came to Berris's chamber the following morning. Carlo was already there, his eyes alight and his voice ringing with the joy of living, as he supervised Berris's toilet, taking meticulous pains to make the most of her undoubted beauty.

He had recovered from the embarrassment of having to explain to his lady that he could never be her lover because his honour would not allow it, but he felt that there could now be a closer relationship between them. He had confessed to her that he desired her greatly, and this knowledge brought poignancy to their relationship which delighted, even as it saddened Carlo. If he and Berris were the only two people in the world, how different things might be.

He lay awake in the night imagining that such a thing could happen, and in his imagination he held her closely in his arms and kissed the beautiful lips and cheeks which he could not only admire from afar. He would make love to her with such delicacy and passion that she would never want any other man.

He sighed for what he could never have, and leaned forward in his chair.

'A small patch on the cheek,' he advised, 'to draw attention to their unusual shape, and the texture of Lady Lora's complexion. It is truly exquisite.'

The young maid who attended to the toilet removed a patch from a jewelled box and held it against Berris's cheek.

'Higher,' said Carlo. 'There, that is better. Now she is ready to face the world and for all the world to admire her. I kiss your hand, Lady Lora.'

He was proceeding to do so when Ninian walked in. He wore the most sober of his garments, with his own hair in a queue, but his neatness and elegance was beyond question. His mouth was set in a hard line and when Berris looked into the icy sparkle of his eyes, her heart lurched. She could see that Ninian was still in a towering rage. Her buttocks still smarted from the spanking he had administered, but Ninian could hardly lay hands upon her in front of Carlo, and she therefore greeted him sweetly.

'Carlo has brought an invitation from Signora Fiorenza that we should take a gondola on the Grand Canal and visit the Accademia di Pittura e Sculptura. I understood you wished to look at paintings by Francesco Guardi, Sir Ninian?'

'I have already done so, Lady Lora,' he replied. 'I will certainly attend Signora Fiorenza if she wishes to make an excursion.'

'That is good,' said Carlo, happily. 'Today we will accompany one another. It is a great delight to have you here, my dear friend, and the beautiful Lady Lora.'

Berris could not prevent her eyes from crinkling with amusement. Carlo was like no one she had ever met. He looked very colourful in his elegant clothes, and his movements were almost that of a dancer as he swept her a bow and turned to Ninian. Then she caught Ninian's smouldering looks and her smile faded. Sooner or later she was going to have to face him alone. How would he deal with her then?

Berris had been satisfied and even secretly delighted by her own looks, but they paled a trifle when the signora made her way to the reception hall on Ninian's arm. Her complexion was like apple-blossom, enhanced by the shell-pink of her beautiful silk gown. Her pale blonde wig had a silvery sheen and the pins which secured it flashed with diamonds and pearls.

She smiled when she saw the admiration

in Berris's eyes, and touched her cheek with a slender jewelled hand.

'You look charming, child,' she said. 'Today we must enjoy the fine weather, then rest when the sun grows hot. My dear friend, Ninian, wishes to look at paintings and we will all accompany him and enjoy learning from his experience.'

Carlo had once mentioned that Fiorenza's experience in the appreciation of paintings was the finest in Venice, but now she was deferring to Ninian. Berris watched carefully, seeing how the Italian lady could build up the stature of her friends, even as she accepted their homage. She wondered if she could ever learn such arts, but sadly decided that she could never learn to be like the signora. She was too forthright. What would the signora say if she knew how she had behaved on the previous evening? Berris swallowed and her eyes flew to Ninian, but he studiously ignored her, and it fell to Carlo to attend her every need.

It was a delightful morning. The Grand Canal was surely one of the world's most beautiful places, thought Berris, feeling like a fairy princess who floated along on a roseleaf, as she sat beside Carlo in the gondola. Such thoughts brought her out of her daydreams sharply, however, when she remembered that other fairy princess whom she had played in *Silver Stardust*. How shocked the signora and Carlo would be if they knew that they entertained a play actress! And if Ninian could suddenly read her past life like an open book, he might be tempted to throw her into the canal.

She swallowed nervously, her confidence beginning to evaporate, then she saw that the signora's searching eyes were upon her, and that her smile was encouraging.

Later Berris forgot to be nervous as they studied the exhibition of Guardi paintings and Fiorenza asked Ninian to compare the work with that of Canaletto. Almost hesitantly, he began to talk and very soon Berris was delighted to see the warm woman who was Fiorenza Michiel shining through the exquisitely beautiful outer shell as they discussed colour, perspective, brush work and the conception of each painting. She listened avidly, not on this occasion because she wished to learn and copy from the signora, but because of genuine interest. Only Carlo was bored and contented himself with staring at Berris, and showing his frank delight in her vivacity and the attraction of her charms.

Ninian, too, had noticed Carlo's absorption with his wife and this time his displeasure was so great that even Carlo drew back with a puzzled frown. Surely his dear friend, Ninian, knew that he was allowed to admire his lady. He must know her honour was completely safe.

When they stopped for refreshment at the fine home of one of Fiorenza's friends, thereby accepting an invitation already extended to the English guests, Fiorenza continued to speak quietly to Berris.

'You must find that Venice is very different from London, Lora,' she said, gently.

'Very different,' Berris agreed, adding with a smile, 'it was raining when we left there.'

'I do not mean the rain. We carry our own weather within our hearts. Sometimes the sun shines, and sometimes it rains.'

'How true,' Berris murmured, feelingly. She had had moments of sunshine with Ninian, but now it seemed as though they were in the middle of a storm.

'It is hard to take up the customs of a country when one is a guest in that country,' Fiorenza went on. 'When I visited London I found that my English friends thought me very cold and remote, but inside my heart I was afraid of making an error which would embarrass my host and hostess. You understand? It is some years ago, and my good friends were the parents of Sir Ninian. Alas, they are dead now. That is sad because I think they would have liked their charming daughter, Ninian's bride.'

Berris coloured with delight. What a gift Fiorenza possessed for bestowing confidence. Sometimes she had wondered about Ninian's parents. Now it was a pleasure to know that they might have liked her.

'And, of course, when one returns to one's own society, and entertains visitors from England, it is easy to imagine how misunderstandings might arise. Carlo makes you a charming companion, but perhaps Ninian grows jealous. Your marriage is very new, unlike my own. My dear husband enjoys his own leisurely pursuits, but he likes me to venture into society and to enjoy what it has to offer.'

'Ninian is not jealous,' said Berris, rather bitterly. 'He is merely angry with me.'

Fiorenza considered this for a moment. She was too well-mannered to ask why Ninian was so angry, and Berris did not wish to tell her.

'You must put your marriage and your English customs before those you have found in Italy,' said Fiorenza quietly. 'One day you will return to England. Perhaps it ought to be soon, if your marriage is not so well-founded that it cannot stand Carlo's attentions to you.'

'Sir Ninian will decide,' said Berris,

rather bleakly. 'I have no influence with him.'

Fiorenza said no more, but her eyes were thoughtful.

Apparently it pleased Fiorenza Michiel to form a party of four wherever they went. She kept Ninian by her side, and encouraged Carlo to attend to Berris's every wish in spite of the advice she had already given. It was as though their conversation had never been, though Berris, as they drove in the fine carriage into the country for a picnic, or attended a gala or reception at the home of one of Fiorenza's friends. Everyone vied with one another to entertain the English nobleman and his bride.

Ninian had not come to Berris's room since that terrible night she had followed him to Sophia Mario's apartment, and sometimes Berris was almost driven to confiding in Fiorenza. She had already seen how shocked Carlo could become at any hint of impropriety, and she felt that although Fiorenza had a breadth of vision belied by her appearance and attention to etiquette, she too would find Berris's behaviour reprehensible.

Then one evening the carriages were delayed as they were about to leave after a visit to the opera house, and Carlo and

194

Berris became separated from Ninian and Fiorenza.

'It is because of some accident,' said Carlo, coming to find her, 'but I have managed to find a carriage for us. I shall take you home, Lady Lora, then return to find the signora and Ninian if they have not yet returned to the Palazzo.'

'I cannot see them in this crush of people, Carlo,' said Berris, worriedly. 'It is certainly best that we return home.'

She was glad to see the warmth of her bedroom once more. The nights could grow remarkably chilly. Maria helped her to undress carefully, and to put on her voluminous white nightgown.

Suddenly the bedroom door flew open and Ninian stood there. He still wore his outdoor clothing, even to the small silver-topped cane which he carried.

'Out!' he commanded Maria.

She threw a startled glance at Berris then scuttled away, shutting the door carefully.

'So you are home, sir,' said Berris with some relief. 'We were anxious about you, Carlo and I.'

'Carlo and I,' he repeated. 'Carlo and I! How easily you link yourself with him. How closely you spend your hours together.'

'I have told you before,' she said, quickly, 'it is the custom as you should know. Your own time is well taken up with the signora,

195

yet I do not complain.'

'No? You did not hesitate to complain when I called upon another friend. I have not noticed that you allow me the freedom you allot yourself. You have no right to oversee my every move, madam.'

Berris's cheeks began to glow.

'I do not mind your escorting Fiorenza, but your lightskirt was different.'

He began to throw off his outer garments, towering over her where she still sat at her dressing table. Slowly she removed her hairpins, and her hair tumbled about her shoulders.

'So my lightskirt was different. I should have made *you* my lightskirt, madam. I should pretend that I do not notice when your eyes smile at Carlo and your lips invite his kisses, even if they cannot be yours. Or so it would seem. But what about the times when you are alone with one another? Is there still restraint between you? He is in love with you, and you ... what do you feel, Lora? Is it love you have for him? Has he taken your heart?'

'You know he has not,' she cried. 'How could I love him, when ... when ...'

She bit her lip and turned her head away. How could she confess her love for him when he did not want her. Sophia Mario supplied his bodily needs, and Signora Fiorenza held his heart.

'When what, Lora?' he was asking, urgently. 'What about your love?' He put a hand on her shoulder. 'I must have the truth from you. Can it be that you love me in spite of the fact that the marriage was forced upon you. I always knew that you had no choice in our marriage.'

She looked at him tiredly. 'Very well, I will tell you the truth. Why should it matter? I do love you, Ninian. I love Italy and find it is a beautiful country with charming people, even if the customs are strange to me, but I could not love Carlo. I could not live this sort of life. You asked me to learn the manners of a noble Italian lady and I have done so for you, but underneath I want to be myself. I do not want to be so ... so full of artifice.'

His shirt was now open at the neck and he had come to sit beside her on the broad stool, pulling her into his arms. His stern face was more tender than she could possibly have imagined.

'My darling,' he whispered, 'my darling Lora, I never knew that it was possible to fall in love with one's own wife. I have been so angered and full of temper when I saw poor Carlo admiring you, and sometimes I could not understand myself. But soon I learned what it was to be jealous, and then I knew that I loved you.'

'But ... but Fiorenza! Surely you are in love with her?'

'In a way, yes I love her. When we met, she was the loveliest woman I had ever seen, but now I know that I admire her as I admire a lovely portrait by Franceso Guardi. I admire her as I admire beautiful sculpture, or the purity of voice of a *castrati*. She is very beautiful and much loved by her husband, but it was only when I saw the two of you together that I realized how much I wanted my wife of warm flesh and blood. I wanted to kill both you and Carlo every time he kissed your hand. Tonight ... tonight when you both left in a separate carriage, I knew that I could stand no more.'

He was removing her white bedgown and Berris could hardly believe what she was hearing. Ninian loved her! His fingers were twining themselves through the warm living softness of her hair.

Then the lamp was turned low and extinguished as Ninian placed Berris gently on the bed. He had made love to her many times, but never before with such tenderness, as he stroked her soft breasts and kissed the whiteness of her throat. His caressing fingers touched her thighs and he whispered to her that she was more beautiful than any woman he had ever known.

Berris felt as though she could scarcely breathe as Ninian touched the most tender parts of her body. Her heart beat loudly and she could feel the blood coursing through her veins as she, in turn, began to caress the smoothness of his skin, knowing as he thrust towards her that he desired her more than he had ever done before.

She called his name and his lips claimed hers, hot and demanding, so that her body seemed to be lifted to a new plane. Then he was taking her in love and Berris's passion was as great as his own, so that once again they lay locked together, their bodies entwined, their ecstasy soaring and leaving them both gasping and trembling with the wild sweetness.

'We will begin our return journey to London and Massingham tomorrow,' said Ninian, 'unless you wish to travel further south to Florence and Rome. There are still beauties for you to see in Italy, but I feel impatient to see our home once more.'

'We will come back,' said Berris. 'Some time we will come back. I will always remember that here I have been happier than I have ever been in my life.'

'We will go home to Massingham and see Aunt Elizabeth,' said Ninian. 'It will give her pleasure that I have found the love she always wanted for me.'

'Oh, Ninian, I am so happy,' she said, softly.

Into her mind's eye there came the image of Fiorenza Michiel and her thoughtful eyes as she talked about the customs of their two countries. She had told Fiorenza that Ninian did not love her, and the Italian lady had, delicately but firmly, insisted upon taking her and Carlo everywhere with Ninian and herself. Carlo's elaborate compliments and open admiration had done the rest. Berris sighed with gratitude towards the beautiful woman who could so easily have taken her happiness, but instead had returned it to her with charm and grace.

Suddenly she was aware that Ninian was shaking with laughter as he lay beside her.

'Why do you laugh?' she asked.

'I was remembering ...'

He tried to find his breath, then once again he was shaken with mirth so that Berris was obliged to laugh with him.

'But what is so amusing?' she repeated.

'Your arrival at Sophia Mario's apartment,' he gasped. 'What a woman I have! When you wrenched her garment from her body, I could not believe it. How amused Sophia was later.'

'Amused?'

'She is a charming woman. You would like her, my dearest.'

'If she takes one small part of you from me, then I should not care for her in the least.'

He kissed her. 'No one will ever take anything from you. I am so happy to be held in these small hands. It is unlikely that I shall ever see Sophia Mario again, but I do not need her any more. In you I have found what I sought both in Fiorenza and Sophia. I never thought to find it in one woman. I love you utterly, my dearest wife.'

With that she was content.

CHAPTER FIFTEEN

It was only after they left Italy to make the long journey home that Berris's happiness began to fade as she realized that she had won Ninian's love, but for Lora, not for herself.

Fiorenza had waved them away with warm entreaties to return to Venice very soon and Carlo had once again kissed her hand, but Berris felt that their relationship had changed. He was very much concerned with the proprieties, and she had offended him by her lack of perception. She should have known that he was a man of honour.

Berris felt relieved to be returning to a life which she understood, but as they entered France and Ninian began to talk to her about plans for their future together, her heart grew cold. She was listening to her sister's future, not her own.

As they spent each night at an inn or coaching house, Berris could only love Ninian with passionate love, made all the more desperate by the thought that each day brought their moment of parting nearer. Sometimes, as they lay in one another's arms, and Ninian whispered that he loved her beyond anything he had ever dreamed, she wondered if she should confess everything to him, and ask him to honour the marriage agreement for her sake, and to see if a marriage could not also be arranged for her sister. After all, she, too, was Sarah's daughter. Surely Aunt Elizabeth would want her for her mother's sake, just as she wanted Lora. Was there such a difference between them? Did it matter so much that she had been brought up to a life in the theatre? It was she whom Ninian loved, not Lora. It was she who loved him. They belonged together.

But Berris could not be completely sure of his reaction to such a confession. Her upbringing *had* been very different from Lora's. At one inn she had walked out into the courtyard where their carriage was being prepared and found Ninian, white-hot with rage, beating a stable boy.

Berris had stopped in her tracks, her eyes full of horror at the violence he had displayed. Then she had quietly withdrawn into the inn and had gone back upstairs to their room, feeling sick and shaken. After a time Ninian had come to find her, the rage still smouldering in his eyes, and when she asked if all was well, he had assured her, rather curtly, that everything was under control. But the sight of his anger had frightened her, and she knew that she dared not tell him she had taken her sister's place.

The weather had grown warm and the journey across France was physically uncomfortable. The Terror was over with the death of Robespierre and the country had swung into the sunlight of gaiety and hope once more. There was no more guillotine, no more fear and suspicion of one citizen towards another, but the revolution against privilege remained and the obvious wealth of travellers, though they be a nationality other than French, was looked upon with disfavour. Hoteliers and inn-keepers accepted their payment for accommodation, but offered as little as possible in exchange. The rich were no better than the poor. Let them live like the poor, even if it be only for one night.

Berris did not care. She hardly noticed the bad food and poor service. She only wanted Ninian—and for her the journey could have lasted for ever. But each day brought them a few miles nearer to Massingham and that moment when she would change places with her sister and would never see Ninian again.

She felt sick and ill when they crossed the Channel and he held her in his arms and tried to soothe her. But her low spirits were because she could not bear to look into the future, a future which would part them for ever.

Back in London, Berris asked Ninian if they could remain in the London house for a week or two before going on to Massingham.

'So you want to go to the theatre,' he said with a smile. 'You want to go to Drury Lane, I suppose. Do you not think you will find the English stage poor entertainment after Italian opera, ballet and music?'

'I shall be able to understand the plays much better,' said Berris, 'and to hear how the great actors play their parts. I can watch how they use the stage and how they appeal to their audiences.'

'Is it not enough merely to enjoy the performance?' asked Ninian. 'Must you take it all apart, piece by piece?'

'I ... of course,' she agreed, rather nervously. 'It will be enough to enjoy the performance.'

'Then we must spend a few weeks in London. I have business matters to attend to, and I must deliver a Canaletto painting which I bought on behalf of a personage of some distinction. Some of my friends like to trust my judgement on Italian works of art. I have also bought that painting you liked by Francesco Guardi. I should like to hang that at Massingham to remind us of Italy.'

'I shall remember it always,' said Berris, softly.

Drury Lane theatre had recently been rebuilt and had been re-opened a few months before under the management of Richard Sheridan. Ninian took a box for a new production of *Macbeth* starring John Philip Kemble and Mrs Siddons, and Berris forgot everything in the excitement of the evening.

Her beauty had a new luminous quality, her eyes glowing as she sat in the box, her hands clasped in Ninian's strong fingers, as she listened with absorption to every word of the play she knew so well and watched every movement of the great actor and actress.

Watching her, Ninian decided that he derived great pleasure from indulging her, but there was a feverish look about her which he found difficult to understand. She seemed to want to savour every moment of every day.

'Where next?' he asked, as they drove back home to the lovely house in the quiet London square. 'The Theatre Royal at Covent Garden, or the Haymarket? You are certainly a great admirer of the theatre.'

Berris blushed. 'You are very patient

with me, Ninian. Perhaps we should go and look at fine paintings for a change. I must take an interest in your pleasures, even as you indulge mine.'

He smiled and shook his head. He must see to it that she did not run off with one of those theatre actors.

Their stay in London had to be curtailed when news was brought from Massingham that Lady Truscott was ill again, and had been forced to take to her bed.

'This time she really is failing,' said Ninian, worriedly. 'Jessop has served Aunt Elizabeth for years and he knows when she is truly ill, and when she has decided to have a rest in order to encourage everyone to accede to her smallest demands. I think we must start for Massingham without delay.'

'I am so sorry,' she said. She had admired Ninian's elderly aunt immensely and had thought how much they might even have loved one another if only ... if only ...

Berris began to feel ill and out of sorts as they made the journey north. The news of Lady Truscott had upset her more deeply than she might have believed, and she felt sickness rising in her. Once again she suspected that it was caused by the fear which was gripping her at every turn of the wheel. She was afraid of what she might find at Massingham, and even more, at Birkridge. She had a mental picture of the Ashingtons and Aunt Louisa's rage because of what had happened. What if Lady Truscott's illness had been caused though her finding out about Lora and herself? Perhaps Mrs Ashington had told her, having been unable to keep Lora hidden away for so long. There were many possibilities and Berris's restless, troubled mind pursued all of them so that she felt ill with nerves and apprehension.

Massingham Hall had looked delightful in early spring, but now it was mellow and charming in the warm sunshine of late summer. Berris's heart ached with love for the beautiful place. If only it were all real, and not make-believe, that she might be mistress of this great house one day. Nor would it be a difficult task for her now that she had learned how to conduct herself and seen how to manage fine property. Large though it was, it seemed an intimate home compared with the great palaces of Italy.

When they eventually drove up to the front entrance, Berris sighed with relief, knowing that her secret was still safe. The Ashingtons had been circumspect and had kept Lora at Birkridge.

Servants hurried out to meet them and

Jessop's relief was plain to see as he welcomed Sir Ninian.

'My lady is brighter because you have been expected home, Sir Ninian,' he said, 'but she is growing weaker. She wants to see Lady Lora.'

'I will go to her directly,' said Berris, 'if Hebe will come and attend me.'

Hebe Jessop conducted Berris to the bedroom which had been re-decorated and furnished for Sir Ninian and his bride, and Berris exclaimed with pleasure as she stood in the doorway.

'It has kept Lady Truscott alive, planning all this,' said Hebe Jessop. 'She was so sure that you would return before autumn. Oh, and your Aunt Ashington has been here to ask for you, my lady. She wishes to see you as soon as you return.'

Berris's face paled. 'Thank you, Hebe,' she said, huskily, 'but first of all, I must see Lady Truscott. I hope we do not excite her too much.'

Ninian had brought the old lady a charming brooch made by Italian craftsmen who were as fine as any in Europe, and Lady Truscott's black eyes filled with tears as he pinned the brooch to her bedgown and bent to kiss her cheek.

Berris had been shocked by Lady Truscott's appearance. On her wedding night, the old lady had looked frail and ill, but her eyes had been bright with interest. Now all that had gone. Now she had to fight for every breath.

'Are you home to stay, my dears?' she asked them.

Ninian held her hand reassuringly.

'We are here to stay, Aunt Elizabeth,' he said, gently. 'Lora and I will not leave you.'

'I am so happy in you both,' she whispered. 'I can see that love has grown between you. I am content.'

Her eyelids drooped and Hebe Jessop bent over her.

'She is asleep,' she whispered. 'She has been unable to rest, but now she is sleeping quietly.'

'We will retire early after dinner,' said Ninian. 'Tomorrow I will interview the staff, and ride round the estate. Our holiday is over, my dear.'

She nodded. For her it was as though her whole life was over. That evening she lay in Ninian's arms, in their beautiful bedroom, and he was astonished by the strength and depth of her passion, and disturbed when he found tears on her cheek after the songbirds had wakened him at dawn. She was murmuring a name in her sleep, and when he bent his ear to hear, he found it was her own name ... Lora. Ninian turned over and slept once more, his fears soothed. Mrs Ashington arrived at ten o'clock the following morning and asked to see her niece. Ninian had already ridden out and Berris had gone to sit with Lady Truscott and to recount small amusing incidents which had highlighted their Grand Tour.

She received Mrs Ashington in the small sitting room and was given no time for further contact with anyone.

'Come,' said Louisa Ashington. 'Pick up your cloak and come with me. I have the carriage waiting at the front entrance.'

'But ... but I cannot leave just like that!' cried Berris.

'Do you wish to go round and say goodbye to all the servants?' asked Mrs Ashington, sarcastically, 'or to Sir Ninian? You have really been very clever about contriving a few more weeks of comfortable living for yourself, but you must face the fact that your part has now been played. So do not argue further. Pick up your cloak and we will drive to Birkridge. Surely it is natural for a loved niece to visit her aunt and uncle. You will return to Massingham this afternoon ... and now, let it be clear ... Lady *Lora* will return this afternoon. You may leave that message with Jessop.'

Berris had no choice but to obey. Her heart was as heavy as lead. It felt like dying a little as she realized she would never see

Ninian again. She would slip out of his life, and he would not even know that she had gone.

'Suppose Lora cannot answer if she is asked a question about recent weeks, and our trip to Italy?' she asked Mrs Ashington, as they drove to Birkridge in the carriage.

'You will tell her as much as you can, and impress upon her the names of the people you have met. Then she must become very fatigued by the journey and the upset of Lady Truscott's illness. She will begin to have headaches and to forget small details about her trip to Italy and other things. It should not be too difficult. Perhaps, even, she could have a slight accident to her head.'

'You have thought of everything,' said Berris, bitterly. 'Have you also decided upon my own future?'

Mrs Ashington shrugged. 'The Meredith Players are performing in Cambridge. You will be taken to the stagecoach so that you can once again join your acting group. I have no doubt that your stepfather will welcome you. He has been well paid for your services.'

Berris turned to look into her aunt's eyes and it was the older woman who looked away from the contempt she saw there. Berris had learned a great deal in Italy and she knew that it was not always necessary to find words to convey her meaning.

'You are not so raw as you were,' Mrs Ashington murmured. 'You might even marry some day. There are tradesmen who are even more wealthy than their betters.'

'I wonder who are their betters,' Berris murmured silkily.

The welcome from her twin sister was a great deal warmer than from the Ashingtons. Lora's blemishes had disappeared some time ago, and she was back to the full bloom of her beauty. She was greatly amused that Berris had been obliged to accompany Ninian on a Grand Tour.

'I should have found it tedious beyond endurance,' she said. 'All those dirty inns and bumpy coaches. I should have been ill every day.'

'I loved all of it,' said Berris. 'I shall never forget how wonderful it all was.'

They had gone upstairs to Lora's bedroom where a gown had been laid out for her. It was plain in style and the material was poor, as befitted her station in life. Slowly Berris removed her lovely gown and fine underwear, so delicately edged with lace. Lora had already discarded her own clothes, and now she dressed in Berris's clothes, using every one of the nether garments. The maids at

213

Massingham must never suspect anything unusual, and they would all be familiar with every garment which Berris wore.

When Lora was dressed, Berris looked at her sister and gasped. How very alike they were! How could anyone ever tell them apart!

Slowly she put on the clothing which had been allocated to her, her lips tightening when she saw the poor quality of the nether garments. She remarked rather bitterly on this to Lora, and the other girl shrugged indifferently.

'Surely it is in keeping with the clothing you are used to wearing,' she said.

She was fastening a patch on her cheek, using a hand mirror, and Berris had a sense of shock. Her sister's welcome of her had been warm and friendly, but now she could see that Lora was too deeply absorbed in herself to worry about Berris's feeling. It meant nothing to her that although they were twins, one sister was forced to live a life quite unsuited to her birth.

Mrs Ashington arrived and after a careful scrutiny, voiced her satisfaction with Lora's appearance and declared her confidence that no one would guess that she had not, all along, been travelling with Sir Ninian.

'Now you must tell Lora about the journey and whom you met in Italy,' she commanded Berris. 'It is essential that she is familiar with all that transpired.'

Berris gave a resumé of the journey and described her stay in Milan and Venice, though it was hard for her to keep the tears out of her voice. Maria had been brought back to the London house, and Berris described every incident about which Maria would know, and tried to teach Lora the few Italian words she had learned.

'Oh that is quite unnecessary,' said Lora, airily. 'I shall forget such things very easily and quickly. My memory is very poor.'

'You will manage very well, my dear child,' said Mrs Ashington. 'No one will expect that there would be another girl involved. And old Lady Truscott is on her death bed. She was always shrewd, but she cannot change events. As for Sir Ninian, he will be tired of his bride by now. When his aunt dies, he will no doubt return to London, and encourage his wife to follow her own devices.'

Berris turned away as tears stung her eyes. She looked on as her cloak was thrown over Lora's shoulders, then with scarcely a backward glance, her sister was conducted downstairs to the waiting coach, and was whirled away out of her life.

CHAPTER SIXTEEN

The stagecoach for Cambridge left early the following morning, and Berris was driven in a closed carriage to the nearest staging post. Mrs Ashington had provided her with a change of clothing, and cleared her conscience with a small purse of gold coins, advising her to seek a steady fellow who might marry her. Her looks were good, her manners improved, and now she even had a little money. It should not be impossible for her to marry, even though the acting profession seldom found favour with people of even the smallest substance.

Berris was feeling ill and upset so that she could only nod her agreement. She would like to have thrown the purse at Mrs Ashington's feet, but common sense prevailed and she persuaded herself that she was entitled to this money. In fact, she was entitled to an equal share of Lora's, though she hardly expected Mrs Ashington to agree with this point of view.

Her trip back to Cambridge was wretched after the comfortable journey she had made in Sir Ninian's coach. The stage swayed and rattled, and nausea gripped her at every turn. The inns were little different from those she had already frequented, but the rooms allocated to passengers from the stage were very different from those offered to a nobleman and his wife. Berris had to share a hard straw bed with two other women and her bones ached so that she continued her journey in great discomfort.

It was not difficult to find the Meredith Players in Cambridge. Berris was well acquainted with the routine and habits of Brendan Meredith, and after asking a few questions at the theatre, she made her way to the lodging house where her stepfather and the rest of the company were staying.

Brendan looked greatly aged. His hair had whitened and he had lost weight, but his joy in Berris's return was heart-warming to her. A great deal of the fire had gone out of him, and only love for her remained.

Mistress Grey also declared herself pleased to see Berris, though this was accompanied by a tirade of complaints. She had missed the worst of all their misfortunes, and things had been very bad for the Players. Berris had been fortunate to be living the life of a lady whilst her family and friends suffered so grievously.

'But I thought you were paid for my

services to Mr and Mrs Ashington,' she said, bluntly.

'To be sure we were,' said Mistress Grey, 'but have you ever known a man who could look after his money? We lived on the best of everything for a week or two. We had fine lodgings, good food and wine, then your stepfather suffered an illness. His heart gave him great pain and he had to rest. Sebastian and I were forced to fall back upon small comedies and recitations for the more discerning. It was not a success.'

'The recitations were not suited to our audiences,' said Brendan. 'I told you so, my dear.'

'But how could you know? You were ill. *I* had to take the responsibility as I still have to, since you are not yet completely recovered.'

'Where is Sebastian?' asked Berris.

'He has gone out for an hour. He likes to seek young company at one of the inns. It is very dull for him with only myself and your stepfather as companions. It will be so much better now that you have returned, Berris.'

She sat down in the dull, shabby room, so much like all the others which had provided a background for her for so many years, and the pain in her heart was like a knife-thrust.

What would Ninian be doing now? Would he be so concerned about affairs at Massingham that he would not have had time to notice that his wife had changed a little? Because surely Lora could not offer him the same love which was in her own heart. Lora cared for herself too deeply.

The door opened and Sebastian swaggered into the room, his legs unsteady and a bawdy song on his lips.

'Sebastian! You promised you would not drink more ale than was good for you!' his mother screeched. 'Now you will have to sober up before we leave for the theatre. And here is Berris returned to us.'

'Berris!'

Sebastian threw out his arms. There was a beaming smile of welcome on his face as he lurched towards her and enveloped her in his arms. The smell of ale on his breath repelled her, and she pushed him away.

'My lady Berris,' he said, thickly. 'So you are a fine lady and too good for Sebastian Grey? Is that it? Instead of kissing Mistress Berris, I must bow the knee and kiss my lady's hand.'

'You are drunk, Sebastian,' she said. 'Sleep for a while, then I will help you. I'll get ready for tonight's performance. I see that we are changing the programme each night, and perhaps we could do *The Miller's Lament*. Mistress Grey enjoys playing Dorcas, and your own part is excellent. You will not need to do a dull monologue.'

'You think you can come back here and everything will be just as it was,' he answered. 'You, a fine lady ...'

'Oh, forget about telling me I am a lady!' she cried, angrily. 'I am no longer a lady. I am a play actress. Now do as I bid you, Sebastian, and get rid of the fumes of ale from your breath. You will give a poor performance if you are drunk.'

'So you *have* come back to us,' Sebastian giggled, 'and you *are* no longer a fine lady! I had forgotten about your sharp tongue. Very well, I will rest and we will do a performance this evening.'

He began to sing again and his mother and stepfather helped him to lie down on a hard straw bed.

'Six months ago he would not have dared to come home in such a state before a performance,' said Brendan, sadly. 'Things have changed, Berris. I am glad you are back.'

She looked at him, feeling love for him.

'I will attend to everything. Do not worry,' she said, consolingly. 'I can handle Sebastian.'

'I wonder if you can,' said Brendan, 'or if already it is too late.'

For Berris the performance that evening was one of the worst of her life. Brendan had been weakened by illness and, to compensate for the lack of voice at his command, he adopted such extravagant gestures that they must surely look ridiculous to an audience. Mistress Grey followed his lead, and Berris could do little else than play her own part in like vein. The contrast with the wonderful acting she had seen in Italy and at Drury Lane was shameful to her. She had managed to sober up Sebastian, but he was dull and lethargic, his stomach soured with ale.

Berris determined to try to change the acting style of the Players and described fully all the great plays she had seen in the Italian theatres and Drury Lane. She demonstrated the natural acting methods which the players there had adopted in order to appeal to their audience.

'I do not see why you should admire the Italian theatre so much,' said Brendan jealously. 'Surely our own Drury Lane is much greater, and Garrick was recognized as the most natural actor of all time. It is from Garrick that I learned my elocution, and have been able to pass that learning to you. Mistress Grey is a very fine actress and no fault could be found with *her* performance, I assure you.'

'I only seek improvement, Stepfather,' said Berris. 'Having had this experience, I think it would be a poor thing if I did not help us all to benefit. Kemble and Mrs Siddons were beyond anything I have seen.'

'You ungrateful wench,' cried Mistress Grey. 'You have been away from the company for months. You don't know how hard I've worked to keep the company together. Yet you come back and within a day we're being criticized.'

'I do not mean it as criticism,' said Berris, unhappily. 'But if my life from now on must be given up to acting, then I would like it to be of the best standard possible.'

She stopped, staring more closely at Brendan. His face was very pale and there was a blue line round his lips. He looked very tired.

'I ... I should not have troubled you with such matters, Stepfather,' said Berris, contritely.

'We are only a small company,' said Brendan. 'We do our best.'

As the days passed and they moved westwards into the Midland towns, Berris began to notice all the differences which had taken place during her absence. Mistress Grey now assumed the greatest control over the company, and the bookings were at the meanest of theatres, with noisy audiences and the poorest of lodgings. The costumes were soiled and badly needed to be mended. Berris felt degraded as she wore them, the rough material chafing her delicate skin.

At first Sebastian had subjected her to heavy teasing which betrayed his resentment of her trip to Italy, and the fact that she had been well-born, even if she had lost her place in society. Then he declared himself happy to have her return to the company. He was as flamboyant and good-humoured as he had always been; but a fondness for drink was beginning to coarsen his features so that he looked very much less attractive now than he had done. Or seemed so to Berris. Was it that he looked a poor specimen of manhood compared with Ninian? Berris thought about Ninian constantly, and when Sebastian would have forced his attentions upon her once again, she pushed him away.

'So I am not good enough for my lady now!' he cried as he tried to kiss her. 'You had better stop sighing for the moon, my dear Berris, and remember that your days as a stand-in bride are over. Our stepfather is no longer a barrier to a marriage between us, and my mother is in favour of such a union. It would make things much easier for the company. Brendan swears it will be yours one day, but you are only a woman. It should be handled by a man. But if we marry, we can run the company together.'

She looked at him unhappily and once again he pulled her into his arms and claimed her mouth with his own, his hands immediately travelling downwards towards her hips. His lips were slack and there was a reek of stale ale from his breath, so that she twisted away in revulsion, and his eyes narrowed again with anger.

'You are determined to act the lady whether it be on or off the stage!'

There was a note of menace in his voice which alarmed her.

'Do not make such conclusions, Sebastian. Surely you must see how it is with me. I do not know whether I am a wife, or not. I took my sister's place and married Sir Ninian Lennox, but I swore my vows before God, and it was my voice which made the vows, and my hand which signed all the documents. Suppose ... suppose I am not now free.'

'Is that what troubles you?'

'Yes,' she prevaricated, 'that is what troubles me. I dare not marry again. That is why I should like one day to become a great actress. I will have to make my own way in life.'

Sebastian looked at her shrewdly.

'You are in love with this nobleman whom you married in your sister's name,' he said, accusingly. 'That is the true reason, is it not?'

Colour stole into her cheeks.

'I mean nothing to him,' she said, huskily. 'He does not even know of my existence.'

'Why does he not?'

'Because always he would think I was Lora. When she was dressed in my clothes and left in the carriage to return to Massingham, it was as though there were only one of us. She is so like me, she could be me. It is so strange to have an identical twin sister.'

'And you did not tell your fine husband?'

'Certainly I did not!' Berris shook her head. 'He was not a man to deceive lightly. He ... he could be terrible in his anger. I was desperately afraid that he would find out the truth. Once I saw him beat a servant near to death. Later I found out that it was because the fellow had ill-treated a young child, and so was deserved. But I was witness there to his fierce rage. I could not tell him or he might have killed me.'

'And you think he does not know?'

'What do you mean?' she asked, as paroxysm of mirth shook him. 'Why are you so amused?'

'I am thinking about the great Sir Ninian,' said Sebastian, 'and how puzzled he must be that his bride of several months suddenly becomes virgin once more. Or can it be that your sister allows lovers to creep up the back stairs to her bedroom?'

'Of course she does not!' cried Berris, indignantly. 'She is always well chaperoned.'

Her hand flew to her mouth. 'Will ... will Ninian know that she is virgin?'

'He *must* know by now. If, as you say, he is easily angered by being made to look a fool, you had better keep well away from York.'

Faintness seized hold of Berris again, but Sebastian put an arm round her and tried to rally her.

'Do not worry about him. I will take care of you, my dear. If you are afraid of marrying twice, why then we will just declare ourselves man and wife here and now, and I will write out two papers that we are married. We shall each sign the papers, and they will satisfy my mother and our stepfather.'

Berris's thoughts were in a turmoil. Was it true that Ninian would know by now that she and Lora were twins? Always she had hoped for a miracle which would return her to him. But now all hope had been shattered. He must surely know about her duplicity.

'Come on, Berris. Surely it is a good plan,' said Sebastian as he looked at her troubled face.

'Not tonight,' she said, quickly. 'Let me think about it and perhaps we will do it.'

'When?' he urged. 'Why not tonight, then we can share a bed.'

'On Saturday,' she said, recklessly. 'We will do it on Saturday, then we can tell Mistress Grey and Brendan that we are married. We will travel together on Sunday. It is not far to our next town.'

'I do not see why we should wait,' Sebastian grumbled, 'but you may have it as you wish.'

He kissed her again and she tried not to push him away in disgust. Every instinct in her revolted against doing this thing, but it seemed to her that she had no choice.

'You are the only woman I could marry,' he said. 'You are pretty and delicate, sweet Berris. How I hate fat women!'

Berris's head ached and she did not feel well, but the reason for her malaise was growing more and more clear to her. She was expecting a child. The worst had happened and she would bear Ninian's child as a bastard unless she married Sebastian.

She bit her lip until it bled. She could not travel back to Massingham and throw herself on Ninian's mercy. If Sebastian was right in saying that Ninian now knew her secret, that she was twin and had deceived him ... and she believed he was right ... then she could not tell him about the child. Perhaps his anger had cooled against Lora who was his wife, but not against her, a scheming actress. He might even refuse to believe that the child was his.

Berris felt tired and the burden of life had suddenly become heavy. Deep in her heart she was glad about the baby. It would be something of Ninian's which she could hug to herself with love.

But should she tell Sebastian that she was with child? Perhaps he would refuse to stand by her if he knew, and she needed the protection of marriage for the child, if not for herself. He claimed to love her, but could she believe him? Could she trust him?

Sebastian lived on the surface of life and everything was gay and amusing to him. Yet, was that really so? Sometimes she felt that there was great depth to him, and dark secrets which she did not understand. Sometimes she felt that his love was already given ... to himself! He loved himself better than he loved her, and he would not want to shoulder the responsibility of another man's child.

Berris thought about the purse of gold which she had hidden on her person. She had decided to share it with Sebastian as a symbol of their union, but now she resolved to hide the purse as security for her child. Her life from now on would be given to the care and protection of that child, and she would say nothing to Sebastian. He could grow used to having a wife, then he could gradually be made to accept the coming child.

On Saturday morning Berris wore the gown supplied by Mrs Ashington and made no further protest as Sebastian took her hand and asked her to follow him to a nearby chapel. It was empty and Berris hung back a little as Sebastian pushed open the heavy door and conducted her inside.

It smelled musty and damp, but Sebastian seemed unaware and led her in front of the altar, and declared in ringing tones that they were husband and wife before God.

Berris's heart almost failed her.

'No, Sebastian,' she whispered. 'Do not say more. It may be blasphemous. We may be punished for what we are doing.'

'I am only saying the words of a priest,'

said Sebastian, 'without paying the fee he would demand. I am an actor. I can be a priest if I wish. See, Berris, I have written out two certificates of marriage and we will each sign our names. Brendan taught us both to read and write and I have brought everything necessary. Write your name there and there.'

'I ... I cannot,' she gasped. 'It is wrong.'

'Why is it wrong? Where is our crime?'

'I do not know, but I do not feel comfortable in signing such documents in this chapel.'

'And I have no wish to go through this ceremony elsewhere. You have said you will accept me in marriage. Well, I have married us. You are my wife. A man of my age should be married, and I have chosen you as my bride.'

Sebastian had laid out a box with the papers, quill pen and ink, and after some hesitation and feeling overwhelmed with confusion, Berris wrote her name. Was the marriage legal? she wondered. Was she truly Sebastian's wife? There was no time for further deliberation. They were due to attend the theatre, and Sebastian held her arm as they returned to their lodgings to find Mistress Grey and Brendan Meredith.

'Berris is now my wife,' said Sebastian, proudly. 'We have just declared our vows in that chapel at the end of the village.'

Brendan's face whitened and he turned to Berris.

'Is this true?' he asked. 'You have no right to marry without my permission.'

'Why not?' demanded Mistress Grey. 'She is not your daughter.'

She turned to Berris and unexpectedly gathered her into her arms.

'I am very happy, daughter,' she said. 'You will be good for Sebastian. It is the best thing which could have happened to him.'

Brendan's heavy frown did not reflect his wife's pleasure. In the old days his anger would have boiled and Berris might have feared him, but now he was too weak to protest too strongly.

'We must leave for the theatre,' he said heavily, after a long silence. 'There is no time now for discussion. But I do not approve of this marriage. It is not right for Berris.'

'She is lucky to be wed to Sebastian,' said Mistress Grey, firmly. 'Tonight we will celebrate. We do not need to travel until tomorrow, and we have several small towns where we have quite a following before we move north to Leicester.'

'We should be in London,' Brendan muttered. 'Berris should be given her chance instead of accepting Sebastian in marriage.'

'I tell you, she is lucky to have him!' screeched Mistress Grey, 'and you know she is not good enough for London.'

'There is no time for such quarrelling,' said Berris, swiftly. 'We will be late for our performance.'

Berris managed to purchase extra food for the wedding feast that evening. In addition to meats and pastries, she bought cheese, fresh bread and wine in a heavy green bottle.

Sebastian fell on the food and wine ravenously. Both he and Mistress Grey were in fine appetite, but Brendan ate little, and Berris even less. The wine was quickly consumed and Sebastian declared that he would buy more from a nearby inn.

'A man's marriage is a very special occasion,' he said, importantly. 'We must celebrate in style, my dear wife, and you did not purchase enough wine to slake the thirst of a mouse. I will be back very quickly.'

They listened to him clattering down the stairs, then Berris slowly ate a pastry.

Nothing was real, she thought. This could not be happening to her. A few weeks ago she had been in Italy, being escorted to galas and theatrical evenings by Carlo, with Ninian ever watchful. Now she sat in a dull dismal room, waiting for her new husband to return with more bottles of cheap wine, whilst her stepfather stared at her morosely, and her mother-in-law beamed with approval.

The falling autumn leaves lay sodden with rain on the muddy streets and the damp air pervaded the badly-structured house. The roof, too long awaiting the services of a thatcher, allowed the rain to soak on to the ceiling and thence to the floor in a steady monotonous drip. The candle began to flicker and Brendan Meredith announced his intention of going to bed. He wanted no more wine.

Mistress Grey archly remarked that the young lovers would prefer to be alone and left Berris to her own devices. Her ears strained for Sebastian's step on the stairs.

Presently the cold clung like a mantle to her shoulders, and she, too, removed her clothing and climbed into the bed she must now share with Sebastian. In spite of her depression, part of her rejoiced that she would no longer have to sleep alone. Ninian had turned her into a warm, passionate woman and as the weeks passed and she tried to forget his lithe, satin-smooth body she would be thankful to try and soothe her aching heart with Sebastian.

Tired out she fell asleep, then woke to

233

the sound of his slightly unsteady footsteps as he climbed the stairs and threw open the door, a half-empty bottle of wine clutched in his hands.

'Oh, show a sparkling eye, and something extra on the sly ...' Sebastian sang, loudly.

'Ssh!' cried Berris, starting up. 'Your mother and stepfather are sleeping. Where have you been, Sebastian?'

'Who's been sleeping in *my* bed?' he bawled, then began to giggle. 'It is my new wife, is it now? My little woman who scolds me and the wedding night not yet begun. Wait there!'

Sebastian had put down the bottle, then he began to remove his clothing except for his hat. Berris felt as though he was a small boy climbing into bed beside her.

'I must have a little wine. It helps the love to flow,' he explained, carefully.

'Oh, Sebastian!' she laughed. 'I must excuse you this night, but it is not good for you to drink too much ale.'

'Be quiet, woman,' he hissed. 'I must love you *now*. Do not try to put me off.'

'I shall not try, dear Sebastian,' she said.

Her life would have been even more dreary and lonely if she had not had this family to whom she could turn.

He did not fondle her, nor would he

234

allow her to touch him, but he started to make love to her, almost hurting her in his urgency. A moment later, however, he turned away from her and lay beside her quietly.

'It is useless, I cannot,' he said, all gaiety gone from his voice.

'You drank too much wine.'

'That is true. I drank too much wine.'

He turned from her and wept for a moment with self-pity, then his breathing grew regular and he slept. Berris tried to stifle her dismay. Sebastian was indeed like a small boy. He was a child compared with Ninian.

In the morning he was still asleep when she woke up, and she smiled mischievously as she tickled his nose with a dried leaf.

Sebastian opened his eyes then turned away from her crossly.

'Leave me alone, Berris,' he complained. 'My head aches.'

'You see what happens when you indulge yourself too much,' she said, her amber eyes alight with amusement. 'Do you not wish to ... ah ... *talk* with your wife?'

'I only wish to be left alone,' he muttered, and she pulled away from him, hurt. He did not desire her, and had never yet taken her in love.

Slowly she rose from their bed and dressed, combing out her tangled curls.

Carlo had not desired her, either. He had made the excuse that a *cicisbeo* was never a lover, but was that true? Or could it have been some sort of excuse? Could it be that she, Berris, was unattractive to men? Ninian had loved her, but Ninian had been making love to Lora his wife, not to Berris. He had claimed to love her, but if she and Fiorenza Michiel had both offered their love, which one of them would he have chosen but for convention?

Quietly she packed her clothing and Sebastian's. It was time to move on.

CHAPTER SEVENTEEN

The cold months of winter were upon them as they began the slow journey north towards the Cheshire towns. Their play *The Deserted Wife* had proved to be a fine success, and once again Brendan Meredith had managed to arrange a series of bookings which ensured a steady income, if small.

Berris found that her costume as the fairy princess in *Silver Stardust* was becoming much too tight for her thickening figure, and she tried to alter it surreptitiously. She had continued to keep news of her pregnancy to herself, unsure as to the reaction of the other members of the company, but Mistress Grey surprised her as she was trying to alter the waistline of the pretty pale blue and silver gown designed to make her look like a moonbeam.

'What are you doing?' she demanded. 'You have cut the tucks at the waistline ...' She paused, then looked sharply at the girl. 'I should have guessed. You are with child! Surely the child cannot be Sebastian's?'

Berris's cheeks flooded with colour and she stared at Mistress Grey wordlessly. The older woman's eyes bored into her own, then narrowed into slits as the girl held her breath.

Brendan Meredith had walked into the room and now he surveyed the two women.

'What is this?' he asked. 'A quarrel?'

'Berris is with child,' said Mistress Grey. 'She cannot deny it. Look at her thickening body. She is too far gone in pregnancy for the child to be Sebastian's and she does not deny it when I accuse her. She has nothing to say.'

Brendan's eyes were bright and sharp as he turned to look at his stepdaughter.

'Is this true?' he asked.

She sighed and nodded. It was useless to withhold the truth.

'I am with child by Sir Ninian Lennox.'

Sebastian had been following behind his stepfather and now he gave a muffled exclamation, then walked forward to stare down at her. The blue and silver gown lay on her lap and he picked it up and threw it into a corner of the room.

'So you thought to offer me a wedding gift,' he cried, 'another man's child! You trap me into marriage ...'

'It was no trap,' she cried. '*You* were the one who wanted marriage, and you persuaded me into it.'

'And you return to us with a child who

must be fed and clothed, and expect us all to wish to bring up your bastard,' cried Mistress Grey. 'You come to us ruined and make use of Sebastian by your very silence. Oh, you are very clever, Mistress Berris.'

'My child is not ... not ...' Berris's voice trailed off. Mistress Grey was quite right. Her child *was* a bastard. If Sebastian did not want to own the baby, it would have no father, and she had made use of Sebastian by her silence.

'You thought to deceive me,' Sebastian was saying, a look of loathing on his face. 'You offer me a body already fruitful by another man, and hope that I shall ...'

He stopped speaking as Berris looked at him levelly.

They both knew that Sebastian could never be the father of her child.

'You hope that I shall say nothing,' he finished, his voice rising hysterically.

'Be quiet!'

Brendan Meredith's voice held more power and authority than Berris had heard since she returned to the company.

'You both forget that Berris earned a fine purse of gold when she took the place of Lady Lennox, and that we all benefited from that gold. Yes, even you, Mistress Grey, though you grumbled about the spending of it, no doubt desiring the whole for yourself! But we were able to

239

make repairs to the wagon and to buy fresh horses. We paid for good food and lodgings, and bought new clothes. Some of it was squandered by Sebastian on reckless living. Do not forget that. He insisted that he had his share. If my stepdaughter is bearing a child because of it, then she will be cared for, *and* her child. They have earned some consideration.'

'If only the child were Sebastian's,' said Mistress Grey, longingly.

Her son flushed. 'I shall say no more,' he said with great dignity.

'There will be other children,' said Mistress Grey, beginning to brighten with anticipation. 'At least she is not barren, and a child is a great draw in the theatre.'

'No!' cried Berris. 'No ... I ... I do not want my child to became a play actor.'

'What is wrong with being a play actor?' hooted Sebastian.

'She will soon change her mind,' said Mistress Grey, 'when she realizes she has no other choice for her child. She should be proud to have the opportunity of entertaining people on the stage, and her child should be brought up to appreciate this.'

Berris listened to the arguments with half an ear. Whatever was said, she had her own plans for her child. It may be a bastard, but it was Ninian's baby. She would see that it grew up to be worthy of its true father.

'We will need another young actress as a stand-in for Berris,' Sebastian grumbled. 'I refuse to go back to stupid sketches and monologues.'

'We cannot afford to support any other,' said Brendan.

'And we cannot depend upon Berris,' Sebastian argued.

They were silent as she put the last stitches into the costume which she had retrieved from the corner of the room. Uneasily she conceded that Sebastian was correct. Yet ... another young actress? A rival for her own parts? A glance at Mistress Grey showed that she was equally displeased and Berris shivered. She had a premonition that her life was about to drift into even more troubled waters.

Sebastian could no longer even try to make love to her.

'I cannot forget that you have been possessed by another man,' he told her, sourly. 'The thought destroys my manhood every time I turn to you.'

Berris hardly knew whether to be relieved or humiliated. Any love she had ever felt for Sebastian had now died entirely. She had been prepared to try to love him again for the sake of making a life together, but she could never forget Ninian, and the child had ensured that she never would. He was constantly in her thoughts, in her dreams, and his name on her lips as she woke from sleep each morning. Her love for him was turning into an all-consuming fire which took charge of her whole being, to the exclusion of everything except for his child.

In the cold winter months they moved into Manchester where they were booked to perform for two weeks each at three separate theatres in the city and from there to small outlying towns. Berris knew a sense of relief. Her figure was already growing heavy, although the child would not be born until early spring. She was glad of a spell without too much travelling.

Sebastian had once again taken to going out to taverns and coming home reeking of cheap ale. But the gaiety which usually accompanied such escapades was missing, and he was inclined to be morose and bad-tempered when he returned to their lodgings. His work was suffering, too, and many times Berris had had to prompt him from the wings when he forgot his words. Brendan had taken him to task, but Brendan was growing older before their eyes, his tall imposing body now gaunt and bent.

Towards the end of their first week in Manchester, Sebastian returned home fairly early one afternoon from his usual jaunt to the inn. Berris was trying to make a small garment for her child, her eyes straining to see stitches in the dull light of a winter's day. She paused in her task when she heard the sound of other voices and a moment later the door of their room was thrust open and Sebastian strode in, his arms once again thrown open expansively.

'Welcome to our splendid lodging house,' he cried. 'Step inside, Miss Hobart, and Mr Hobart. The lady dozing by the poor miserable fire is my mother, that famous actress, Mistress Grey, and here is my wife, Mistress Berris Meredith. Mr Brendan Meredith will no doubt already be at the theatre. The rest of us will leave very soon and you may accompany us, Miss Hobart and, of course, Mr Hobart.'

Berris scarcely listened to Sebastian's introductions. Her eyes were on the young woman who was being pushed into the room by Sebastian and another young man whose face was in shadow. She could guess quite easily why Sebastian had brought them home, even before he explained that he had met them at a nearby tavern frequented by theatrical people.

'Mr and Miss Hobart were members of the Dobson Theatrical Group which, alas, has just broken up,' Sebastian explained

243

looking first at his wife, then turning to his mother. 'They plan to go to Liverpool. I have invited them to travel with us. It is not easy for young members of the profession to travel alone without inviting a certain amount of disrespect.'

What would Brendan say to that? wondered Berris. Sebastian had taken a lot upon himself.

Mistress Grey acknowledged Sebastian's introduction awkwardly, and the girl eyed them both sullenly and made a small curtsey. Then the young man, who was introduced as her brother, stepped forward and Berris almost gasped aloud. He was surely the most exquisite young man she had ever seen. Surely she had seen someone like him before? His face appeared to float somewhere in her dreams. He was as tall as Sebastian and very slender, with an abundance of golden hair, dainty features and the lightly controlled step of a dancer.

'I am honoured, ma'am,' he said to Berris, and swept another bow towards Mistress Grey, though it seemed to her that he hardly looked at either of them. Sebastian must have entertained him with some private joke, and the amusement of it was still in his eyes as they regarded one another from time to time.

Perhaps it had been at the expense

of Miss Hobart. She bore a family resemblance to the young man, but her features were heavier, and the golden hair was more straw-coloured on her. Her expression was dull and sulky, and she hung back uneasily when Sebastian would have had her sit down beside the ladies.

'Miss Polly and Mr Deryk Hobart,' said Sebastian. 'They have both been brought up in the acting profession. He is a student of Sheridan and Rich whilst Miss Polly admires Kemble and Mrs Siddons, as does my wife.'

Polly Hobart flushed. 'I do not claim to be an actress,' she said, defensively.

'We were brought up to it by our parents,' said her brother, smoothly. 'It is a great profession.'

'Just wait till you meet Brendan Meredith. He will be most grateful to me that I have found you.'

Sebastian could hardly contain his delight, and devoured young Mr Hobart with his gaze as though he might vanish before his very eyes. But it was Miss Polly who held Berris's interest, and she knew that Mistress Grey shared her own mixed feelings.

The girl looked too withdrawn and sulky to be a great attraction as an actress, but at the same time, she did not look like the kind of girl to attract Sebastian. It was easy to see Sebastian's motives in befriending the brother and sister, but Miss Polly did not look as though she was likely to usurp Berris's place permanently in the company.

A short time later they all prepared to leave for the theatre and Berris saw Polly Hobart's gaze resting on her heavily pregnant figure, and she blushed as she turned away. Her brother, too, had noticed and was suddenly so still that she sensed his surprise and wondered why this should be so. Surely Sebastian had introduced her as his wife?

It was as though this man could see into her soul, and knew that the child belonged to another man! She stared into the actor's pale blue eyes and something in them repelled her, even though he smiled and bowed pleasantly.

'I am looking forward to meeting Brendan Meredith. His name is a famous one. I understand he is your father, Miss Meredith.'

'My stepfather,' she said, briefly.

'Come, my dear,' said Sebastian, with elaborate courtesy. 'Take my arm. Fortunately we do not have to walk far.'

Berris hesitated then did as she was bid. Mistress Grey escorted Polly Hobart, and Deryk Hobart walked beside them with his smooth graceful step. He was just behind Berris and she had a sudden impulse to pick up her long skirts and run as far from the Hobarts as she could go.

But her pregnant body was too ungainly for such wild fancies, and even before they reached the theatre, she knew that her stepfather would accept the brother and sister as members of the Meredith Players. An actor who could play Sheridan must be an asset, and they greatly needed an extra girl player.

Brendan Meredith acknowledged the introductions briefly. He spent much longer over his make-up these days and he was intent upon darkening the bushy white of his eyebrows when they arrived at the theatre. He listened politely whilst Sebastian sang the praises of his new friends, saying that he had merely asked them to join them until Liverpool was reached.

'You are welcome to travel with us,' he agreed.

After the show, however, Brendan Meredith was practically forced into discussing remuneration by Sebastian, and he was too tired to prevaricate. The Meredith Players acquired two more members. Only later did Brendan look back to this moment of decision. If only he had not been so tired ...

CHAPTER EIGHTEEN

Berris's disappointment in the two new players was great as they started to rehearse new plays which Deryk had recommended. She had hoped for support for her own ideas on how to present a play, but the Hobarts had been brought up in the old school, and Deryk over-acted his parts at every turn, inviting the enthusiastic approval of Mistress Grey and Sebastian, who thought him a great asset to the company.

Brendan Meredith shook his head. He had hoped for an actor who could adopt the heavier roles which were his own particular métier, but Deryk was even more mercurial than Sebastian. Brendan was tired and would so have welcomed an actor who could understudy his own demanding work.

Polly, on the other hand, was dull and solid in her parts and spoke her lines in a monotone. She had taken over some of Berris's roles, but she was unhappy acting a principal character and begged to be allowed to play supporting roles only. To compensate she took over the job of wardrobe mistress, exclaiming at the condition of some of the costumes, and soon these were being repaired and refurbished, much to Berris's relief.

'But you *must* play the young female roles,' Mistress Grey told Polly. 'There is no one else now that Berris is indisposed.'

Berris was now very great with child and spent much of her time in the travelling wagon, now shared by two more people. Fortunately the journeys between the Lancashire towns were short and the Players were not greatly inconvenienced, but a second wagon was now essential. In the meantime Berris strove to make the wagon more attractive by keeping it clean and neat. She also liked to rest there whilst the Players were at the theatre. Her heavy body made it advisable for her to withdraw from public view.

Her appearance revolted Sebastian. In spite of his acceptance that she was bearing another man's child, he could no longer bear to look at her, or to drop a quick kiss on her head as he had once done.

In this he was aided by Deryk Hobart and Berris often suspected that Sebastian had told Deryk the true circumstances behind the child's paternity, because there was a look of amusement and even contempt in the light blue eyes whenever she was obliged to consult or talk with him.

This proved to be quite often after Deryk had declared himself willing to play young female parts. At first Brendan Meredith had raised his eyebrows, then Deryk had quickly borrowed one of Berris's old gowns and a wig. The gown was much too short and could not be fastened since Deryk was not quite as slender as Berris had been, but after he had drawn the wig into place, and held the gown together with a ribbon, he quickly minced on to the stage in front of Brendan and began to recite the lines to perfection. His natural voice was high-pitched and he would have little difficulty in convincing an audience that he was a very attractive girl.

Grudgingly Brendan agreed that he could play the female parts, and for once Berris was enthusiastic over Deryk's acting ability. She remembered that men had played women's parts in the Italian theatre and she saw no reason why Deryk could not be equally successful. He was a great deal better than Polly.

She agreed to help Deryk as best she could as he learned her parts, but often she felt his eyes resting upon her with a strange unreadable light in them. His blue eyes would become very intense as he looked at her face and for no reason which she could define, she began to detest him. He repelled her. She wondered if he was becoming attracted to her as he sat in front of her, watching her every move with deep intensity, but she sensed that he was merely learning his parts and listening carefully to everything she had to tell him. He intended to copy her every mannerism.

Sometimes Sebastian would come to sit beside them and would smile approvingly at Deryk, gently slapping him on the back when he repeated his lines to perfection. He was full of pride and self-congratulation that he had been the one to find the Hobarts who, he claimed, would revolutionize the company. In a few months they would be truly famous.

His praise delighted Deryk, who smiled almost shyly in return, then caught Berris's eyes upon him. His expression slowly changed and once again she could see that strange glowing light in his eyes and her mouth felt dry as she ran her tongue over her lips. She was afraid of Deryk Hobart. She must ensure that they were never allowed to be alone together.

'I do not think there is anything further to tell you, Deryk,' she said, stiffly. 'You can play all my parts, except for *Silver Stardust*. I do not think it would suit you.'

His lips curled. 'It is not a part I would wish to play.'

'It is greatly appreciated by audiences.'

'*Some* audiences, perhaps. I know several plays which are even more appreciated by audiences, but Mr Meredith will not countenance anything rich and full-blooded. He prefers the wishy-washy material which will be a great bore some day not far distant.'

'Rich and full-blooded?' she repeated. 'Perhaps you mean bawdy, sir. If so, then my stepfather most certainly will *not* countenance such entertainment. Our standard of work is perhaps not as high as it might have been once upon a time, but neither has it sunk so low.'

'That depends upon one's point of view. I like to see a nice pile of coins at the box office. It makes life so much more comfortable.'

'Then I am at a loss to know why you joined the company, Mr Hobart.'

His eyes narrowed to slits.

'I had my reasons.' He turned to smile at Sebastian. 'We will leave your ... your *wife* to her stitching.'

Berris's cheeks flamed as they sauntered out, one of Sebastian's arms carelessly thrown over Deryk's shoulder. There was no mistaking the emphasis in his words. How dare Sebastian! So he had told

Deryk Hobart about their strange marriage ceremony. No doubt they had laughed uproariously over the fact that Sebastian had claimed to be his own priest, and had performed the ceremony himself. How *could* he!

Yet the marriage was legal and binding. They had both signed certificates and she guarded hers carefully. She was Sebastian's wife, whatever Deryk said, or however much amusement he derived from it.

But her hatred of him grew like a weed in her heart.

As the winter months passed and the snowdrops began to bloom once more, the Meredith Players moved through the Lancashire towns and into Yorkshire. Their progress was slow because they were managing to be booked for two weeks instead of one in some of the bigger towns where theatre-going was looked upon with favour, even if audience participation was also more highly developed and anything displeasing was met with a volley of cat-calls, followed by a variety of objects thrown on to the stage.

Berris spent her waiting time either in the lodgings or the wagon. She fell asleep there one evening after looking out at the clear midnight blue of the sky and the sparkle of silvery stars. Memories of her life with Ninian had come crowding back to her, and the evening stars bobbed and shimmered through a mist of tears. Where was he now? What was he doing? Was he happy with Lora and had she come to love him as she, Berris, loved him? Was Lora also bearing his child, a child who would inherit Massingham one day, a child who would be brought up by his own father?

Gradually the hard knot in her heart eased as the hot tears soothed her, and she slept. When she awoke she was conscious of a change in her body, and even as she lay confused and bewildered, a fierce pain shot through her, so deep in intensity that she was left gasping. Her baby was about to be born.

Berris lay back and tried to fight down a sense of panic. Mistress Grey and the rest of the company would go back to their lodgings after the performance, which would surely be over by now. How long would it be before she was missed, and would Mistress Grey think about coming to the wagon just to make sure she was well, or would she be too tired? Brendan was often tired these days as was Polly, who was obliged to play small parts. There might be no one to help her, thought Berris. The wagon was placed in a disused yard, and there were no houses nearby.

The next pain caused her to gasp for breath and she moaned audibly, then relief swept over her when she heard Sebastian approaching the wagon and talking excitedly to someone, then Deryk's high voice answering him. They had not forgotten about her after all.

'In here, Sebastian,' she called weakly as she heard him clambering into the other section of the wagon, then Deryk Hobart's high-pitched laughter rang out as he, too, climbed in.

'In here,' she repeated, though the words were choked as another pain seemed to rip her body apart. Clearly she could hear sounds from the other side of the partition and however much she tried to attract attention, she gradually became aware that the two men were too busily talking and laughing as they shared bottles of wine to pay her any heed. Sebastian had started to sing, and Deryk joined in with a surprisingly clear tenor voice.

Berris was dimly aware that she would have no help with the birth of her child, and tried to do what she could for herself, arranging her petticoats and pieces of linen which she had prepared to the best advantage. Then a pain of such ferocity gripped her that she screamed like an animal. There was silence from the other side of the partition, then Sebastian's face, scarlet with drink, peeped from behind the curtain.

'God in Heaven, it is Berris giving birth,' he said. 'The child is arriving. We had better fetch my mother.'

She was scarcely conscious that neither of them tried to help her in any way. The baby's head was struggling free of her body, then with another wave of pain, the child was born, and Berris feebly tried to reach it and to protect it with a covering of linen. But her body was still expelling the afterbirth, and she was too weak to help herself.

The child began to cry feebly, then the flap of the wagon was thrust aside as Mistress Grey arrived with Polly Hobart close behind.

'Oh, gracious lord,' said Mistress Grey. 'Here is a fine to-do. It is a wonder that there is life in either of them. See to the child after I cut the cord, Miss Polly. Berris has borne a son, but she will be lucky if she lives to raise him. She has lost a deal of blood.'

Their voices seemed to come from far above Berris's head and she was aware of hands helping her, but they were a great distance away.

'Thank you,' she tried to whisper, but the words would not form properly. She could hear Polly crooning over the child, and the pride in Mistress Grey's voice as she claimed the baby for her grandson. Berris wanted to snatch him to herself, and to say that it belonged to no one but her, but she was too weak and ill.

'She must not be moved for a few days,' said Mistress Grey. 'Brendan must bring a doctor. She looks feverish, poor child.'

The next few days were filled with dreams and nightmares when Berris called constantly for Ninian to help her and not to beat the servant at the inn, whatever his crime. Neither must he inflict more pain upon her for deceiving him.

Mistress Grey and Polly were in constant attendance, talking to her and trying to soothe her with reassuring words. Brendan also came to lay his hand upon her forehead and to call her his dear child. Of Sebastian and Deryk Hobart, there was no sign at all.

'They are ashamed of what happened,' she heard Brendan saying clearly. 'They were roistering and drinking together and they made no attempt to help Berris even though she is Sebastian's wife. I mislike this friendship between them. They take too much upon themselves, and if they try to put forward any more ideas which I do not like, they go.'

'Sebastian cannot go,' Mistress Grey protested. 'He is husband to Berris. Part of the company belongs to Sebastian.'

'It is *my* company,' roared Brendan with a great deal of his old fire. 'It belongs to no one but me.'

But anger and upset had tired him and he slumped back, exhausted. Mistress Grey drew herself up in stature.

'You make too much of it, Mr Meredith. Sebastian stays and we need Mr Hobart. They have a great love of life and wish to enjoy themselves whilst they are young.'

Brendan had no energy left for further protest, but he bitterly regretted that he had not followed his instincts and the initial impulse to turn the brother and sister away when he first set eyes on them. He did not like Deryk Hobart's influence over Sebastian. It might harm Berris and Berris was the only human being left in this world whom he loved as dearly as life itself. He had loved her mother, and now he loved her. Somehow he must try to secure her future.

But how could a sick old man achieve such an ambition? Wearily, he had to own that it was beyond his powers.

CHAPTER NINETEEN

Berris had never truly loved Sebastian, but she began to hate him and Deryk as she slowly regained her health and strength. Polly Hobart had appointed herself nursemaid to Andrew Brendan Grey. Mistress Grey had insisted that the child was born in wedlock and entitled to Sebastian's name, and Berris accepted this, but had chosen the baby's names herself, calling him by one of his true father's Christian names. Brendan was pleased that his name had also been chosen.

She was slow to regain her strength, and as she nursed the child, her eyes were often bleak as she tried to look into the future for both of them. Andrew Brendan Grey was not a beautiful child. He had a large head and adult features which were quite distinctive in so young a baby. He did not resemble either of his parents, though his well-formed nose and broad forehead reminded Berris of someone she had seen at one time, but the memory was tantalizing and she could not recall who it was.

Andrew was a good baby, however, well

nourished and his every other whim was granted by his adopted Aunt Polly.

Polly Hobart loved the child. Having come to them withdrawn and sullen, she began to flower under the absorption and interest of caring for a small baby. She grew softer and more feminine, though she still avoided playing a stage role of importance. She had no desire to become well-known as an actress, and Berris suspected that she hated the stage.

But she was happy to mend the costumes, washing and ironing the frills and flounces carefully and replacing tattered feathers and ribbons. From material which she declared superfluous, she made small dainty garments for Andrew, stitching them lovingly and patiently.

'You need a great many more costumes,' she said to Berris, 'if you plan to take over your parts once more from Deryk. Your gowns have had to be altered to fit him, but he has torn most of them so that they are not even fit to be mended. There is only your costume for *Silver Stardust*. It is still in good condition.'

'Then we must play *Silver Stardust* next week,' Berris decided, 'when we reach Huddersfield. I must return to my work, Polly. We will see Mr Meredith regarding the costumes. Do you think you could make new gowns if I managed to purchase the materials?'

She thought about her small hoard of gold coins, and decided that one of them might be well spent in this way.

Polly nodded. 'Certainly I could, though I must also look after Andrew when you are busy and have rehearsals. I can take care of him, and sew a little whilst he sleeps.'

'I too will be spending as much time with him as possible,' said Berris, quickly. She did not want anyone to touch her baby but herself. Polly was much too high-handed with him at times.

It was quite a task to persuade Sebastian to play his role in *Silver Stardust,* and Brendan looked too tired to insist that Berris should have her way.

'It is a demanding part for me,' he said. 'I would prefer not to do it, my dear.'

'I have thought about that also,' said Berris, 'because I wondered if you might not find it too much for you sooner or later. Sebastian could play your part and Deryk could play the Water Prince. We need new costumes. Deryk has ruined most of mine, but I might manage to buy new materials and Polly can make them up more appropriately.'

'We also need to decide on whether or not to play the same old boring routine,' said Sebastian, scowling. 'Deryk has a few ideas which should be a great deal more fun.'

The two stood side by side leaning against one another, and Brendan's eyes were full of contempt as he stared at them. He could no longer hide the truth from himself, nor could the rest of the company. Whether Sebastian realized it or not, he and Deryk had more regard for one another than Sebastian had for his wife. Brendan considered that his stepson was not a true man. Even Mistress Grey could no longer pretend that Sebastian was merely having an hour's amusement with Deryk Hobart. She was forced to acknowledge the truth about their relationship, though it cost her dear to do so, and she was inclined to blame Berris for not making herself attractive to her husband.

'The costume for *Silver Stardust* is the only one which fits me,' Berris pursued.

She glanced thoughtfully at Deryk. She loathed him, but had to acknowledge that in some plays he was a dynamic figure who could hold an audience in the palm of his hand.

As well as Sheridan, plays by George Lillo and Richard Cumberland had been entertaining audiences for a number of years, plays in which kings, heroes and princesses, beloved by Brendan Meredith had no part, but audiences were changing even as society was changing, and Berris might have welcomed new ventures if only Deryk was willing to co-operate.

A new play by Thomas Holcroft, *The Road to Ruin,* might be well within their capabilities if only Deryk would play young Harry Dornton. Brendan would be needed for Old Dornton and there was little left for Sebastian other than Silky or Goldfinch, but Mistress Grey might do well as the Widow Warren.

'If Deryk would prefer some good new plays which we could learn easily, then I would be happy to co-operate,' she said. 'Polly could soon make the costumes for any particular play and it could be performed in every town. It would be well worth the effort. What do you think, Stepfather? I was thinking of *The Road to Ruin* in particular.'

'Very appropriate title for you, my dear wife,' Sebastian snorted. 'A familiar road for you.'

Brendan stared him out of countenance. 'I think your idea for Sebastian to take over my role in *Silver Stardust* is a good one. We will play that this week, and perhaps we can rehearse a Sheridan for next week. I do not think we can be more ambitious. What do you say, Hobart?'

He could not bring himself to use

Deryk's Christian name.

'Well ... I have other plays in mind, too, Mr Meredith,' said Deryk, turning to look into Sebastian's eyes. They laughed together, low laughter, as though they shared a great many private jokes. 'I will prepare them for rehearsal next week. Meanwhile I will play the Prince for Mistress Meredith.'

Berris wished she could open the door and push him out into the street. She was suffering the presence of the Hobarts because she had very little choice, and she was grateful for Polly's help with the baby, and her skills with her needle.

But she loathed Deryk so much now that she felt a deep revulsion every time he stood near to her, and she suspected him of deliberately making loving gestures towards Sebastian in her presence, just to cause her anger and annoyance.

As for Sebastian, he seemed to grow more foolish yet more brutal and aggressive towards her every day. He had wanted to marry her to safeguard the company, but she could see now that it had also been in a desperate attempt to behave as other men. But his natural instincts had now surfaced and he openly showed his contempt for her as well as all women. Together he and Deryk made a veritable sore on the well-being of the rest of the company. Berris knew that she could never allow her child to grow up in such an atmosphere. Something must be done before baby Andrew was old enough to be influenced by his environment.

Surprisingly Deryk played the part of the Water Prince in *Silver Stardust* to perfection and his delicate slender beauty made a perfect foil for Berris as the fairy princess. She put personal feelings aside, and their absorption in the play communicated itself to Sebastian and Mistress Grey, so that the whole production was one of such charm and delicacy that the theatre audiences were moved each evening to tears as well as laughter, and the applause was loud and long.

Deryk took Berris's hand as they made their curtain calls and it was only after she had changed her costume that she felt compelled to wash her hands to free herself of the strange musky perfume which clung to the man. She thought about Ninian and shivered. Ninian's contempt for such an exquisite as Deryk, might overflow on to herself for even breathing the same air.

The following week was one of tension and quarrels. Having played the Prince to please Berris, Deryk claimed co-operation with the new plays he had chosen and wished to introduce into their repertoire, but when Berris realized the degrading quality of the bawdy plays, she refused to accept any part of them.

'You will honour your promise to Deryk,' cried Sebastian angrily, when she showed her scathing contempt for the first play he chose to read. 'So what is wrong with a little bit of bawdy humour? The audiences will love it. Their noses will not be so wrinkled up as yours, my lady Berris. And what have you to be so high-minded about, anyway? If I did not protect you with my name, you would need to earn your bread in the streets. *That* might not encourage you to be so full of pride!'

'Playing this part would make me no better than a street woman,' said Berris.

'Then perhaps it will suit you very well,' said Deryk, coming into the room. He leered at her so that she lifted her chin and deliberately pulled in her skirts to avoid contamination.

'I might have known what sort of play you would choose, Mr Hobart,' she said, very quietly. 'Your standards do not appear to be very high.'

'High enough for you, madam,' said Deryk, silkily. 'Leave us, Sebastian. I rather think Mistress Meredith requires a little persuasion in order to play her new roles.'

'You will not touch me!' cried Berris

as Sebastiain slouched out of the room and she was left alone with the man she hated.

'No? Perhaps it would amuse you to know that I have often been tempted to touch you, my dear Berris. I do not always admire the softness of a woman, but you are slender, with lean flanks and good limbs. Perhaps you do not understand that I can be roused by a woman. I have a great desire to take you and remove some of that haughty dignity behind which you retreat from time to time. What right have you to be so unapproachable? What is so special about you that no one must touch your body?'

Her eyes showed their horror as he began to advance towards her.

'No!' she whispered, her voice heavy with loathing. 'No! I will not allow you to touch me! You cannot!'

'I cannot?' he asked. 'Oh, but you are wrong, Mistress Berris. I could, and I can. You will see that I can, and there is no reason why I cannot have you. Sebastian might be a little jealous, but of you, my dear, not of me. But he is not difficult to handle, and he has great regard for me, very great regard.'

The words tripped delicately off his tongue. Berris had backed away until she was leaning against the wall, and now

Deryk grasped her arm and pulled her so that his arm encircled her neck. His grip was like a band of steel and she was unable to move within his arms. Deliberately he kissed her mouth and she made a small moaning sound of protest as she tried to break free of him. She was almost sick at the feel of his scented lips enclosing her own.

'You are very beautiful,' he whispered. 'Oh God, how beautiful you are! I have watched you many times, but always your eyes tell me that you consider yourself far above my reach. Yet I could love you ... Do not resist me and I will not hurt you.'

She shook her head wildly. Deryk was slender and only a little taller than she, but he was lithe and sinewy and even though she fought like one demented to free herself from his grasp, she knew that sooner or later her strength would be unequal to his.

Almost venomously he bore her down on to a couch, his body imprisoning her own even as his hands were busy pulling at her clothing. She felt his fingers reaching for her private parts and she almost fainted with the horror of what was happening. She lay quiet for a moment, drawing a deep breath before making her final bid to be free of him, and he gave a small grunt of satisfaction.

'I knew you would want me sooner or later,' he whispered. 'I have seen you looking at me, and I know that you are looking at the man in me. Am I not the Water Prince to your Princess? There are many kinds of love, my Berris, and an actor can be many things to many people.'

He relaxed his hold for a second in order to adjust his clothing so that she was left in no doubt that he intended rape. Bitter sickness rose into her mouth and she brought her knee up suddenly, hitting him in the groin and his face contorted with pain and rage. Words poured from him, vile words which were offensive to her ears, and she felt soiled by his invective. Then he began to call out for Sebastian who hurried eagerly into the room.

'She is about to receive what she deserves,' said Deryk, in his high-pitched voice, 'but she wriggles like an eel. Hold her down, Sebastian, and I will oblige you if you want her later. You can have sport with her if I am here to help you.'

Berris could no longer utter a word because of her rage and humiliation. She was so angry that she longed for a weapon with which to strike dead her tormentors. At that moment she could have killed both of them. But it needed all her concentration to try and free herself from the grasping hands of the two men. Her nether garments were torn and Sebastian's eyes were wild with excitement and laughter. What fine sport Deryk could provide, though he certainly did not want Berris for himself. She no longer held any attraction for him whatsoever. She was dull and lifeless after Deryk.

He held her legs, thinking that she must tire soon from her wild threshing, and besides Deryk was on top of her now, and would soon have his way with her.

Suddenly the door flew open and Brendan Meredith's great bulk filled the doorway. The two young men froze in their efforts to rape the girl, then slowly Deryk Hobart rose to his feet as Brendan Meredith walked into the room.

'Animals!' he roared with all the old ringing passion in his voice. 'Get out! You are no longer part of my company. Go before I kill you, both of you. You are swines of the lowest order. You have brought nothing but disgrace and dishonour to the Meredith Players, so get out of my sight. I never want to see either of you ever again.'

His face, which had been pale and drawn in recent weeks, was now suffused with colour. Berris was swiftly putting her clothing to rights and trying to pin up her loosened hair. She ran to her stepfather and he held her closely in his arms, even as the sobs began to rise in her throat.

Sebastian was looking at Brendan Meredith with disbelief.

'You cannot show me the door, sir,' he blustered. 'The company is as much mine as yours now. You forget that my mother and I have contributed as much as yourself in recent years to building it up. As for bringing dishonour to the Meredith Players, your stepdaughter has done that with her bastard child. Do you forget that it was I who protected her by giving her my name?'

'Enough!' Brendan Meredith's face was black with anger.

Mistress Grey sidled into the room, attracted by the noise of argument. 'What is the cause of the upset this time?' she asked. 'Berris, as usual?'

'These two ... gentlemen ... were about to rape my stepdaughter,' he said, roughly. 'I have ordered both of them to leave my company.'

'Sebastian will not leave!' cried Mistress Grey. 'He is my son and the company belongs to us as much as to you now, Mr Meredith. You forget yourself, sir. We have worked hard to build it.'

'And now you would destroy it,' he raged. 'You would ruin a good name and a good reputation. You would draw the crowds, but at the cost of our integrity. And already we watch the influence at work as you lay hands upon my stepdaughter. Mr Hobart, sir, you are contemptible!'

Deryk Hobart tried to laugh.

'We were merely enjoying a little amusement, sir, as young people will do. I am sure that Mistress Meredith would not hold it against us. It was a change of circumstances for her since she is greatly tied to looking after her child. Perhaps ...' he looked at Berris and she heard the hard steely note creeping into his voice, '... perhaps we should have taken care of the babe instead of trying to amuse Mistress Berris.'

He stared into her eyes and cold shivers again shook her. He was evil, this exquisite young man. His beauty came from the power of evil and was not a gift of God. He was telling her that she had better co-operate with him and Sebastian, or he might harm her child. And she could not shield the baby every hour of the day. It was Polly who looked after him while she was busy, and Polly always agreed to whatever her brother suggested. She would soon give up the baby to Deryk if he asked her.

'I ...' she stammered, trying to find the words, 'they were merely being playful,

Stepfather, but thank you for ... for offering to help, even if you did not understand.'

Her eyes turned again to Deryk, striking the bargain. She would say nothing, if he did not harm the child. Her fear was reaching to the very depths of her heart, but for the moment she was powerless to fight his evil.

'I am not a fool,' said Brendan Meredith, 'and I recognize a rotten fruit when it is placed in a basket of apples. I tell you that you will go. Now! At once! At ...'

Suddenly his voice began to croak and he leaned over to take hold of a chair. Immediately Berris rushed to his side once more, guiding him on to the couch as he clutched at his chest and his breath came in laboured gasps.

'Get a doctor,' she cried to Mistress Grey. 'He is ill. He may be having a seizure.'

'He should not lose his temper so easily,' said Deryk Hobart, nonchalantly.

'He *must* have a doctor,' Berris insisted, loosening the scarf at his neck.

'I will go,' said Polly Hobart.

Silently Berris prayed that her stepfather would not die, as she sponged his forehead and tried to make him as comfortable as possible. Over the past few weeks she had watched him anxiously and it had

273

occurred to her that she might lose him one day soon. The thought had been hard to bear. Now his breathing was heavy and laboured, and he could not speak to her.

'His heart is growing weaker,' said Mistress Grey. 'He was ill in just this fashion before autumn, when you were a fine lady travelling in Italy. He would like to force his will upon other people, but he cannot do so any longer. Sebastian and Deryk must stay with the company. We cannot manage without them.'

'They will not touch me again,' said Berris and stared Mistress Grey in the eye. The older woman looked away.

A moment later Polly Hobart returned with an elderly man following closely behind. The old doctor shook his head over Brendan Meredith's condition.

'He may live for a few more weeks, or he may have another seizure at any time,' he said, turning to Mistress Grey.

'But will he not recover his strength?' asked Berris with alarm.

'Perhaps. Who knows? I do not play God, and if he rests who can say if he will recover. Try to keep him free of excitement.'

'We will do our best to look after him,' said Berris.

She saw that Brendan's eyes were open

even though he could not whisper to her. She saw his lips moving, but no sound came.

'We will look after you, Stepfather,' she said, taking his hand. 'Do not worry. I shall always be here if you need me.'

Brendan's illness removed the biggest obstacle to putting on the bawdy plays which Deryk promised would make them all rich. Berris was given her parts to learn, and with the veiled threat of harming her baby now a very real one, she learned the lines which were distasteful to her, and had no choice but to agree to play the part.

Mistress Grey was foolish enough to believe in the large income she had been promised, and threw herself wholeheartedly into her part in each play.

Had the performances been lightly amusing, Berris might not have minded, but they were merely degrading and at times immature. But she saw real anger in Deryk's eyes when she described the plays as only fit for those adults who had minds like children.

'They are rich and full-blooded,' he cried, 'not like the poor milksop stuff you have always played. I could select scenes from the plays of Mr William Shakespeare and you would be complaining that they were bawdy and not worthy of your great acting talent and finer sensibilities. It is you who are childish and immature, Mistress Berris, not I.'

She did not argue. She had looked around for a weapon to conceal about her person in case she was once again molested by Deryk or Sebastian, but there was nothing which could be concealed easily, other than a handful of pepper in a square of linen. If she threw that in their faces, they might decide to leave her alone in future.

Or the evil Deryk might press her baby's face into his pillow and say that a cat had slept in his basket. She believed him to be capable of such a thing. Also Sebastian. Sebastian hated the child and constantly remarked upon how ugly he looked.

Berris believed that Polly was also deeply aware of the baby's danger because she watched over him constantly and lifted him out of his basket at every turn. Berris had grown tired of telling her that she spoiled the child with too much attention. Polly merely held the baby against her thin chest and grudged the times when Berris nursed him to sleep. His strong features were still dominant, though there was a new baby prettiness to his cheeks and he now looked less like a miniature adult. But Mistress

Grey no longer looked at him with such pride. Sadly she felt that she could no longer pretend to herself that he could be her grandson.

CHAPTER TWENTY

It was Deryk who decided that they should include Leeds and York in their new bookings, laughing with amusement when Berris pleaded with him to forego York.

'So you think your fine relatives might come to the theatre,' he sniggered.

'I do not think my sister would attend any theatre where we were playing, especially now that our standards have dropped so low, but I do not wish to take the risk,' she said.

'It might be amusing if your brother-in-law watched one of our performances,' said Deryk. 'How entertaining *that* could be. Sebastian told me how you tried to fool him into accepting you as your sister. I laughed until my eyes were blinded with tears. I declare I would give the performance of my life if he were sitting in one of the boxes. Perhaps I could call at the ancestral home and leave a few complimentary tickets.'

'No!' cried Berris, a great lump in her throat. 'Please do not, Deryk. Please do not.'

'Why should I not?' he asked, silkily.

'You have not always been generous towards me. I might even have possessed you when the mood was upon me, but it is upon me no longer. You are not attractive to me now, so you cannot throw yourself at my feet and offer to please me. I think I would find more amusement in York.'

She said no more and hoped, wearily, that Ninian and Lora would ignore the theatre. She knew that Deryk was quite capable of carrying out such intentions, but she could imagine Lora instructing one of the servants to throw the invitations into the fire. She had little fear that they would come to the theatre, but if they did ... if they *did*, how humiliating it would be! She hated their present repertoire of plays and if Ninian saw her tripping around the stage with a shoulder bared and a skirt lifted suggestively at the ankle, she could imagine his curled lip and the derisive look in his eyes. Or would he still want to punish her more severely for tricking him into believing she was her sister?

Then there was the child. She must try to hide the child from him, for he would not believe that Andrew was his. He would accuse her of pleasuring other men. She could not bear that he would think so ill of her. She pressed her hands to her temple as her thoughts whirled round in her head, unable to be free of them even

279

as she tried to sleep.

Brendan Meredith was no longer strong enough to make decisions for the company. Leeds and York were included in the new bookings.

As the company travelled eastwards from Bradford, Beris began to feel that each day was a lifetime through which she must live. Since her earliest memory, Brendan had been a father to her, giving her help, advice and education. Sometimes he had been stern and even cruel if he had been drinking, but he had been the mainstay of her life. Now Berris had to face the fact that he was dying and the knowledge bit deeply into her heart.

Mistress Grey refused to believe that he was any more ill than on previous occasions, and made plans for when he would once again be back to full health and strength, and in charge of the company once more. It was left to Berris to look after her stepfather, and gradually she allowed Polly to take charge of her baby so that she could devote as much time as possible to the sick man. She no longer cared about the parts she had to play. It was poor-quality work and Berris was glad that Brendan Meredith could not see what the Meredith Players had become.

She sat beside his bed one afternoon,

trying to coax him into drinking a few spoonsful of nourishing soup, but she could see that he was weakening fast. His eyes had been closed after he had rejected the food, then suddenly they were open again and bright with awareness.

'Berris,' he whispered, urgently. 'Can you forgive me?'

'There is nothing to forgive,' she said, taking his hand in her own.

'Much to forgive,' he whispered. 'Take the child to Massingham. You must see Lennox. You are his legal wife, whatever name you used at the wedding. The child is his legal heir.'

Berris's expression did not change. Gently she used a piece of damp linen to mop his forehead. Brendan often had fancies, believing himself to be appearing at Drury Lane or Covent Garden. He spoke about the old days with Mr Garrick, and now Mr Kemble and his sister, Mrs Siddons as though he were close in friendship to all of them. Now he believed her to be the true Lady Lennox!

'Do not worry about it,' she said, soothingly. 'I will take care of it.'

He gripped her arm. 'I was afraid for you when you married Sebastian, but he told his creature that he had acted his own priest. You are not his wife and have broken no law. You are the wife

281

of Lennox. You must go to him and take the child.'

She drew back a little. So often his ramblings were disjointed sentences which trailed away into nonsense, but now his eyes were brightly feverish. Now it seemed that he was well aware of his words and that he truly believed what he was telling her.

'I did not want to lose you,' he whispered. 'I would never have seen you again. Sebastian and Hobart have ruined my company. It is best that you should not be part of their degradation. He is a weak man ... Sebastian ... He was a weak boy and I never wanted him to have you ... always knew what he was ... no man ... no man ...'

Again the words were mumbled and his breathing became heavy, then he caught her hand and held it in his grasp.

'Promise me!' he cried. 'Promise me you will take the child when I am gone.'

'I promise,' she said, as he stared at her beseechingly, and his hand like a claw holding her arm.

Brendan Meredith died whilst the company was playing at a small shabby theatre in Leeds. Berris had thought herself prepared to lose him, but her grief was like a sword-thrust into her heart. She was too hurt for tears and listened, unmoved, to Mistress Grey's noisy weeping. Even Sebastian grew quiet and more sober as arrangements had to be made for burial. But Deryk Hobart reminded them that they were still theatre players and were expected to play their parts.

The performances were a nightmare to Berris and she no longer cared that they were travelling to York and that Massingham was now so close that she could quite easily walk to the gates, carrying her child.

The thought came, unbidden, into her mind as they once again settled into their cheap dark lodgings near to the river. Berris had pleaded that their new repertoire would be unsuitable for York audiences, but Sebastian had overruled her. He had officially declared himself in charge of the company though it was easy to recognize the true identity of the new actor-manager. Sebastian never made a move without first consulting his other self. He and Deryk were inseparable.

Mistress Grey was prostrated with grief over the loss of her husband, and Berris did her best to comfort her, then found that Mistress Grey had been reaching out blindly for another prop to her life, and that the older woman clung to her as though she were a lifeline. Berris's heart was touched, but she had never loved

Mistress Grey enough to want to fill such a gap in her life. And she herself longed to be left alone to mourn her stepfather in her own way.

Thankfully she had her child to care for. Berris turned to him once more, but found that Polly was always there before her, whisking him into her arms and offering to attend to his needs. Tiredly Berris allowed her to help, and spent her evenings on the stage, always fearful that one of the boxes would be occupied by Ninian and Lora, then relieved when she saw they were not there. It was just as she had supposed. Lora would not come, even out of curiosity.

But her own promise to Brendan still rang in her ears. He had made her promise to take baby Andrew to his father, and she had agreed. Now she could feel his presence all round her, urging her to keep that promise.

Confiding in no one, Berris dressed quietly in her most sober clothing on the day before they were due to leave York, then picked up her baby shortly after Polly had laid him down to rest and had gone to wash some of the tiny garments.

Silently Berris left the lodging house, the child well wrapped in a fine shawl, and began to walk towards Massingham. She had little money left from the purse of coins which Mistress Ashington had given her, and she had no wish to hire a coach. She was afraid that it would draw attention and that questions would be asked.

Baby Andrew was thriving, but it was only as Berris began to walk along the winding dusty road which would take her to Massingham Hall that she realized how much heavier he had become. She began to recognize landmarks and had to fight down the threatening tears as she remembered driving along the road in the Massingham carriage with Ninian close beside her, his hand covering his own. Now she had to press close to the hedgerows as farm carts rumbled past. She did not invite any of them to stop and give her a lift on her way. This was Massingham land, and the farmers could well be familiar with the sight of Lady Lennox attending church, or visiting them if they were sick. Their curiosity about her appearance could be harmful. Instead she drew up the hood of her cloak to hide her face, and walked on doggedly, knowing that each step was one nearer to Massingham.

The driveway from the wrought-iron gates seemed even longer than she remembered, and she was exhausted by the time she reached the oak door of the great house. How big it seemed. Was Lady Truscott still alive? She had been mistress of Massingham for a great many years, but now it must surely be Lora who was mistress of this great property.

Jessop opened the door, his rheumy eyes peering out at Berris short-sightedly. She wanted to sob with fatigue and to thrust her baby into his arms, asking him to take the child to Hebe, but she dared not show signs of recognition until she had seen Ninian and Lora. She felt sick with nerves as the elderly butler peered out at her.

'I wish to see Lady Truscott, please,' she said, huskily.

'Lady Truscott is dead and gone, ma'am,' said Jessop. 'Dead and gone she is. You are too late to see her, ma'am.'

He bowed and stepped back into the gloomy depths of the hall, then started to swing the door shut. The woman with the child was probably a beggar.

'Sir Ninian Lennox!' cried Berris, desperately, 'or ... or Lady Lora.'

The door slowly opened again and the faded eyes peered at her again.

'Sir Ninian is in London, ma'am. I will enquire about Lady Lennox. Who shall I say?'

'Mistress Meredith. Mistress Berris Meredith.'

Jessop disappeared and Berris stood on the doorstep for an eternity. The child started to whimper and she began to walk along the wide drive at the front of the house, gently rocking him to hush his fretful cries. Heavy clouds had blown up and the day had become dark and ominous with the threat of thunder in the air.

Berris caught a glimpse of something pale and ethereal from behind a window in the main upstairs bedroom, but when her eyes were immediately drawn upwards, the fleeting movement had gone and the windows remained blank.

Presently the old man shuffled back again and stared out at her.

'Lady Lora is indisposed, ma'am,' he said. 'She can see no one.'

'Oh, please!' cried Berris. 'I am very tired. I ... I have walked from York and I would like to rest with my baby. I ... I appeal to Lady Lora.'

The old man hesitated, then he stood back. He had been given his orders by the mistress of the house.

'I am sorry, ma'am. Lady Lennox does not wish to see Mistress Meredith. Her instructions were quite clear. I am sorry, ma'am.' His voice lowered. 'There is a flat stone near the main gates, ma'am. It can be restful to sit there for a while.'

'Thank you, Jessop,' said Berris and heard his sharp intake of breath. He stared at her more closely, but this time it was Berris who turned away, her feet now swollen in her heavy shoes, and her arms aching as she clasped the baby who was growing more and more unsettled. She would have to hurry if she were to reach their lodgings again before dark and she would be late for her performance. There were one or two plays where Polly could take her place, but she knew she would have to explain her absence, and she had a sudden fear of what Sebastian and Deryk might say or do when they knew that she had been to Massingham, and had been turned away.

Holding the baby close she stumbled down the drive, then had to stand aside as a carriage hove into view. Berris walked on to the grass, expecting the carriage to sweep past her, but she saw that a man's head had appeared at one of the windows and moments later the carriage was pulled to a halt within a few yards of her.

Berris looked up and slowly the hood of her cloak slid from her head as she found herself staring into Ninian's eyes. How much older he looked! she thought and how stern and cold the expression on his face. She was too tired to be afraid as he scrutinized every inch of her, and a small sound escaped his lips when he looked at the child in her arms.

'Who are you and why have you come here?' he asked.

Berris quickly pulled the hood over her dark chestnut hair once more, and grasped the child more tightly. She was acutely aware of her soiled and rather tattered appearance, also the reason for the child's growing discomfort. She felt dirty and dishevelled and she could see no kindness in the hard face of the man who looked at her from his carriage. She must look very different from that day when she had walked out of his life.

'It ... it is nothing, sir,' she said, hurriedly. 'I ... I only wished to rest.'

'Then you must rest in this carriage,' he said, opening the door and jumping to the ground. She had no choice but to enter the carriage, whereupon he leapt back inside and ordered the coachman to drive to the house.

Berris tried to hide her face in her hood, but Sir Ninian's dark eyes never left her face, except to stare at the child as he whimpered restlessly.

'Wait here,' he said to the coachman when they drove up to the main door. 'And you, madam, you will come with me and bring the child.'

He took hold of her arm and at the contact with his fingers, her heart began to beat loudly. She could hardly believe she was standing so close to him once again, yet his whole attitude told her that they might have been thousands of miles apart. The Ashingtons had been quite correct. Already he must clearly see the truth, but his anger would be terrible. But her fatigue had now taken all her strength. She could only accept what was to come.

'I wish to see Lady Lennox in the drawing room immediately, Jessop,' he told the butler as he escorted Berris into the large square hall. 'Tell her I will not listen to any excuse.'

Once more Jessop gave Berris a long look, then he shuffled away to do his master's bidding.

Automatically Berris moved forward towards the drawing room, then Ninian walked ahead of her, holding the door open. Once again his eyes held hers, and she saw the feverish light of excitement beginning to burn as he ushered her into the room.

There were faint ominous rumblings of thunder and the light was poor in the room. He lit one of the oil lamps on the table, then asked her to sit near the fire. He stared at her in the soft orange glow of the lamp, then began to light a few candles without uttering another word. Berris was too tired to say anything now. Gratefully she sat down on the soft cushions of the sofa and laid the baby on her knees.

Then Lora's soft light footsteps sounded outside the door and Ninian went to open it.

'Come in, my love,' he said pleasantly. 'We have a visitor. I think I am owed an explanation, but I warn you, both of you, that only the truth will do.'

His fist suddenly banged on the table, so that the baby woke and started up in fright.

'And, by God, I shall have it!' he shouted, to the accompaniment of the thin wailing of the child.

CHAPTER TWENTY-ONE

When Lora Ashingtoon drove away from Birkridge to return to Massingham, she had been completely confident in her own ability to take her rightful place as Lady Lennox. The exchange of clothing with Berris had been accomplished very easily, though she had seen the distress on her sister's face when she was forced to relinquish her fine nether garments, replacing them with those of poor quality which Mistress Ashington deemed suitable.

Berris whispered, 'They will chafe my skin.'

Lora shrugged. 'Aunt Louisa bought new clothing for you. She thought them finer than the clothing which you wore when you first arrived here.'

She leaned forward to peer closely into her looking glass, fixing a patch on her cheek on exactly the same place as that which Berris had worn. She turned to look at her sister, and saw her eyes widen. No doubt Berris was surprised to see her dressed in the clothing which had so recently been her own. For a moment, Lora's heart softened, feeling sympathy for the other girl, then she turned away. If she spent too much time worrying about Berris, her own future could so easily be jeopardized. Berris had been brought up as a play actress. It was a life she knew and understood. Far better that she returned to it than that Sir Ninian discovered he had been tricked.

Lora's looks were indifferent as she picked up Berris's small silk purse which contained a few coins and a small lace handkerchief. She hesitated over returning the handkerchief, then snapped the purse shut. Aunt Louisa was already inviting her to hurry, and a moment later she ran down the broad stairs, receiving Aunt Louisa's kiss on her cheek as she was helped into the Massingham carriage. She was on her way to her new life.

It was only when she leaned back in the carriage and realized that she was now entirely on her own, that Lora's courage began to waver. She had scarcely listened to all Berris had to tell her about the Grand Tour of Italy. They had met Italian people named Fiorenza and Carlo, but she could not remember any surnames. Then there had been a lightskirt. Lora's lip curled. Berris had not held Sir Ninian's attention for long when he turned to a lightskirt so quickly. What was her name? Lora's brows wrinkled and wondered if it was Maria. But surely that was the name of the maidservant? How could she be expected to remember so many people? she wondered petulantly. Aunt Louisa had been too hurried in making the exchange, but she had been fearful that Sir Ninian would ride to Birkridge to look for his bride, and would discover Berris as well as Lora.

Her head began to ache intolerably, and she put up a hand to her temple. Perhaps that was the answer. Perhaps she ought to have a slight accident, with her head striking the side of the coach. Her memory could so easily be impaired.

Lora sighed with relief because she had found a solution satisfactory to herself, though by the time the carriage reached Massingham and she saw Sir Ninian walking forward to greet her, her nerves took hold of her once again and she pressed Berris's handkerchief to her temple. She stumbled a little as she descended from the coach, and Ninian was quick to take her into his arms.

'What has happened, my darling?' he asked, anxiously. 'You look very pale.'

'It ... it was the coach ride, sir,' she said, nervously. 'I seem to have hit my head. The coach lurched, though I ... I do not remember ...'

'My sweet Lora!' His voice was very

concerned, but Lora was not comforted. Aunt Louisa had always said that Lennox would hardly be a loving husband. His reputation amongst women was not of the best and this had been borne out by Berris's tale about visiting his lightskirt in Italy. But now he was behaving like a lover! Panic began to swell in Lora's heart. She was not yet prepared to live *so* closely to this man who was practically a stranger to her. They had talked together when the marriage was first arranged, and Lora had felt that he was indifferent to her and even had a bored tolerance of her background. He had left her in no doubt that he was not a man to be trifled with, and would expect high standards from his wife.

Lora had been taught the social graces, and how to manage a large household by Aunt Louisa, who then decided that with Lora's beauty and accomplishments, Sir Ninian Lennox was very fortunate to have such a bride. She had impressed upon Lora that she should never feel inferior to Lennox or any of his friends, even though the marriage settlement favoured the Ashingtons. It was Lady Truscott's express wish that she and Lennox should marry, and he stood to gain almost as much from the marriage as she.

'Do not be intimidated, child,' Aunt Louisa had said, repeatedly. 'Remember that you are of excellent family, as good as that of Lennox. Remember who you are and all will be well.'

But Aunt Louisa had not allowed for the fact that Sir Ninian might behave amorously towards his bride. Berris must have encouraged this, thought Lora angrily, just to embarrass her. She was a play actress and used to professing love for the entertainment of onlookers. She must have encouraged Sir Ninian to believe in love between husband and wife, and now she, Lora, was being placed in a difficult position. He felt that he was entitled to take her into his arms when she would vastly prefer to behave with decorum and dignity, especially before the servants.

'We are not alone, sir,' she muttered as he held her tightly in his arms and guided her into the huge drawing room where a fire had been lit.

'What is this?' he asked, astonished. 'Who has accompanied you? Surely your aunt does not intend to call on us freely. You are a Lennox now, my dear, not an Ashington.'

'I ... I mean the servants,' said Lora.

His eyebrows drew together.

'You know that the servants do not require to be consulted. What is wrong, Lora? You have already learned that our servants are here to serve us, not to stand in judgement.'

'I know how to handle servants,' said Lora stiffly.

'But naturally you do. Now tell me, little one, what has happened to upset you so? You are so stiff and unyielding in my arms, you who are my love and my wife. You say your head aches?'

His lips sought her temple as he held her lightly but firmly in his arms, then his long sensitive fingers stroked her forehead lightly. Lora's fear of him and her revulsion caused her to stand perfectly still, though hysteria was beginning to rise in her. Soon she would be forced to push him away. She could not bear to be so close to him.

But Sir Ninian must have sensed her lack of response because he looked at her closely.

'Perhaps the injury is greater than I supposed,' he said, thoughtfully, his fingers running lightly over her forehead. 'Perhaps we ought to have the doctor to examine you. He will call shortly to see Aunt Elizabeth.'

'No!' she protested, sharply, then slid out of his arms and smiled at him warmly. She would plead fatigue, and perhaps that would satisfy him. 'It ... it was fatiguing to see my aunt and uncle once again.'

'Nevertheless the doctor will examine

you, Lora.' He came once more to draw her into his arms. 'You are not with child, are you?'

'No!' she cried, then more gently, 'no, of course not. Not yet.'

This time his eyes gleamed with amusement as they looked into her own.

'Those two words are more like my Lora than any I have heard since your return from Birkridge. Perhaps it is time we gave thought to an heir. But we must make sure you have not been injured in that accident. You are very precious to me, sweet one. I cannot allow even a hair of your head to be injured.'

He pulled at her soft curls playfully, then helped a maidservant, Hebe Jessop, to settle her on to a large couch with a tray of tea and delicious sweetmeats for both of them to enjoy. Lora remembered that Berris had found it difficult to preside over the tea table and she was more than happy to show her own competence. She would have enjoyed eating the sweetmeats but she caught a gleam in Ninian's eyes as he watched her and once again she complained of her bad headache, and pushed away the plate. His expression sobered.

'My poor beloved,' he said, tenderly, 'then it is true that you have been injured. You have lost your appetite. I will see that

Jessop calls the doctor for you.'

Lora had no choice but to agree and professed a desire to rest. Later an elderly man with kindly but shrewd eyes came to examine her, and to ask her questions which she would have preferred to avoid. She left him in no doubt that there was still no heir to Massingham on the way and that her only complaint was a recurring headache, having hit her head when her carriage bumped over rough ground. The elderly doctor examined her head carefully then shook his own with perplexity. He and Sir Ninian walked out of the room, their voices low, then Ninian returned, walking briskly.

'It would appear that any injury is only of a temporary nature, my dear,' he said. 'You are not in such need of care as Aunt Elizabeth. There is no good news of her. She has been asking for you, and perhaps when you feel better, you will sit with her once more.'

Lora pouted petulantly. How dull to be asked to sit by the bedside of an old lady who was dying. Yet she dared not antagonize him further.

'Very well, but not this evening. I would like to retire to my room and remain there quietly. The doctor cannot see my headaches, but they are very real to me.'

'I will call Jessop,' said Ninian, then

once again he took her gently into his arms. 'Rest well and I will attend you later.'

The next two weeks brought long days of boredom and nights of sheer torture for Lora. When she had day-dreamed of becoming Lady Lennox, she had imagined herself wearing beautiful, becoming gowns with flashing gems round her neck and on her wrists, but the reality could not have been more different. Because of Lady Truscott's illness, few people called except to enquire for the invalid and to leave small gifts which she was obliged to acknowledge on Lady Truscott's behalf.

But even more harrowing were the nights when Sir Ninian came to their bed, sometimes rather late, and insisted on making love to her.

Lora was afraid of giving her body to a man. It had happened to her once before, and she had dreaded Aunt Louisa finding out. Aunt Louisa had always guarded her so closely when her beauty began to attract admiring but respectful glances from the younger men who worked around Birkridge estate.

John Lamont, whose family farmed an independent property bordering Birkridge, had begun to make his own deliveries of the cheese in which they specialized instead of sending a farm servant, and once or twice he had found an excuse to talk to her. Lora had been pleased by the admiration in his eyes, and the deference he had shown, though one warm spring day he had walked beside her for a step or two, admiring the display of daffodils under the old beech tree.

'They are very beautiful,' said Lora.

'They are as nothing compared with your own beauty, ma'am,' said John Lamont and blushed at his own temerity. Then Aunt Louisa had caught sight of her pale pink gown and had hurried out to hustle her indoors once more and to chide her for talking to young Lamont.

But the brief conversation had sewn a seed in her heart, and she began to look forward to seeing John Lamont and to incline her head graciously when he looked towards her. The Lamont farm was large and well stocked, and John had received an education and wore better clothing than that of a farm labourer. He was tall, with curling dark hair and his teeth gleamed like pearls in his bronzed face.

After recovering from her chicken pox, Lora had become bored and lonely. She had expected to be married and living at Massingham, but instead she must be kept in hiding at Birkridge. Her only excitement lay in finding ways to exchange a few smiles and looks which gradually became languishing, with John Lamont.

Then one warm day Aunt Louisa had declared her intention of visiting a friend and had given Lora permission to walk in the rose garden if she remained out of sight of would-be callers. If she heard a carriage, she was instructed to sit in the small garden house until the visitor had gone.

Lora had waited until John Lamont had arrived, but this time she had encouraged him to walk with her and to admire the roses.

'I cannot see them when you stand beside me,' he told her, his dark eyes sparkling. How handsome he looked as he walked beside her, tall and splendid. Lora's heart fluttered wildly, especially when John invited her to sit with him in the garden house.

'It may be our only opportunity,' he entreated her. 'Your aunt would never allow you to talk to me ...'

'She is out until tea-time.'

Lora put all other thoughts behind her. Her days were so long and so full of boredom and now it was exciting to have this handsome man looking at her with such adoration in his eyes.

'If only your aunt and uncle would countenance me as a suitor,' he said. 'My father has bought more land and plans to rebuild our farm house. I would have much to offer.'

'No, no, it is impossible,' she whispered. How could she explain that she was already 'married'? He was drawing her into his arms and she could almost hear his heartbeats through the thin silk of his shirt.

Then his lips had claimed hers, and Lora's body lost all resistance to his demanding mouth and his probing hands. His skin was soft in spite of being weather-beaten and his hands, though slightly rough, were the hands of a strong man. He had pulled her down on to the wide bench built all along one wall of the garden house, and Lora had a moment of panic when she remembered that she had removed a few of her nether garments against the heat of the day.

Then, somehow, it did not seem to matter. Nothing mattered except that she and John were young and desired one another. At least she had thought she desired him, but when he began to take possession of her, Lora was jerked awake as though she had been douched with cold water.

'No!' she cried. 'You must not!'

But it was too late and her body began to throb with pain, even as she struggled to be free.

'Dear God,' John Lamont whispered as he pulled away from her. 'What have I done?'

'You have raped me!' she retorted, struggling free.

'That I have not!' he denied. 'You know you wanted me even as I wanted you. I love you, Lora Ashington. I would have you for my wife if it could be arranged.'

'That can never be,' she cried, 'and you took advantage of me. You hurt me.'

He stared at her then, his teeth flashed in a smile.

'I would not hurt you the next time, Mistress Lora. We could be happy together, we two.'

Lora adjusted her clothing then pushed open the door of the garden house to find Aunt Louisa staring in at her. She almost fainted with fright.

'Go and do not come back,' Louisa Ashington said in a terrible voice to John Lamont who, for a moment, stood his ground, holding his body tall and straight. Then with another searching glance at Lora he disappeared through the rose garden to find his pony and trap.

Lora had been terrified that her aunt would know everything. Surprisingly she had not been punished as severely as she had expected. Her aunt had questioned her closely and at first Lora had lied valiantly, declaring that only a brief kiss had been exchanged. But her aunt had worn her down and she had thrown the truth at her in desperation. Only then did Louisa Ashington stop questioning her, though she made it clear that Lora would be soundly whipped if she ever acknowledged the presence of John Lamont again.

Later, when Lora reflected on the matter, it surprised her how lenient Aunt Louisa had been, and how strange that she should change her mind about making the purposed visit to her friend. How could she have known that she would find Lora and John Lamont in the garden house?

Shortly afterwards news came that Sir Ninian and Lady Lennox had returned to Massingham, and Lora was told by Aunt Louisa to prepare to make the exchange at a moment's notice. But it had all happened too quickly, she thought, as Sir Ninian came to her bed that night. She was ashamed that she had ever allowed John Lamont to possess her, yet she knew that if he had changed places with Sir Ninian, she might have become reconciled to pleasing him. John's body had not revolted her as did Sir Ninian's. He seemed impatient and almost angry with her for not removing her bedgown, and participating in the love-making. Again she gave silent angry thought to Berris, who must have loved him with such abandon that he now expected the same from a lady.

Lora lay quiet and acquiescent when he took her, and most certainly she did not suffer the same pain but neither did she derive any pleasure or excitement. With a grunt Ninian turned from her and lay breathing deeply for a while, then he turned to her once again.

'Are you ill?' he asked. 'Have I displeased you in any way?'

'I ... I do not feel well,' she complained.

He sighed. 'Very well, I shall not trouble you further this night, but I trust you will feel better soon. You know that I am not a patient man and you know what you and I be to one another, my love.'

She said nothing and he turned away. She had not denied him. Why should he complain? Perhaps she might have a child?

Lora's heart misgave her. Suppose ... suppose she bore John Lamont's child. For a few days she lived with this nightmare, but that was resolved when the rhythm of her body proved to be normal. Her spirits lifted and she saw that Ninian was looking at her with relief.

'That is better,' he said one morning. 'I see a smile in your eyes once more. You cannot know how it hurts me to see you withdrawn into yourself where I cannot reach you. I have told you how much I love you, Lora, and I know you love me. That is something precious. We must not destroy it.'

But although she tried hard, Lora could not give Ninian the love he craved, neither could she bear to sit very long with the old skeleton of a woman who kept trying to tell her how much Lora's mother had meant to her. She could scarcely remember her mother.

Ninian took to remaining with his wife longer each evening, and one night he came to her bed smelling strongly of port. This time he was brutal in his treatment of her, shaking her in his frenzy to make her respond to his love-making. She could not hide the revulsion and he threw her aside.

'And to think I put Sophia Mario aside for you!'

'Who?' she asked, startled. The name was a vague shadow upon her memory.

He grew very still, lying beside her in silence.

'Surely you remember the Countess Sophia Mario Bellini?' he asked.

She caught her breath. He was talking about his friends in Italy.

'But certainly I do.'

'Where did we meet her? Was it Milan or perhaps Rome or Venice?'

'I ... I do not remember. I was confused by all those Italian cities and the people we met. Why do you question me? My head aches after that blow I received.'

'There is no such person as Countess Sophia Mario Bellini. But we *both* ought to remember Sophia Mario, Lora. You cannot have forgotten her.'

She was sobbing as she sat up in bed, cowering away from him.

'I cannot remember *anything*. I have told you so.'

Again he sighed gently.

'Very well, Lady Lora. I shall trouble you as little as possible.'

But his voice was distant as he turned away from her.

Ninian listened to Lora's short sigh of relief with a bitter taste in his mouth. For a short while he had glimpsed something wonderful in his life. He'd thought he had found a woman who could match his love with equal passion and delight, and whose mind and personality were a constant delight to him.

But it had all been an illusion, a delusion. Perhaps she had never existed. Perhaps the excitement of the journey had animated her into believing that she loved him. The real Lora was exactly as he had

308

always expected; a dull, immature young lady who was the perfect product of her upbringing. She would bear him children and no doubt run his household after he had given her a sharp lesson against leaving it to the servants, but he would find no companionship in her.

The blow she had received to her head had not appeared to be of a serious nature, but she now had blanks in her memory. She could not even remember Sophia Mario! It seemed incredible that this girl who lay so quietly beside him had ever had the courage to enter the apartment of a woman such as Sophia.

Lady Truscott grew very weak, and Ninian laid all other considerations aside and sat many hours by her bedside. She welcomed him with love, but her disappointment in Lora could not be hidden.

'She has become so unlike my dearest Sarah,' the old lady whispered, 'who was like my own daughter to me. Foolish Sarah. Yet I would rather see her making mistakes because of love than living entirely for herself. She loved that actor.'

'Who was the actor?'

Ninian's eyes had sharpened.

'Tell me, Aunt Elizabeth, no one ever would. Tell me what happened.'

Lady Truscott shook her head. She had

grown tired once again and her eyelids drooped so that she slept. Ninian tried to question her again, but the old woman's mind had started to wander and she confused him with his father, then with her husband. Sometimes she asked him to go and find Ninian because she wanted him to sit with her.

'I am here, dearest Aunt Elizabeth,' he said. 'It is Ninian who sits with you.'

'I have made a mistake,' she whispered. 'I married you to that girl. She is not for you. I ... I thought she would be like my Sarah, but she is an empty shell.'

He had to lean forward to catch her words.

'She was a poor mother. She left one child motherless and took the other to the actor ...'

Ninian's eyes sharpened, even as he wondered if he had heard aright.

'Which other one?' he asked. 'Did you say there was another child, Aunt Elizabeth?'

But the old lady's breath rasped in her throat. That evening she died and the house was thrown into mourning. Ninian forgot about the whispered words and when he remembered, he could not be sure of what he had heard. Later, when the house returned to normal routine, he sought out Lora and began to question her about her mother. He had stopped sharing her bed and made no secret of the fact that he enjoyed other women, so that she had withdrawn from him even further. Nor did she blame him for his lack of fidelity. It was almost as though she thought it a normal state of affairs.

'Have you a sister?' he asked her one evening, as remembrance came back.

'A ... a sister? What can you mean? Why do you ask?'

There was fear in her eyes as she stared at him.

'Your mother caused a scandal by leaving your father to live with an actor. That much is common knowledge. Did she take a child with her? ... your sister.'

'How dare you question me like this!' cried Lora, her eyes blazing like lamps. 'Surely you must know that my mother is never mentioned in my family. When she left my father she ceased to exist and my aunt forbade me to speak of her. I do not even remember her. I was a child when she left Birkridge. I know nothing.'

Ninian sighed and nodded. He did not question her further. A few days later he left for London and asked one of his closest friends whom he could trust to make a few discreet enquiries from those who might have remembered Sarah Ashington; but although some of

311

them remembered the scandal, he learned neither the name of the actor involved nor whether or not there was another child.

Ninian did not pursue the matter. He did not wish to risk his private affairs being bandied about. Soon he was obliged to return to attend to the Massingham estate and to a wife who had begun to assume the duties of Mistress of Massingham, but only after he had insisted upon her support. He had learned that she was lazy by nature, and this, too, was a puzzle. No one had had more vitality than Lora when they first married.

Lora, indeed, had little vitality left. She had never imagined that marriage could be so dull. She hated the marriage bed and being forced to consider someone other than herself at every turn. Also she was afraid of the mistakes she had made which had caused Ninian to question her closely about her sister. She was afraid that he might find out everything, then what would happen to her?

Aunt Louisa would not be here to save her from the wrath of Lennox.

The house was also dull and boring. Now that old Lady Truscott was dead, the servants no longer took pride in keeping Massingham clean and well polished, nor did they afford her a great deal of respect when she was forced to check up on the standards of cleanliness when Ninian was expected home from one of his frequent trips to London. He had asked her to accompany him, but she was afraid of meeting the maidservant who had accompanied them to Italy. Berris had told her to be careful with the woman.

As time dragged on, she knew she ought to become more relaxed and more confident in the fact that she was Mistress of Massingham. Instead she grew more frightened as she looked into her husband's cold eyes. He had called her a cheat when he had drunk too much wine and he had reviled her for allowing him to think her a real woman when she was only a shell.

'My loss is worse than death,' he complained, bitterly. 'Death is final and such bereavement can be healed, but you tantalize me like a festering sore.'

Ninian had returned to London then as the anniversary of their wedding drew near and the weather began to grow warm, he was almost sick with longing once again for their wonderful days in Italy. Lora *must* remember, he told himself almost savagely. She must be *made* to remember.

He purchased a delicate china figurine of a dancing girl which had been exquisitely painted. Perhaps, when she saw it, she would remember the nights they spent in the theatre. With renewed hope in his heart, Ninian was impatient with his coachman on the trip back to Massingham. He would brook no delay and his horses were lathered when he stopped overnight on the road.

As his carriage turned in at the gates of Massingham, his eyes had grown hard and bright with resolution. Then he saw the figure of a woman, burdened with a small child, walking slowly and awkwardly away from the house.

Ninian called for his coachman to slow his pace and as he drew level with the woman, his heart leapt, then hammered. It was Lora! Yet ... it was *not* Lora! He looked at the child in her arms and again his breath rasped in his throat.

'Who are you and why have you come here?' he demanded.

He watched the woman pulling the hood of the cloak over her hair, then he leapt down from his carriage and practically forced her to enter. She claimed that she had only wanted to rest at Massingham, but he scarcely listened. Asking the coachman to wait, he escorted the woman to the drawing room, his mind registering the face that she already knew the way.

Then he sent for Lora.

As she walked slowly into the room, a fierce anger began to boil up in Ninian.

Who had been the perpetrator of this joke? Who had thought him such a fool? Yet he *had* been a fool in that he had not pursued the matter straight away, since even then he had known somewhere deep in his mind that he had been duped. Superficially the two women were as alike as peas in a pod, yet it would take an idiot of a husband not to see any difference under the skin. And he had been turned into that idiot!

Lora's face was pearly-white in the glow of the lamplight. Her hair had been arranged to perfection and she wore a new lilac silk gown cut in the latest style from France, its soft exquisite folds clinging to her slender figure.

Berris had thrown back the hood of her cloak and was bent on pacifying her child. She felt wretchedly unhappy. At the sight of Ninian, her whole being craved his love, yet her pride made her want to rush from the room so that she could not see how much he despised her.

He pulled Lora forward to stand in front of Berris, and the two girls gazed at one another. Berris could see the horror and disgust in her sister's eyes. She, on the other hand, could only look on Lora's beauty and wonder that she had ever taken her place.

'I want you to tell me again that you

have no sister, madam,' Sir Ninian was saying.

Lora's lip curled and her head was thrown back.

'Are you suggesting, sir, that this ... this woman is *my* sister?' she asked. 'Why, she is no better than a beggar who had to be turned away from the door.'

'You admit that she was at our door?'

'Certainly. She is an actress from one of the theatres. She was begging bread and milk for the child. If I hand out food and money to every beggar, we will find ourselves supporting every theatrical company who travels in the vicinity of Massingham. Her child is no doubt a bastard ...'

'That is not true!' cried Berris, goaded.

She could listen to slighting remarks about herself, but no one would sneer at her baby.

'My stepfather said he was born in wedlock and is heir to Massingham,' she said, her head thrown back. She turned to look at Sir Ninian.

'Aye, sir, it is true we are sisters, twin sisters. Our mother was Sarah Ashington, and when she left our father to go to Brendan Meredith, she took me with her. She left Lora with our father. When she died, my stepfather, who became her husband, looked after me. I was known as Berris Meredith, and became an actress with his company. A year ago we played in York and Mistress Ashington asked me to take Lora's place at the betrothal party because Lora had chicken pox. They ... Mr and Mrs Ashington ... did not want to postpone the betrothal party. I took her place and ... you know what happened, sir. I was obliged to stand in for my sister at a wedding, also, and to go with you to Italy on a Grand Tour. It was only after our return from Italy that we changed places once more, but by then I was with child. The boy is your son, sir. I have named him Andrew since it is one of your names. I have come to ask you to take him. He needs a father.'

'He has a father!' cried Lora, wildly. 'She lies. It is all lies. She tried to obtain money from my aunt and uncle with her lies because she happens to resemble me. They set a man to ask about her. She is married to another actor and this is their child. Now she is trying to foist the child upon you. Cannot you see what she is?'

Ninian's face was in shadow and only the dark eyes gleamed as they stared at one girl, then turned to the other.

'I can see what she is,' he said, very softly.

'Then she must leave my house,' cried Lora, imperiously, 'and, if she returns, I shall have the law on her. As it is, I shall require the servants to clean the room, or I shall be quite sick of the odour and not even a pot pourri will help. The child disgusts me.'

Berris scarcely heard her. Her eyes were full of longing and appeal as she stared at Ninian.

'I beg you to take the child,' she said. 'My stepfather is dead, but he says the child is legally your heir, sir. Perhaps you can establish what the law says on this matter. In the meantime, you can do so much more for him than I. His life will be spoiled if he remains with me. I cannot prove to you that the child is yours, but I beg you to believe me since I am telling the truth.'

Silently Sir Ninian held out his arms and Berris rose and, wrapping the soft shawl round the baby, she prepared to put him into his father's arms.

Lora had been silent for a moment, then suddenly she was screaming loudly with rage and fear. Her life as the wife of Lennox was tedious and she had no love for the dark-faced man with the black brooding eyes who demanded so much of her. But if he acknowledged her sister's child as his heir, then it was possible that he might also wish to acknowledge Berris as his true wife. What then, would

318

become of her? Would she be deprived of her rightful place at Massingham?

Lora's thoughts became uncontrollable. Rushing forward she picked up a heavy silver candlestick, and before Berris could stop her, she held it high above her head, and aimed it at the child. Ninian reacted swiftly. Pushing Berris back on to the sofa, he managed to grasp the candlestick even as the blow glanced off one of his arms. Berris saw his face contort with pain. Then he was wrestling with a maddened woman, as Lora searched frantically for another weapon.

'Liar!' she screamed. 'The child could belong to anyone! She is trying to usurp my position, and to make her child heir to Massingham ...'

Her arms flailed wildly as Ninian tried to control her, but suddenly she knocked over the oil lamp which he had lit. The flames spread rapidly across the table and Lora shrieked as her gown caught fire. Horrified Berris pulled off the baby's shawl and began to beat at the flames. Ninian threw Lora to the floor, then bent down to stifle the flames with the shawl.

Servants began to run from all directions and the baby screamed at the top of his lungs.

Silently, her eyes wide with horror, Berris withdrew towards the door as the servants thrust her aside and began to obey Ninian's shouted instructions. Smoke was filling the room and the baby's cries were mingled with coughs so that Berris turned and ran down the corridor towards the main door. She felt sick with fright, but her first considerations was for her child. There were enough people able to deal with the fire without her help.

The carriage was still standing outside with the coachman still waiting his instructions. Berris looked up at him.

'Sir Ninian desires that you take me to York,' she said, swiftly.

She had wrapped her screaming baby in her cloak and, after a moment's hesitation, the coachman acknowledged the instructions.

Inside the coach Berris had to fight against nausea. So much had happened in such a short time that she felt numb with shock, her thoughts jumbled and confused. Should she have fled from Massingham? Was her sister badly injured? She did not think so. Sir Ninian would very soon have the fire under control.

Had he believed her story? She had been unable to read his thoughts, nor had he acknowledged that the child was his. The whole visit had been one of humiliation beyond belief. How ugly and soiled she had felt beside her sister. It was as though the dark sordid aspects of her life were wrapped round her like her cloak. The smell of her own body odours was also the smell of the corruption which surrounded her. Her eyes were no longer young and innocent. They had seen too much of life. She had no place at Massingham. The servants had jostled her aside as they went to assist Sir Ninian and Lady Lora. They had no thought for her welfare.

'This will do,' she said to the coachman as they drove along the main thoroughfare at York. The others must not see, or recognize, the coach. There was still time to get to the theatre and she could claim to have taken the child for a walk, and to have lost her way. They need never know that she had gone to Massingham.

The coachman did not offer to help her down from the carriage. He watched whilst she alighted and took a firm hold of her baby who was now whimpering monotonously, then he drove back towards Massingham.

Berris turned down one of the mean streets and made her way back to the hovel where they lodged. Her attempt to give her child a home, and a better life, had been a complete disaster.

CHAPTER TWENTY-TWO

Over the next few days Berris felt that her spirits were lower than they had ever been in her whole life. When she returned to their lodgings, Polly Hobart rushed towards her like a small tornado and almost wrenched the baby from her grasp. He had been whimpering continuously for some time, but now he began to cry loudly and lustily.

'Where have you been?' Polly cried, her eyes almost feverishly bright. 'What have you done with him?'

Polly and Mistress Grey were alone in the room, Sebastian and Deryk having already left for the theatre, and Berris sank tiredly on to a rickety uncomfortable chair.

'I went walking,' she said, briefly.

Mistress Grey's eyes travelled over her cloak and gown. Although plain and shabby, they were Berris's best clothes, and the older woman eyed her thoughtfully.

'You have walked too far, Berris,' she murmured.

'I forgot the time.'

'The baby is starving,' cried Polly, and

began to feed him sops.

That night Berris put on the worst performance of her career. She had no interest in the lifted skirts and suggestive posturings or the bawdy dialogue which so amused Sebastian and Deryk, and it was Deryk's steely fingers which gripped her arm until it hurt.

'Try to do better, my charming Berris,' he hissed. 'Try to remember you are a woman, and you know what women are for.'

'For the most part, you do not know what women are for,' she said through her teeth.

'Why, then, perhaps it is time I showed you once more,' he countered, and her heart plunged. She should not have provoked him. Since Brendan Meredith had died, Deryk Hobart had assumed more and more authority in their lives. Soon she would be unable to lift a finger without asking his permission. Yet always, for the sake of her child, she must not defy him. Always she had the terrible fear that he would use the child to injure her.

Their stage performance proceeded, but the audience were quick to sense the half-hearted attitude of the young female lead, and their shouts of encouragement turned to censure. A piece of disgustingly rotten fruit landed on Berris's gown. She hesitated, then slowly she walked forward to stand perfectly still at the front of the stage. Other revolting missiles bespattered her, but she appeared to be oblivious of them.

Slowly she began to sway, her body twisting and turning, her steps becoming dainty and precise. It was a dance which Brendan had taught her many years before, and gradually the noise in the theatre subsided and the audience grew rapt as they watched her beginning to twirl this way and that around the stage, so that she was no longer a cheap actress, but a talented entertainer.

Sebastian had been moving forward to stop her, but Mistress Grey grasped his arm.

'She knows what she is doing. Leave her alone. They want to be entertained and she is entertaining them. We can all learn a lesson from this.'

At the end of the dance the audience began to cheer and to call for an encore, but Berris was almost dropping with fatigue. She dropped a curtsey and ran from the stage.

In the wings Mistress Grey waited for her, her eyes brimming with tears as a tall man stepped forward out of the shadows.

Berris pulled herself up sharply. She was totally exhausted after the strain of trying to hold her audience with a performance completely at variance with any she had previously given.

The shock of her sister's attack on her child had also made her feel weak and ill, but now she was no longer blaming Lora so grievously. How easy it was to lose one's reason when one's very life was beset by fear. Lora's eyes had reflected that fear, the fear of losing all she possessed.

And now panic rose in Berris as the tall dark figure moved towards her, then her heart leapt with hope when she saw that it was Sir Ninian. He had followed her to the theatre. He was going to acknowledge the child as his own.

'Fetch the baby, Lady Lennox,' he said, quietly. 'This is no place for my wife. You will return to Massingham with me.'

'Your wife!' she repeated.

Her eyes widened. Surely they had been married in Lora's name. Could it be true that she really was Sir Ninian's wife? Brendan Meredith had told her that it was so, but she had not dared to believe him.

'How can I be your wife when the name of my sister was used in the ceremony?'

Sir Ninian stared at her with the eyes of a stranger.

'But certainly you are my wife. I married you, not your sister. Whatever name you used for the ceremony is of no consequence. Please do not waste my time further, madam.'

Sebastian and Deryk had come to gaze on the scene with disbelief and Sebastian walked forward and would have taken Berris's arm but for the menace he saw on the face of the tall nobleman wearing the great black cloak.

Berris stared at Sebastian. Their marriage could not be legal. She was free of this man whose name she had come to hate.

'Go with the gentleman,' Mistress Grey whispered.

'But the company?'

'I will attend to the company. Tonight I have seen how it must be run. It does not yet belong to Sebastian or anyone else, and you no longer have need of it. The company is mine. I will see that you will have no cause for shame that you were a Meredith Player. Give the child to Lady Lennox, Polly.'

Polly Hobart's face was crumpled with grief, but she handed the boy into his mother's arms and a warm cloak was wrapped round them. Sir Ninian escorted his wife and son to a carriage where a maidservant was waiting to take the child out of Berris's arms.

'What has happened to my sister?' Berris asked, fearfully, as they made the journey to Massingham Hall.

Sir Ninian stared at her and his mouth drew into a hard straight line.

'Your sister is well enough, madam.'

The anger in his eyes forbade further questioning though Berris's hands clenched with nerves and fear. If only she were returning to Massingham because Ninian loved her and desired her. But his eyes told her that his anger against her and Lora was too great.

'I ... I am truly sorry, Sir Ninian,' she whispered.

'You deceived me,' he said very quietly. 'You told me nothing. I cannot forgive you for not telling me that you had taken your sister's place. I suppose that you enjoyed being the play actress with me.'

She was too tired to try to make him understand and a few minutes later the carriage pulled up in front of the great broad entrance to Massingham Hall.

Once again Berris was escorted indoors by Jessop then Hebe was there to put her arms round her mistress and to escort her upstairs to the master bedroom.

'My baby?' Berris asked.

'The nursery has been opened for him and all has been made ready, my lady.'

'I see. He will no doubt be well cared for.'

She was barely conscious of having her

clothing removed and of climbing once again into the huge soft bed. Maidservants were tidying up after her toilet and for a while Berris relaxed and lay looking at familiar cracks on the ceiling, then turning to watch the flames from the log fire casting long shadows against the walls.

'I am glad that you are home, my lady,' said Hebe as she snuffed one or two candles.

'Where is my sister, Hebe?' Berris asked, and the serving maid drew in her breath sharply.

'She is being cared for, Lady Berris,' she said, quietly.

Lady Berris! How strange to hear one of the maidservants address her by that name. Was she truly Lady Berris? She lay awake, wondering rather fearfully yet with inward excitement if Ninian would come to their room. But the house grew quiet and she was left alone. Exhaustion finally overcame her and she slept.

CHAPTER TWENTY-THREE

Berris woke in great fear, having been pursued by strange Harlequin-like creatures in her dreams. Sebastian and Deryk were forcing her to act in a play which she found degrading. Deryk held up a china doll, then smashed it at her feet when she refused to do as he wished. Berris screamed then woke as Hebe walked into the room, and pulled back heavy curtains.

'Sir Ninian desires that you remain in bed for a day, ma'am,' she said, brightly. 'You were very fatigued yesterday.'

'I am perfectly all right,' said Berris, throwing back the covers.

'I think you had better heed Sir Ninian,' said Hebe, coming over to her swiftly. 'The house servants are very busy. They are cleaning the drawing room after the fire accident. It is best that you remain here, my lady. I will bring breakfast for you.'

'I am not hungry,' Berris whispered.

Yet it was not true. In spite of her nerves and her fear as to her future place at Massingham, she was conscious of a gnawing empty feeling inside. When Hebe brought a tray of food, she ate sparingly at first, then with growing appetite so that the maidservant smiled her approval when she came to take the tray away.

'I will also attend to your toilet, ma'am,' she said. 'The master will come to see you shortly.'

'And my sister?'

Again the closed look dropped over Hebe's face.

'Perhaps you can ask the master,' she suggested.

Berris felt better after eating breakfast. She decided that there was no reason why she should be forced to remain in bed and was about to swing her legs over the side when the door of the room opened and Sir Ninian strode in, shutting it behind him.

Slowly he crossed over to the bed twirling a small ebony cane in his hands, and stared down at her.

'So you have rested, madam,' he remarked, pleasantly.

'Yes, sir. There is no reason for me to remain in bed. I ... I would like to get up now.'

'You will remain where you are for the present,' he said, slapping the cane against his hand. 'Your sister is similarly confined to another room. She has superficial burns on one of her arms. They are not serious, and no worse than my own.'

Berris saw that one of his wrists had been carefully bandaged. She longed to take his hands in hers and to ask him if he suffered any pain. But he had built a great wall of reserve between them.

'What are your plans for Lora and myself, sir? What of my sister if ... if you wish me to remain here?'

'She will be returned to the Ashingtons at Birkridge,' he said, indifferently.

Berris pulled herself up in bed. How cold he was! She had already explained exactly what had happened when she first took Lora's place, but her explanation had been made to deaf ears. There was no charity in him, and no attempt to understand anyone else's thoughts and feelings other than his own.

Berris's temper began to rise.

'You *cannot* send her back to Birkridge as though she were a sack of potatoes,' she protested. 'She is a human being with thoughts and feelings. Her life will ... will be untenable if you merely return her to her family without more thought and care.'

His lips once again compressed into a hard straight line and his eyes flashed with anger.

'And how much care and thought went into considering *my* feelings when you undertook this charade, madam?' he asked, tightly. 'How much consideration did the Ashingtons afford *me?*'

She was silent. The hurt in his voice was finding an echo in her heart. She loved him. She wanted to reach out and touch him, then pull him into her arms and hold his head against her breast, stroking the crisply curling blackness of his hair. But he had cocooned himself in ice and she could not reach him. The love which he had once felt for her seemed long since to have died completely.

He stopped prowling around the room.

'Remain where you are, madam,' he told her. 'A great deal of my home has been ruined by smoke damage. Perhaps you have not thought about the fire so I will remind you that I have many pictures which now require to be cleaned, as well as precious ornaments and hangings. For that I must thank the Ashingtons. And you expect me to be grateful for their generosity, that they have given me *two* wives instead of one. I must be generous and understanding. Perhaps I am even expected to keep both of my wives? Is *that* what you wish, Lady Berris?'

Again she was silent but fear of him was lessening and she was aware of the deep unhappiness behind his words. She had agreed to take her sister's place for the money it would bring to the Meredith

Players. And the Ashingtons had made no secret of the fact that Lora must marry Sir Ninian in order that Mark Ashington's debts be paid. Even Lady Truscott was determined that Ninian should marry Sarah's daughter.

But what of Ninian? Who had considered his feelings? Had he been hurt so that, like an injured dog, if anyone touched him he was liable to snarl and bite? She felt as though he had bitten her until her body writhed with pain, but she could not reach him to comfort him.

She remained with her jumbled thoughts after he had left her. From far away she could hear the noises of activity as furniture was moved and floors and walls were cleaned.

She asked about her baby and a plump nurse in a starched white apron and cap arrived with the child in her arms. Andrew slept comfortably and Berris knew a sense of relief. He was no longer under the shadow of Deryk Hobart. Whatever punishment lay ahead for her, it was worth all to see her child safe and properly cared for.

That night Berris settled more easily for sleep. She had to acknowledge that the rest in bed had been beneficial and her courage began to return. Even if Sir Ninian no longer loved her, she would try to find happiness in watching her child grow up to take his rightful place in the world.

It was very late, and the fire had died down into glowing embers when the door suddenly opened, and a dark figure walked silently into the room. Berris's heart hammered as Ninian walked over to the bed. She could see that he had been drinking more than usual and that his eyes glittered in the light of a flickering candle as he stared down at her. Then he began to shed his clothing, and moments later he was again beside her in the great bed.

'Take off your bedgown,' he commanded and without a word, she pulled it over her head, even as he clasped her against his chest.

'You denied me,' he told her so softly that she could scarcely hear the words. 'For almost a year you have denied me.'

'No,' she protested. 'I did not. I have not. You know I could not come to you.'

His hands, softly stroking her body, were all that she remembered; yet how very different was his treatment of her now. Then there had been joy between them, but now all the trust had gone, and all the deep true intimacy, one with another. She might have been Sophia Mario as he explored her body, but her own need of him began to grow and in spite of her resolution not to reach out to him, thereby giving him every excuse to spurn her, she cradled his head in her arms and sought to soften his hard stern face with her kisses.

She knew that he desired her greatly, but his desire was a need for a woman, and she began to suspect that any woman would do.

Berris felt that her whole body cried out in protest. Surely he must remember what they had been to one another? Surely he must know that their love was something which could not be given to anyone else?

She stroked his body as she had done so often in the past and sought to remind him of her own sweetness as he pulled her towards him.

Then he was making love to her violently, with no tenderness between them, and Berris cried out because he was tearing her tender flesh.

'You are hurting me!' she cried.

He turned her over and gave her a stinging blow across her buttocks, so that she had to bite the edge of her pillow to keep herself from crying out.

'There,' he panted. 'Perhaps you are now on familiar territory, madam. I have no doubt that your theatre actors used you in just this way.'

'They did not!' she cried. 'Do you think I would allow myself to be used in this

335

way? Sebastian ... Sebastian *could* not, even though he thought himself my husband. We did not know that I was still Lady Lennox ... and Sebastian married me in church, but was his own priest. Brendan Meredith said it was not a legal marriage, but we thought it was binding.'

Swiftly she explained all the circumstances and he scoffed at her ignorance in thinking the marriage legal. Then his anger rose against her once more for going through such a form of marriage with another man.

'You chose *him* for a husband! That sop was your own choice. How unfortunate that you had already married me as a result of an accident,' he said, bitterly.

'No!' she cried, again.

'A play actress,' he said, scathingly. 'A play actress and a rag doll without feelings. Those are my two wives. How can I ever believe what you tell me, Lady Berris? How will I ever know whether or not you are still in the theatre in your heart, acting a part for my pleasure? How shall I ever know you are telling the truth if you say you love me?'

'I do,' she whispered. 'I do love you.'

He was climbing out of her bed once more. He stood in the middle of the floor, his shoulders hunched instead of standing tall and straight.

'How will I ever know?' he repeated, his voice low.

She heard him walk slowly out from the room and her pillow grew wet with tears. He had used her roughly, but for a few moments she had loved him once more, just as she remembered in her dreams. But in her dreams she had always imagined that she would find him again one day. Now she felt that she never would.

CHAPTER TWENTY-FOUR

Berris did not wait for Hebe to tell her to remain in bed next day. She was already up and wearing simple clothing when the maidservant walked into her room.

Once again breakfast had been prepared for her, and now she ate ravenously. She had slept well and had woken early, finding that a great deal of her courage had returned with her strength. Perhaps she deserved punishment for what she and the Ashingtons had done, but she would not accept it meekly. Sir Ninian would have to learn that the sister he had married was far from being a rag doll.

Having finished breakfast Berris walked along the corridor towards the main staircase. The door of the room in which she and Ninian had spent the first night of their marriage was slightly open and she could hear a woman's voice raised in anger, and Hebe Jessop's low soothing placatory tones answering her.

Berris paused, then pushed the door open. Lora lay in the large bed, her hair dishevelled and her eyes reddened. Her wrist was being dressed in a fresh bandage and Berris's eyes were distressed when she walked further into the room. So Lora had been burned; and burned rather worse than Sir Ninian would have had her believe. How distressing it must be for her.

'Have you come to gloat?' her sister asked, sharply. 'You come here, depriving me of my home, bringing a child, and now you wish to show me what a fine lady you are. But I know what you are, even if your husband does not. You are a play actress and nothing more. Lennox has turned a play actress into the Mistress of Massingham.'

She began to laugh and Berris walked forward and picked up a cloth which had been wrung out in cool water. She laid it upon Lora's forehead and the shock of the cold water sobered her.

'I may have been a play actress, Lora, but I am also your sister,' she said, quietly. 'You no longer humiliate me by throwing me back into a life which should never have been mine in the first place.'

'Yet now you would throw *me* back,' screamed Lora. 'What of me? This should be *my* life, not yours. It was only intended that you take my place for one night.'

This time Berris paused and her heart ached with compassion for her sister as she sat down on the other side of the bed. Hebe Jessop had removed the tray of dressings and had quietly left the room. Berris was alone with her sister.

'It should not have happened,' she agreed huskily. 'Mr and Mrs Ashington were wrong to do such a thing. It has been hurtful to ... to Sir Ninian.'

'Sir Ninian! What do I care about him? It has been hurtful to *me*.'

Berris drew back. She, also, had been hurt but Lora's petulant face showed clearly that she was only concerned for her own feelings.

'Do you love Sir Ninian, Lora?' she asked, quietly.

Lora's eyes flickered. There had been an anxious note in Berris's voice and she bit back the ready retort that she hated him. He had had no compunction in showing his contempt for her when he had found out how he had been deceived.

'I will not discuss it,' she said. 'Ladies do not share their private feelings with anyone outside marriage.'

Slowly Berris rose to her feet, her eyes on Lora's face. She watched the tears welling in her sister's eyes.

'Do not let him send me away,' she pleaded. 'I am ruined and my wrist is scarred. What is to become of me?'

Her voice was piteous and Berris's heart was touched.

Leaning forward she kissed her sister's forehead.

'I will do what I can,' she promised, and did not see the distaste on Lora's face as she turned towards the door.

CHAPTER TWENTY-FIVE

The drawing room was once again clean and fresh, the draperies having been laundered and the furniture polished. One or two small ornaments were missing, ones broken in the agitation caused by the fire, and Jessop remarked that Sir Ninian was arranging to have the pictures cleaned by an expert.

'Where is Sir Ninian, Jessop?' asked Berris.

She had already gone to the nursery to kiss and fondle her child, glad to see that he was now being so well cared for, and the nurse had told her that Sir Ninian had spent some time admiring the child, but had now gone downstairs. Berris's heart beat more quickly as she looked for his tall figure.

'He has gone riding, my lady, as he usually does in the morning. He may still be at the stables. Sometimes he inspects the horses.'

Berris nodded and made her way to the large cobbled yard at the back of Massingham. Ninian was talking to the stable boy, and he turned to stare at her, the smile leaving his eyes as he waited for her to approach.

'Good morning, sir,' she said. 'I would like to speak with you when it is convenient.'

Her eyes challenged his and he nodded sombrely.

'Very well. Later in the morning. At this time I am accustomed to riding out to the farms. You may accompany me, madam.'

'I do not ride,' said Berris, clearly, and she saw a hint of amusement in the dark eyes.

'At least you do not offer excuses as you did once before. You will learn to ride, Lady Berris. It is essential that you are able to sit a horse. Roberts will arrange for you to be mounted on a quiet beast and I will teach you myself.'

Berris nodded. She recognized that her inability to ride might prove a handicap in the future.

Her heart warmed as she wandered round the old house. She was close to Ninian once more. She loved him passionately, and he had loved her once. Surely she should be able to win that love again? He was angry with her, and he had been badly hurt by the ruse which had been played upon him, but she began to grow confident that she could make him forget that they had ever been separated.

Her confidence was short-lived, however, when she went to talk to Ninian in his business room later that morning.

'Well, Lady Berris?' he asked, coldly. 'What do you wish to say to me?'

She stared into his cold eyes and her hopes began to fade. It was not going to be easy, yet she had promised Lora that she would plead her cause.

'My ... my sister,' she said nervously. 'I wanted to talk to you about Lora. Please do not send her home without making some other arrangement for her.'

'Other arrangement? What would you have me arrange, madam?'

'I hardly know, sir,' she confessed. 'Her life has been ruined by these events. Cannot you understand that? She is neither wife or maid. Her aunt and uncle will not welcome her now. She would be an object of ... of gossip. Only consider her feelings, sir.'

His eyes raked over her from head to foot.

'My own feelings do not appear to be worthy of your consideration,' he said, evenly. 'Perhaps you would inform Jessop that we will dine fifteen minutes later this evening. I have an engagement and may be delayed. I will expect you to join me for dinner. Your sister may dine in her room.'

She was dismissed. His nod of dismissal was that of a master to a servant and her cheeks grew scarlet with humiliation as she was obliged to leave the room. His attitude made her position very plain to her. She had become his wife because of a trick, and had borne him a son. She would be acknowledged at Massingham as Lady Lennox, but the position was an empty shell for her. In fact her whole life had become empty except for her son, thought Berris, as she walked along the corridors and wondered how she would plan her day. She, too, was neither wife nor maid, nor yet play actress. And Sir Ninian had ensured that their son was receiving such excellent attention that she was no longer necessary to him either.

Berris wandered into the sewing room and took up some mending, trying to control her tears, then her mouth firmed. She had not sought this position. It had been forced upon her when old Lady Truscott desired to see her and Ninian married. She would *not* be thrust out of Ninian's life and given the role of housekeeper. He had gained much from their marriage. She would remind him of that when the opportunity arose.

In the evening Berris did not leave her room until the gong sounded for dinner. Some of the gowns which she had purchased in Italy were still hanging in her bedroom. Lora had not cared for them, as she told Berris poutingly. They were too elaborately fashioned for Massingham.

Eyes glinting, Berris asked Hebe to iron the flounces of a beautiful oyster satin gown and to help her to dress her hair in a style which resembled the blonde wig which she had worn in Italy.

Since the birth of her child, her figure had become even more rounded and Berris's eyes glowed like jewelled amber when she saw the results of her labour. Perhaps the extreme elegance was missing, the elegance which came from attention to the smallest detail which Carlo had dictated, but at first glance she had changed little from the girl who had shared those enchanting evenings with Ninian.

She had heard the sounds of his arrival and knew that he was engaged in attending to his own toilet. Later he descended the stairs once more, and when Jessop sounded the gong which announced that their evening meal was now prepared, Berris picked up her oyster satin reticule and descended the stairs to the drawing room.

Holding a glass of wine in his hand, Ninian stood in front of the great tall window, gazing out into the garden. For a few moments Berris watched him, admiring the set of his shoulders and the strength in his fine body, then as though aware of her presence, he turned to look at her. She saw the familiar flame leaping into his eyes and her heart began to race madly. Would he forget everything that had happened between them except for those wonderful days when they had rejoiced in love for one another?

She did not trouble to hide the love in her eyes as she moved towards him. The answering gleam in his made the colour steal into her cheeks, then slowly he began to turn away, carefully placing his glass on a wine table before offering her wine, which she refused. He kicked a log in the fire, sending up a myriad sparks followed by a leaping flame which seemed to dance in her eyes.

'We will go into the dining room, Lady Lennox,' he said, formally, and rather stiffly. 'We dine alone this evening.'

'That will be pleasant,' she said, warmly, and once again he stared at her.

'It is only a quiet supper. It is useless to dress for the opera at Massingham.'

'I dress for a quiet supper with you, Sir Ninian,' she returned equably. 'That is as important to me as a night at the theatre.'

'Ah yes ... the theatre,' he said, heavily, and she bit her lip. She should not have reminded him about the theatre.

Berris longed to ask if he had made any new plans for Lora, but instead she tried to remember everything Fiorenza had taught her about pleasing Ninian. She talked about various topics as intelligently as she could. Travelling the country, she was better versed in social conditions than many ladies who were obliged to remain at home, and soon Ninian's interest was caught.

Having finished supper, Berris returned to the drawing room to be joined shortly afterwards by Ninian, his mood greatly lightened. To her delight, his laugher rang out more than once.

Later she rose quietly and excused herself in order to retire to bed. He gave her leave to go, though his eyes gleamed as he watched her leave the room.

It was almost an hour later, after the old house had settled into silence, that the door of Berris's room opened quietly and Ninian stepped inside.

Without a word he threw off his clothing and climbed into bed beside his wife, where she waited for him as she had waited so often in the past. Without a word she went into his arms, then held him close to her in love. She felt the gentle touch of his fingers as he explored her body, and her murmured name on his lips. This time it was her own name and not her sister's.

'I have missed you,' he told her, huskily.

'And *how* I have missed you,' she told him, her arms creeping round his neck.

His body was satin-smooth and more beautiful to her than any other man. She felt his kisses upon her neck and the warm rich blood flowed through her veins so that once again she became a different person, and her desire for him was like a living thing, as great as his for her.

He kissed her, smoothing the long tendrils of hair away from her forehead, and she held him close and murmured his name, her arms creeping round his neck. He stroked her soft breasts, and the long slender length of her thigh, then he was possessing her like one who had thirsted for a long time. Berris had already known the wild heights of ecstasy with Ninian, but never more than now. She lay fulfilled in his arms, and he pulled idly at the curls on her forehead, then kissed her gently.

She sighed, then remembered her sister whose room was at the end of the corridor, yet who might have been placed at the top of a tower, so far apart was she from their lives.

Berris had promised to plead her cause with Ninian. Lora should not be sent home to Birkridge. Surely some other plan could

349

be made for her future.

'What are you thinking?' he asked, playfully tickling her nose with one of her own curls.

'I was thinking about Lora,' she said, honestly. 'I promised her that I would speak to you ...'

Even as she spoke the words, she could hear the hiss of his indrawn breath.

'Lora!' he cried. 'You think to use our ... our marriage bed to talk to me about your sister!'

'No, Ninian!' she cried. 'How could you think such a thing? You know I love you.'

'I know you *tell* me you love me,' he said, roughly.

In the pale light of a flickering candle, he stared down into her face and she pulled away. How could he spoil such a moment of intimacy? Yet ... perhaps she had spoiled it by reminding him about Lora?

'Ninian,' she said, gently. 'I ... I should not have spoken about my sister. Cannot ...?'

'No,' he said, harshly. 'For a while you made me forget, but how can I forget?'

'What cannot you forget?'

'That you are a play actress. You would use your wiles to your own ends, and extract promises from me which would be easy to give as you offer your body like a drug. But I *will* not be used again! You *will* not make a fool of me another time.'

'Ninian, it is not so.'

She sat up and the bed covers fell away from her body so that she looked unbelievably beautiful to him. But already he was leaving her bed and his eyes glittered in the faint light.

'I shall deal with your sister in the morning, madam,' he said, harshly. 'Perhaps you have forgotten that she tried to attack our child.'

'I have not forgotten, sir. She was greatly upset. She will not do so again.'

'I do not wish to discuss it. I wish you goodnight.'

The door slammed and Berris lay down again, her whole body shaking uncontrollably. How could such a thing have happened? She had been so sure that everything was as it had once been between her and Ninian. Their lives were again bound together as though this past year had never been. But how easily he could be hurt by the slightest word carelessly spoken. How could he think she would use their love for Lora's benefit? Yet she had done so, she thought with sickness in her heart. She had not realized how much his life had been disrupted by her sister. His trust in her had been broken.

Berris shed unhappy tears then, having worn herself out, she sank into a troubled sleep. She woke up to the sound of voices underneath her window and the noise of carriage wheels. Shortly afterwards Hebe Jessop walked quietly into her room.

'Has Sir Ninian gone out?' Berris asked.

'Yes, my lady, he left a short time ago.'

'Oh.'

Berris hardly knew whether to be glad or sorry. She was torn between her love for him together with understanding and sympathy, and anger that he could believe her to be play acting when she was not on stage. She was always entirely herself when she was not acting out one of her roles. How could she make him understand this?

'Is my sister improving in health?' she asked Hebe. 'I would like to see her shortly. How bad is the wound on her wrist from the fire?'

'It is almost healed, my lady. My mother knows a great deal about herbs and she prepared a soothing lotion for Mistress Lora. I have given her a supply to take to Birkridge.'

'To Birkridge?'

'Why yes, my lady. That is where Sir Ninian has gone. He has taken Mistress Lora home and he said you must not be disturbed too early. I ... I thought you knew ...'

'Of course,' she said, swiftly, though her lips firmed with anger. So this was how Ninian was treating the matter. She had thought that, given time to consider, he would realize that she had offered herself to him without reservations. She had given him all she had to give—her heart. But now he was removing her sister to Birkridge despite her wishes. Could not he understand that she and Lora were twins? Ever since she had met her sister once again, she had been conscious of a special bond between them. It had superseded all other considerations in her relationship with her sister, though she recognized that Lora had not experienced this same instinct. Despite the selfish and even violent behaviour of her sister, Berris could only feel pain for her. Lora's sufferings were her own.

'I have no appetite for breakfast, Hebe,' she said quietly. 'I wish to see my son.'

'Very well, my lady,' said Hebe, and her eyes were concerned as she looked at Berris's white face.

CHAPTER TWENTY-SIX

The next few weeks were amongst the most unhappy Berris had ever known. She had tried to see her sister but Louisa Ashington had not received her at Birkridge with any degree of warmth, and had left her in no doubt that she held Berris completely responsible for all that had happened at Massingham.

'Lora has been trained for years to be Mistress of Massingham,' she said, harshly, 'and now her place has been usurped by you who are nobody. I blame myself that this could happen. I should have known that you have not been bred to recognize right from wrong, and that you would find some way of turning everything to your own advantage.

Berris closed her eyes against the harsh words. She knew now that Louisa Ashington had hated her mother and some of that hatred was now being reflected on her.

'I only called to enquire for my sister's health, ma'am,' she said, with dignity. She could not rest until she knew how Lora fared.

'She is well. She plans to marry the son of a local farmer,' said Mrs Ashington. 'I am sure that must please you.'

'I insist that I see her before I go.'

Louisa Ashington shrugged. 'Oh, very well. It cannot matter now.'

Lora looked younger than she had done when Berris last saw her. Then she had been confined to bed with a peevish expression and had complained bitterly about her fate and the wound on her wrist. Now her bandages had been removed and the flounces of her pretty dress fell away to reveal a faint pink mark on her wrist.

Her expression sobered when she saw Berris, but there was no longer hostility in her eyes.

'So you have paid us a call, sister,' she said, lightly.

'I had to see you ... to see that you were well and ... and had accepted your return to Birkridge.'

Berris stumbled over the words. She could not express her feelings to her sister. Lora shrugged, then smiled faintly.

'You are kind, Berris. You bear me no malice for attempting to injure your son. For a little while, I think I was mad. Lennox turned me into a mad thing. I tell you, sister, I would not exchange my life for yours were I offered the kingdom. I am going to marry John Lamont. He loves me and will be kind to me. You are very welcome to Massingham since you must also accept Lennox. He has always been abhorrent to me.'

'You did not love him at any time?'

'He is not an easy man to love. Thanks to him I find the prospect of becoming the wife of a farmer very attractive indeed.'

'Then you are happy, Lora?'

Berris's eyes were anxious. Lora looked up at her. 'Why should you concern yourself? You have got what you wanted.'

'Perhaps I wanted a sister,' said Berris, quietly. 'Our lives might have been very different had we been brought up together instead of separately. Cannot we be friends, Lora, even if we cannot be sisters?'

Lora pushed a strand of hair out of her eyes.

'The Mistress of Massingham and the wife of a farmer,' she said, heavily. 'Yes, sister, perhaps we can be friends. But only when Lennox is from home.'

Berris nodded. It was enough for now.

She drove home from Birkridge, thinking deeply about her sister. She could not imagine Lora the wife of a farmer. Could it be that she really felt affection, or even love for this man? Lora had been more animated than Berris had ever seen her. Perhaps she was happy at last.

Berris grew lonely at Massingham, though she spent many hours in the nursery with her son. Ninian was away a great deal on business, but he always came home again and sometimes he even came to her bed; but it was a cold-eyed stranger who used her, left her bed, then rode away again from Massingham as though he could neither bear to be near her, nor yet away from her for too long.

The weeks drifted past, then once again the notices were put up in York that the Meredith Players were performing at the theatre, and that a Sheridan play was to be performed. Visiting the city with Hebe, Berris commanded the coachman to stop whilst she read the advertisement, then her eyes grew very thoughtful as she drove home.

Sir Ninian had arrived from London on the previous day and so far he had treated her with the greatest courtesy, his joy and lightness of spirits being reserved for his son, whom he loved devotedly. Berris had watched that love growing with time, but as Ninian closed his heart against her, she had found herself even a little jealous of her own son. If only Ninian would rush home and clasp *her* in his arms as he did Andrew! Her joy and laughter would be as great as the child's who adored his father.

However it was not to be. She was given every courtesy as Lady Lennox, but the years seemed to stretch bleakly ahead, years in which she could only foresee loneliness and isolation.

Berris considered the matter carefully that evening. If she were to be given the status of a play actress by her husband, then perhaps it was time for her to become a true actress once more. She had no real place at Massingham. Her son was well cared for and had his father's love, and the household ran smoothly even without her care and attention. Or so she believed. Nor had Sir Ninian any real need of her. He no doubt had several mistresses in London.

Berris's heart ached as she pursued her thoughts. How could she give up her son? And she loved Massingham and took more and more interest every day in affairs of the estate. She had learned to ride and she was now a familiar figure in the villages and hamlets, taking a personal interest in the affairs of the tenants.

The greatest blow, however, would be to lose Ninian once again. She saw little of him, but she treasured what she had. How could she bear to lose the smallest sight of him? But the pride and dignity, inherent in her nature, was an integral part of her being. Ninian had made his choice and it was apparent to her that she had no part in his future.

Berris thought deeply before packing a small bag in preparation for leaving Massingham to join the Players. She began to write a note for Ninian, then pushed her notepaper aside. It would not do. It was not in her nature to give up so easily, nor did she run away. She would confront Sir Ninian, face to face, and tell him of her decision.

Berris made her plans accordingly, choosing a selection of her simplest gowns and a plain hard-wearing cloak to take with her. She would accept no jewellery from her husband, not even the personal gifts which he had made to her.

On the following day Berris requested an interview with Ninian in his business room. He had made the nursery his first port of call, and had met Berris in the corridor as she made her way downstairs. Immediately he stiffened, his eyes raking over her, then he bowed politely.

'I would like to see you as soon as is convenient, Sir Ninian,' she said, quietly.

'I must refresh myself, madam. I bear the odour of horseflesh.'

'I will see that everything is made ready for you, after which I should like to talk with you when you are free. It is important.'

'Very well, since it is so important ...'

His voice trailed away and he stared at her searchingly. She bobbed a small curtsey, then continued on her way down the long staircase which had been thronged with guests on their wedding night. How rarely they entertained nowadays. How sad and empty their lives had become.

Berris wore a simple white gown sprigged with lilacs for her interview with Ninian. Her hours of riding had brought a warm rich pallor to her complexion and her hair glowed with dark coppery lights.

She had spent little time on her appearance, however, and did not know that her own natural beauty was breathtaking to Ninian, after the painted women he had sometimes visited in London. Berris vibrated with life. No one could compare with her. But how could he ever trust her with his heart? How could he know that her love for him, which she had professed so openly, was really true and not merely an act in order to use him for her own ends?

Ninian stared at her sombrely as she walked into the room. What did she require in order to add to her comforts? He had lavished clothing and jewels upon his wife, and his son had been given every possible luxury. The boy was so like his own grandfather whose portrait was hanging in this very room, that he had developed an even greater love for the child than he had ever thought possible. And in his most secret heart he knew that part of that love was also because of the child's mother. More and more, he found that he could not stay away from Massingham for longer than a few days at any one time. It held all that was most dear to him; his son and ... and his wife. Deep in his heart Ninian knew this was so, but she had the power to hurt him more than anyone in the world, and he refused to be hurt again.

Storm clouds had gathered and the sky was almost black as night as Berris walked towards Ninian. She refused to sit down and he turned away to light one or two candles with a taper which he lit from the fire.

'It grows dull, madam,' he said, easily. 'I am fortunate to have avoided a storm when I rode out. Unless ...' He quirked an eyebrow, 'Unless a storm of a different nature is upon me. Have you saved your complaints for me? Have you been paying calls upon your sister once more? Am I yet again expected to admit her into my household?'

'No, sir. She has arranged her own life and is happy. She marries John Lamont.'

His eyes glinted. 'It has been my experience of life that, given their independence,

361

people are quite capable of arranging their own affairs.'

She nodded. She had been wrong to plead Lora's cause with him. He had been wiser in removing her from Massingham. Her presence in the house would have cast a shadow, perhaps in time as black as the clouds which now gathered over their lives.

'I am glad to hear these sentiments, sir,' she agreed, 'because now I wish to arrange *my* own life. You remind me constantly that I am a play actress. Very well, I accept that and I wish to return to the theatre. You ...' her voice faltered, '... you do not need me and you can give our son the life he deserves. I had thought to join the Meredith Players and leave a letter for you, but ... but that is not my way. I thought it more honest to come to you, and to tell you my intentions.'

The firelight flickered on his dark face, but she could not see his eyes. He wandered over to the window then came to stand in front of the fire once more.

'That is not your way,' he repeated slowly. 'You desire to be completely honest with me. Is that what you are saying? You did not call the carriage and leave me a note because it would not have been honest and straightforward. That is the truth?'

Colour had crept into her cheeks. Was

362

it the truth? she searched her heart and knew that it was not.

'Not the whole truth,' she whispered.

'*Another* ploy?'

'Why do you always scrutinize my motives so minutely?' she asked, suddenly angered. 'Perhaps I have made a mistake, sir. Perhaps I should not have wished to see you. I only wanted to see you once more.' Her voice trailed to a whisper and she turned to leave the room.

'I shall leave in the morning, Sir Ninian.'

Before he could say a word, the room was suddenly alight with a great flash of lightning and she started with fright, then put her hands to her ears as the thunder crashed a moment later.

Ninian had moved forward and put his arms round her so that she cowed against him.

'I am afraid of thunder,' she said. 'Travelling in the wagon, I have sometimes seen trees struck by lightning and people and animals have been killed.'

'There is no need to fear, my little one,' Ninian said, tenderly. 'I am here to care for you. Berris, I cannot let you go out of my life. I see clearly now that you do love me as much as I love you, my dearest wife. I could see the honesty in your eyes when you told me that you remained here in order that you might see me just once

363

more. That makes me very happy, but I am not proud of myself for doubting your love. I have wasted so much time, and have put myself into agonies of mind and heart.'

'You were not to blame, Ninian,' said Berris, leaning her head on his shoulder. 'We almost destroyed you, my Ashington relatives and I. Oh yes, I was also to blame. I should never have agreed to take Lora's place.'

'If you had not, then our lives might have been ruined; mine, Lora's and perhaps even yours, my Berris.'

Great happiness was beginning to glow in her heart. She thought about the Meredith Players and shivered. She had never really been a good actress. Brendan Meredith had always known that, but he had done his best for her. He had made her promise to find Ninian once more. Perhaps he had known that they might one day find happiness together. Until now she had thought that was beyond her reach.

The storm still raged but Berris no longer cared as Ninian held her tightly in his arms, as though he would never let her go. He bent to kiss her, feeling the immediate response of her vibrant young body. The ice-hard protection which he had built round his heart melted completely away, leaving him warm with love once more. In his arms he held that which was more

364

precious to him than anything he had ever known.

'The sun is breaking through the clouds,' he said as the room began to glow with light. 'Shall we look for the rainbow?'

'It is already here, my dear love,' said Berris, and her arms slid round his neck.

The publishers hope that this book has given you enjoyable reading. Large Print Books are especially designed to be as easy to see and hold as possible. If you wish a complete list of our books, please ask at your local library or write directly to: Dales Large Print Books, Long Preston, North Yorkshire, BD23 4ND, England.

This Large Print Book for the Partially sighted, who cannot read normal print, is published under the auspices of

THE ULVERSCROFT FOUNDATION

THE ULVERSCROFT FOUNDATION

. . . we hope that you have enjoyed this Large Print Book. Please think for a moment about those people who have worse eyesight problems than you . . . and are unable to even read or enjoy Large Print, without great difficulty.

You can help them by sending a donation, large or small to:

**The Ulverscroft Foundation,
1, The Green, Bradgate Road,
Anstey, Leicestershire, LE7 7FU,
England.**
or request a copy of our brochure for more details.

The Foundation will use all your help to assist those people who are handicapped by various sight problems and need special attention.

Thank you very much for your help.